COMING TO TERMS

By

KA Moll

2015

Coming to Terms © 2015 KA Moll
Triplicity Publishing, LLC

ISBN-13: 978-0996242936
ISBN-10: 0996242937

Printed in the United States of America
First Edition – 2015
Cover Design: Triplicity Publishing, LLC
Interior Design: Triplicity Publishing, LLC
Editor: Lauren Weiler - Triplicity Publishing, LLC

Acknowledgements

People often ask which character in the novel, is 'really' me. My answer is always the same. None, but a piece of me is in each and every one. Their story isn't my story though—not even close. I've worked with cops like Sawyer. I've practiced alongside social workers like Sage. Although Sage and Sawyer are fictional characters, they do possess some of the qualities that I most respected in the people who were once my colleagues.

Coming to Terms allowed me to follow along behind Sawyer and Sage as they walked the snowy streets of my childhood. I'm not usually nostalgic, but I must admit, during the writing of this novel, I was.

My thanks go out to my beta readers—Jennifer, Rebecca, Paula, Maureen, Valerie, and of course, Kay. You suffered through multiple readings of early drafts and didn't complain, but it had to be painful. Your input helped to shape this work into what it is today. My thanks also go out to those who taught me this craft—the writing of fiction. You know who you are.

Most of all, I thank my wife, Kay. You've learned to live with a house full of characters—me included. I can tell that you've come to terms. Our thirty years together have flashed by in an instant. Our marriage is the wind beneath my wings. *Amo te.*

Last, but certainly not least, I offer thanks to my publisher; And to my editor, Lauren Weiler. Your insight and attention to detail were amazing.

<u>Dedication</u>

For Irene.
She was my mother-in-law and my pal.
I was her Mechanical Genius.

Chapter One

Amber heard the hum of hushed whispers, moving desks, and scooting chairs in her normally quiet and orderly classroom. Somewhere deep inside her mind she knew what to do to regain control. She was a master teacher, for God's sake. This was simple classroom management.

"What's up with her?" one kid whispered to another. "Look…the way she's twisting at her hair."

"I know. Weird, right?" He tucked a long, slightly greasy strand of hair behind his ear. "Look at her expression. Friggin wild. Scary." He swallowed and spoke up. "Ms. James?"

Amber gaped into the wide eyes of her students. "Shhh," she said, "he's listening to us." She was petrified and wanted to scream. She didn't dare. "We have to be quiet." She crouched down below desk level. "He can hurt us. He's done it before. Shhh…we have to hide."

A kid in the front row spoke up. "Who can hurt us, Ms. James?"

"Shhh," Amber said. "He can…and he's coming…now…bzzzzzzz." She galloped like a wild filly to the rear of her classroom. "We have to run."

The long haired kid leaned over again. "That's it. We need help." He nodded toward the door. "You keep her talking while I slip out."

1

KA Moll

***

Sawyer tipped back in her leather chair, a victim statement in one hand and her second cup of steaming black coffee in the other. She was in a couple hours ahead of schedule trying to review statements and consider evidence while the usually chaotic bullpen was still quiet. Soon, the other detectives would trickle in and it would be all over. She took another sip of coffee, adjusted her Glock 9mm shoulder holster, and reached into the cardboard box for her second chocolate glazed donut.

Sawyer loved everything about being a cop. She thrived on it–solving the crimes, incarcerating the criminals, and that intoxicating rush of adrenaline that always accompanied danger. This job was who she was; she did it well, and it was all she had. She had the intellect and edge of a great detective, which is the main reason that all the nightmare cases gravitated to her load. She growled with each new assignment, but the growls were a smokescreen. Sawyer loved the heavy load–loved the challenge. It kept her mind engaged enough to stay sober–at least during the workday.

This case was complicated, probably the most complex of her career. It was the reason Sawyer was in so early. She had to figure out how all the pieces fit together and she had to do it quick. The attacks were increasing in frequency and severity. It was only a matter of time before rape led to murder. She had to catch him, the rapist, before that happened. Sawyer dropped her forehead into her palm to think just as the phone on the corner of her desk rang. It snapped her to her senses and she answered.

Coming to Terms

"Detective James," Sawyer said as she brushed donut crumbs from the front of her freshly pressed blue trousers. The caller was the principal at Tampa High. "A nervous breakdown…Amber?" Her breathing quickened. "You called an ambulance?" She flew forward in her chair. "Oh my God…I'm on my way."

Sawyer hung up and darted out the door. It was 65 minutes from Sarasota to Tampa General unless she ran with lights and siren, which of course she did. She squealed into an emergency vehicle parking space in less than 45, right on time. She'd been monitoring the communications between Amber's ambulance and the hospital on her police radio and knew it should have just arrived.

Sawyer shoved her keys into her pocket and ran. She was scared breathless by the time she skidded to a halt at the rear of the vehicle. Her heartbeat was wild in her chest. It was a struggle to hold it together, but she did…at least until the paramedic opened the rear door of the ambulance and she caught a glimpse of the straps that held Amber to the gurney. With clenched fists, she catapulted over the edge. "What the hell?" Her eyes glared fury. "You get those fucking straps off my sister."

Spit splattered in the paramedic's face. She looked up, but didn't remove the straps or engage Sawyer.

Amber surged. She twisted, struggled, and jerked frantically against all her restraints until one loosened. As quick as a flash of lightening, she had a grip on the paramedic's waistband. The woman gently pried her fingers loose and her partner re-secured the strap.

"Your sister was swinging and clawing like that when we got to the school this morning," the paramedic said. "She had those school folks scared half to death." The woman met Sawyer's gaze. "We had to strap her down for everyone's safety." She gave the gurney strap an extra tug. "Don't worry, they'll give her something pretty soon. It'll settle her right down."

Sawyer looked away from the paramedic, trying to hold onto her sister's gaze. Amber's wild frenzy, most likely psychosis, made her look so much older than her 35 years. They were identical twins, and yet at this moment, Amber didn't even look like Sawyer's distant relative. She was virtually unrecognizable to her, even though she'd seen her just yesterday. A wave of nausea overtook Sawyer as she flashed back to all they'd been through together—their secret—their shared experience.

"Shh, you're okay," Sawyer choked as she reached to brush away a wisp of tangled hair.

Amber screamed the scream of an injured animal caught in a trap.

Sawyer jumped back.

Amber's eyes widened. Her face contorted unnaturally and she began to froth at the mouth. She grunted and squealed the squeals of a wild boar.

Chills shot down Sawyer's spine. Her teeth chattered. She clenched her jaw to still them and met the paramedic's gaze. "Please help her."

The paramedic responded and whisked Amber away. "Good luck," she said with a nod to Sawyer.

Sawyer watched the gurney zip down the hallway and into an exam room. She started to follow, but didn't. Instead, she headed for the ER admitting desk to provide the required information. It was a necessary nuisance. Afterward, she reluctantly took a seat. Knots squeezed the contents of her stomach into her throat by the spoonful as she waited.

Eventually, the striking redhead appeared and extended her hand. "Sage Carson, I'm a social worker on the psychiatric unit. I'll be Amber's therapist while she's here."

Sawyer shook the offered hand and held on. By that point, both barrels were loaded and ready. "Well, it's about time! Do you realize that I've been sitting here for well over an hour without a single update?"

Others in the waiting room turned their heads and took notice.

Sawyer glared. "Do you people not get that part of your job is to communicate with family?" She dropped the social worker's hand. "You're all fucking incompetent."

Sage locked eyes with the obnoxious family member. "Please lower your voice. I do apologize for the length of your wait. However, our first responsibility is to our patient and she kept us fully occupied this past hour. I came with an update as soon as I could."

Sage took a breath and tried to control her temper. "It's important to remember that this is not about you, it's about your sister." She turned to head down the corridor. "Now if you'll come with me, I'll take you to see Amber's psychiatrist."

"Lead the way," Sawyer said as she ran her fingers through her hair. "I'm right behind you."

Sawyer twiddled with her Smartphone in one hand and drummed the glass top table with the other. Waiting again. Finally, a soft knock and the door opened. She watched without a word as the squinty-eyed man in his late 40s and the attractive redhead laid their manila folders on the table and sat down. Her volley of questions and list of demands launched like torpedoes.

"Your sister is resting comfortably," Dr. Perry said, "but only with the aid of a potent tranquilizer. She'll need a thorough medical examination, a psychiatric evaluation, and of course, hospitalization. It may take days or weeks for us to make progress. You'll need to be patient."

Sawyer felt a vein twitch in her neck. Fear and anger consumed her. Self-control slipped through her grasp. What a condescending bastard. She broke into a sweat. "My sister's not crazy." She glared at the psychiatrist and then Sage. "Amber's smart, witty, and totally sane. If you people are trying to say she's schizophrenic, you're the ones who are crazy!"

Sage scooted closer and gently laid her hand on Sawyer's arm. "At this point, we're not trying to say anything other than we need to do a work-up for possible schizophrenia. We're doing that because Amber's symptoms would be consistent with that diagnosis." She saw terror flicker in Sawyer's cobalt-blue eyes and felt an urge to ease her fears. "Schizophrenia is just one possibility. We'll know better what we're dealing with in a few days. Let's not place our total focus on worst-case scenarios. There are many less serious conditions that could explain your sister's current symptoms."

"I want to see her," Sawyer demanded.

Sage shook her head slowly. "We can't allow you to do that right now. Amber's fearful of virtually everyone, including you. We need to give her some time and space to calm down and let her medications take effect." She pursed her lips. "I'm very sorry, but you'll just have to wait until she's ready."

Sawyer clinched her fists. "You people can't stop me from seeing my sister. I'm her medical power of attorney, for God's sake."

"I'm afraid we can, if it's in her best interest," Sage said as she gazed into the defiant eyes. "I'm sorry, but we can."

Sawyer shoved back and her chair almost took a tumble. "Well then, I guess I just won't admit her."

Sage stood and again met her gaze. "I'm sorry, but that's not something that you have control of at this point either. Amber's been assessed to be a danger to herself and possibly others. It's our responsibility to assure her safety as well as those she might come in contact with."

"Fine!" Sawyer spun and flung open the door. Once she'd exited the building, she broke into a run.

***

"They're identical twins?" Dr. Perry asked in disbelief.

Sawyer's manner and style had thrown Sage off too. She'd checked the record just to be sure. "It's hard to believe, but they are."

"If we are dealing with schizophrenia, Detective James will be at a significantly higher risk for developing the disorder," Dr. Perry said. "You'll need to address that issue with her during your sessions."

"Yes, Doctor," Sage said with a shake of her head. "That is, if she'll meet with me." Her eyes widened. "The detective is quite volatile."

Dr. Perry picked up his folder. "Then let's hope that she does."

7

Sage was exhausted by the end of her day. It seemed like all she'd done was run between new admissions and fires on the unit. She dropped into the bucket seat of her blue Mustang just a few minutes after 5:00, cranked her radio loud enough to rumble the dash, and did what she always did on a Wednesday night. She headed for Sarasota to have dinner with her parents. The difference between her drive to Sarasota this evening and all the others, was that she couldn't seem to get the angry detective with the short brown hair and the intense blue eyes out of her mind.

***

Sawyer jerked the driver's door of her cruiser open and flopped onto the firm leather seat. She was pissed off. It'd been an unproductive day during which she'd felt almost totally out of control. She jammed down the accelerator and backed with a squeal out of her reserved space in the Sarasota PD parking lot. The cruiser just naturally headed for one of the few places that she felt comfortable.

"Hey there, SD," the bartender called out as the bell on the front door announced the new arrival. "You aren't usually in here on Wednesdays."

"Hey there, Butch," Sawyer sighed as she slumped onto her favorite bar stool. "No, not usually, but my sister's not available for dinner tonight, so here I am." She flashed a sham of a grin and laid the first of several five-dollar bills on the counter. "Give me the usual."

"Miller Lite with a lemon-lime twist coming right up," Butch called out as he popped the top on the bottle and slid a bowl of freshly cut lemon and lime slices down the worn mahogany bar.

Sawyer squeezed several slices into her beer and took a quick swig. She closed her eyes and enjoyed the sensation of the ice-cold beer as it slid down her throat. Then, she tipped the bottle back and chug-a-lugged the rest. "Mmm, that was good. I think it calls for another." She knew a row of empties would be lined up in front of her before she'd call it a night.

Chapter Two

Sage was thankful to have been blessed with wonderful parents. She tried never to take their unconditional love and support for granted. Bob and Jenny Carson had raised her to be a kind and responsible daughter. They'd cared for her grandparents and now it was her privilege to care for them.

"So, you never did tell me what you think about your daddy's condition," Jenny said the moment her husband shuffled into the next room. "You being a clinical social worker and all, I know you know a lot more about this than you're letting on." She gazed into her daughter's eyes. "I'm already worried, sweetie. Just tell me what you think we're up against."

Sage's eyes filled with love and tears. "I think daddy's getting more confused and his short-term memory is almost gone." She heard her words and felt a catch of emotion in the back of her throat. "It's almost gone and he's already on the strongest dosage of medication the doctor can give him. There's nothing more that can be done for him beyond that, which means that it's only a matter of time before he gets a lot worse. You're doing a good job taking care of him now…but I think you need help. You look tired Mama and I'm worried about you too." Sage stroked her mom's cheek. "I could help you arrange respite if you want."

"Not yet," Jenny choked as she looked into her only child's eyes. "Soon maybe, but not yet. We're just not ready."

Sage nodded. "Okay, whatever you say. I trust you to know when it's time." She fought back insistent tears. "Alzheimer's is an awful disease, as hard on caregivers as it is the patient. Please don't wait until daddy's disease makes you sick too."

Jenny jumped up. "I'd better see where your daddy's gotten to. Lately, he's been getting lost on his way back from the bathroom." She ran down the hall.

Sage heard her mom locate her dad in the back bedroom. "You need any help?" she called out.

"No," Jenny said as she led her husband back into the living room, "I've got him. We're fine."

Sage looked up and smiled. "Hi, Daddy." She patted the seat of a second chair at the card table. "How about you come sit with me. We can work on a jigsaw puzzle."

Bob Carson's kind brown eyes looked into his daughter's, first with confusion, then with a spark of recognition. "Okay, honey." He smiled a warm, but distant smile. "I like jigsaw puzzles."

Sage hugged his neck. "I know you do, Daddy." She enjoyed their Wednesday night 100 piece puzzle. It was one of very few activities that her dad could still almost do on his own. After they'd finished, she kissed the top of his balding head and announced that it was time for her to head back to Tampa. She grabbed her purse, kissed her mom, and headed for the door. "See you guys next Wednesday." She met her mom's eye and paused. "Unless you need me sooner. I love you both."

"We love you too," Jenny said as she followed her daughter to the porch. "Drive carefully and call us when you get home."

"I will," Sage said as she tossed her purse into the passenger seat. She waved one more time, turned on her music, and headed for the interstate. By the time she entered the ramp she was lost in thought about her life, her failed marriage, her parents, and for some strange reason, those gorgeous blue eyes that had stared her down.

***

Sawyer stumbled onto the elevator. She leaned against the wall and rode up to the third floor of her building. The doors opened and she stepped off, dizzy. She leaned again until she felt steady enough to resume a forward stagger down the hall that led to her two-bedroom condo. Snoop met her at the door.

"Such a good boy," she slurred as she patted the head of her big German shepherd. At one time, he'd been her partner on the K9 Narcotics Unit, the best partner she'd ever had. After he was injured and retired from active duty, she'd transferred off the unit. It just wasn't the same without him. "Sorry big guy, but you have to wait until I can see straight before you get your supper. I had a few too many–again." She shook her head in disgust. "This is it, though. No more. Starting tonight, I'm turning over a new leaf." She made it to the living room couch and collapsed. Snoop dropped to the floor beside her. The worn leather felt soft against her skin. That, combined with her current level of intoxication, knocked her out.

Coming to Terms

After several hours, Sawyer stirred to Snoop's cold nose nudging her hand. She sat up and dropped back down. A splintering headache had come out of nowhere. Her brain was exploding. She pressed her thumbs deep into her temples. It didn't help.

Snoop nosed her again.

"Okay, okay…just a minute…I'm getting up…just give me a minute." Finally, Sawyer stood on sea legs and stumbled toward the kitchen. She reached for the can of Alpo on the shelf, opened it, and plopped the cylindrical chunk into the bowl. The dog food smell made her nauseous and she hurried to the toilet to throw up.

***

It was sunrise before Sawyer awoke in bed, still hung over. She squinted and tried to see the digital clock on her nightstand, but her eyes refused to focus. She swung her legs over the side of the bed and stumbled to the shower. The steaming hot spray felt good, but it didn't solve her biggest problem, the damn headache.

Snoop sat outside the bathroom door. It had become his morning ritual to watch his master dress. Sawyer knew he was disappointed that he couldn't go. "Sorry, buddy. You have to stay home and guard the house. I'm headed up to Tampa today and it's too hot to leave you in the car." She pulled on her blue trousers, buckled her belt, and slid her Glock 9 mm into her shoulder holster. With a finger combing of her damp hair and a scratch of the big dog's ears, she was on her way. "See you tonight. You be a good boy."

***

Sawyer paced as she checked her smart phone for messages. Waiting again. What a pain in the ass. "Come on, Ms. Carson. Get to work." She'd arrived at the hospital early in hopes of seeing Amber before her shift started. If the social worker didn't get here soon, that wasn't going to happen. "Come on. Some of us don't have all day."

As if on cue, Sage came around the corner. "Well good morning, Detective. You're here bright and early."

"Morning," Sawyer growled. "I want to see Amber."

Sage pursed her lips and inhaled. "She may or may not be able to receive visitors yet." She unlocked her office door. "Have a seat if you want. I'll check on her and be right back." Sage looked into Sawyer's eyes. "Don't get your hopes up."

Sawyer considered sitting down, but couldn't. The blood pounding inside her head was too loud. Instead, she paced in and out of the doorway. After a few minutes, she reached for her Smartphone. Distraction was her best hope of maintaining control. Five minutes turned into 25 before she spotted Sage come back around the corner. Her expression was clear. She had no intention of allowing a visit. Sawyer clenched her fists and jaw.

"I see you're upset," Sage said. "Come in. I'll fix us a cup of coffee and we'll talk."

Sawyer positioned herself, angry and defiant by the door. "No, thanks."

"You want to see your sister this morning," Sage said softly. "I get that. Amber's just not ready for visitors yet. I'm sorry, but she's just not. She's my patient and I have to put her needs first. Be angry at me if you must, but I just can't let you see her, not today." Their gazes locked. "I cannot set Amber up to lose ground just to please you."

Sawyer stepped inside the door. She immediately felt confined, like a wild colt must feel after being tied to a hitching post. Panic gripped her and she began to pace. "When? If not today, when?"

"Soon, but I can't tell you exactly when. Hopefully, we'll get Amber more grounded in reality as we titrate her medication levels. She's still immersed in the terror of her psychosis and very fragile. We have to protect her. You want her safe and protected too. I know you do. Why don't we just agree to work together to help her? You might find that approach to be more helpful to Amber and a lot less stressful for you."

Sawyer blew out a breath. "I do want her safe and protected."

Sage smiled. "I know you do."

*"*We need you to help us, so that we can help Amber," Sage said softly. "Do you think you could meet with me a few mornings this next week? Maybe help me get to know who your sister was before the psychosis? We need to figure out what triggered Amber's psychotic break. Once we do, we'll be able to work together to help her find her path back to reality."

Sawyer began to pace again. This time, her hands were fisted tightly in her pockets. A couple beads of sweat trickled down her face. "I can do that. When?"

"How about I come in a bit early for a few days. That way, our meetings won't interfere so much with your work schedule. Would 7:00 work?"

"Yeah, that's good," Sawyer said with a turn toward the door. "I'll see you tomorrow."

***

Sage leaned onto her elbow and propped her head in her palm. She had a lot to think about–personally and professionally. Never before had she fought so hard to keep professional distance, to maintain control. From the moment she saw Sawyer trembling in her doorway, she had an overwhelming urge to hold her. God, they were both so fragile. Amber might be her patient, but Sage knew without a doubt that she'd have to help them both.

It was a most unproductive workday and Sage was glad when it was finally over. All she wanted, no, needed, was to slip into her riding clothes, hop on her bike, and ride. Every therapist needs a therapist. The bike was hers, and she had a serious need for therapy time. At almost 40, Sage had been taken aback by a tidal wave of new and unsettling feelings. Her stomach fluttered like it did during her first junior high crush. She planned to peddle until she understood how the obnoxious detective, a woman no less, had not only caught her eye, but also had stolen her heart.

***

The crushed shells crackled between the rows of coconut palms as the white cruiser came to a stop in front of trailer #5. It was one of the oldest trailers in the park, but well maintained.

Sawyer knew she couldn't go to the bar two nights in a row and this was as good a place as any. She'd be with people she cared about, people who cared about her. It's funny how years can make such a difference.

"Hey there good-lookin," the sexy blonde called out through her front screen door. "What brings you over our way?" Laurie assumed her most provocative stance. "I'll bet you came to see me."

Sawyer grinned. "Watch it now. You're gonna get us in trouble again."

"Aw, Jo don't care," Laurie said loud enough to be heard inside the trailer. "Do ya, baby?"

"I'm used to it after 10 years," Jo said as she stepped onto the porch.

She nodded to Sawyer. "Hey there, SD. Want a beer?"

Laurie glared.

Her partner paid her no attention.

"Love one," Sawyer said. "How'd ya know?"

"Just a lucky guess," Jo called out as she headed back inside.

Sawyer cruised Laurie's skimpy attire with her eyes. Her full breasts and round ass always did command full attention. "You're as beautiful as ever."

Laurie adjusted her stance and short shorts with a wink. "Even at 55 with all my wrinkles, huh?" She gave her bikini top a tug. "I'll bet you say that to all your ex-girlfriends."

Sawyer shook her head. "Now you know there aren't any other ex-girlfriends. You were my first and only." Her smile was tender as she brushed Laurie's cheek. "You know you'll always be special to me."

Sawyer caught a whiff of cigarette smoke as Jo stepped onto the porch. "Here you go," she said with a toss of an unopened bottle of Miller Lite. Jo's gaze turned to Laurie. "Did I give you two enough time? If not, I can go back inside and let you finish up."

"That's enough," Sawyer said. "It's not as funny as it used to be."

Jo grinned and slapped Sawyer's back. "Just kidding, pal. I know you two wouldn't mess around right under my nose."

Sawyer pinned the smart-ass to the wall with her eyes. "And you know we haven't been together in over a decade."

Jo shook her head and laughed. "Drink your beer. I'll throw three steaks on the grill."

***

It was a fun evening except for Jo's smart remarks and her constant scowl. She always managed to dampen a good time, especially if it looked like Sawyer was relaxed and having fun.

"It's been good," Sawyer said, "but I need to be on my way." She stood and headed for the door. "Thanks for the hospitality."

Laurie got up to walk her out. "I know you came for a reason. You don't just socialize and you never stop by unannounced."

She met Sawyer's beautiful blue eyes. "Sometimes I think I know you better than you know yourself. What's wrong, honey?"

Sawyer shook her head. "It's nothing. I just needed to be with people tonight and you guys are my people. Kind of sad, isn't it? The woman I dumped 15 years ago, her partner, and my sister are my only people."

Laurie touched Sawyer's cheek. "Aw, sweetie. You were just a 21-year-old baby back then. You didn't know what you were throwing away." She winked. "Now you do and that's all that matters to me." She straightened Sawyer's collar. "How about you take me to lunch one of these days? I've been itching to try that Mexican restaurant, the new one over on University. Jo won't go, but I'll bet you will."

"Uh-huh," Sawyer said. "You know my weakness and you use it against me." She smiled. "Sure. I'd love to take you to lunch." Her brow furrowed in concern. "You sure Jo won't mind?"

Laurie made a face. "No way. She'll be fine with it."

"I'm not so sure you're being totally honest with me about that," Sawyer said, "or with yourself for that matter."

Laurie knew she wasn't either, but didn't care. She rose up to kiss Sawyer on her cheek. "It'll be fine. We're just friends now and Jo knows it."

Sawyer met her ex's gaze. "You do know that I know that we're going to lunch because you think I need to talk, right?"

"I know," Laurie said with a smile. "But I care about you…that's okay, isn't it?"

"Yeah, it's okay. I'm glad we made it through our rough patch." Sawyer brushed a lock of hair from Laurie's eyes.

"Yeah, me too," Laurie said. "And Sawyer…whatever it is, it's not as bad as you think. It'll be okay. You're strong and you'll get through it."

"You know me too well," Sawyer said as she dropped into her cruiser.

Laurie touched her arm. "Yeah sweetie, I do." She watched until Sawyer was out of sight and then went back inside.

"SD seemed different tonight," Jo said as she wiped down the yellowing laminate kitchen counter. "Preoccupied or something." She looked up to meet Laurie's eye. "So, is dropping by unannounced gonna become a regular thing with her now or what?"

Laurie assumed her perturbed stance and expression. "No, tonight was different. She's got some kind of problem right now. Even you know that she's got to be really troubled before she seeks out companionship. Sawyer always thinks she's got her shit hidden under that shell of hers, but she doesn't. I can see right through it."

"Oh yeah," Jo said with a hint of sarcasm. "You see right through it, don't you baby?"

Laurie loaded the last glass into the dishwasher, a luxury that many of her neighbors didn't have. "What's that supposed to mean?"

"I don't know," Jo said. "You figure it out."

"Sawyer's taking me to lunch next week so we can talk about whatever's going on." Laurie pushed the button to start the wash cycle.

"Of course she is," Jo snarled. "I'm sure she'll talk really well when you two are all alone in some secluded corner of a nice restaurant." She threw her rag into the sink. "I don't get how you can still be around her after the way she treated you when you guys broke up. She beat you up, for God's sake—treated you like a piece of garbage. Now you rub all over her like a cat in heat. It makes me sick to my stomach."

"I do not," Laurie sneered. "We're just friends."

Jo rolled her eyes. "Yeah, right."

Laurie added a plate and slammed the door hard enough to rattle glasses. "SD got mean back then because she was scared. I understood that then and I understand it now. She was just a scared kid when we were together. I forgave her and we moved on. That's all there is to it."

"Well, I guess it's just lucky for me that she got tired of you," Jo said as she yanked Laurie into her arms and began to roughly feel her up. She squeezed Laurie's breasts and grabbed her crotch. "I'm so lucky I got her sloppy-seconds."

Laurie pushed away. Her upper lip curled in disgust. "You're drunk, Jo. Get your hands off me!"

"I thought you liked drunks," Jo said as she grabbed another bottle of beer from the refrigerator. She twisted off the cap and headed for the door. It slammed as she stepped onto the porch.

Laurie didn't follow. It was good to have some peace and quiet.

Chapter Three

Sleep was one of many things that had always come easy to Sage, but not last night. Last night, she'd tossed and turned until she'd finally given up. Her body and mind just wouldn't stop, wouldn't let her sleep. She rolled out of bed just before dawn and tottered to the bathroom. Sage stepped into the shower, immediately sticking her head under the spray. The hot water pounded, but it didn't help. Nothing did. She just couldn't get those mesmerizing blue eyes, that low authoritative voice, out of her head. Sage went ahead and dressed for work. The sooner she got there, the sooner she'd have the chance to see the woman who singlehandedly was driving her crazy.

Sage arrived over an hour early. She was glad. Early meant she had extra time to prepare for what she expected would be a difficult session. She heard footsteps and looked up to find Sawyer standing in her doorway. Sawyer looked so scared. Sage wanted to hold her, but instead she just smiled. "Come in. Can I fix you a cup of coffee?"

Sawyer nodded. "Thanks…black."

Sage poured the steaming beverage into her favorite mug and handed it to Sawyer. "I appreciate your coming in."

Sawyer took a sip. "I had to, didn't I? You said Amber needed me. I didn't see any other choice or I wouldn't be here. I can assure you of that. I don't do shrinks." She sat down on the end of the couch, stiff and edgy, in a constant state of motion.

Sage had practiced long enough to know that today would not be easy. Sawyer was one high-strung, skittish, and oh-so rude detective. She expected that considerable patience would be required to get her to the point she trusted enough to open up and share the details of her life.

"So, Amber's a teacher," Sage said as she settled back into her chair. She took a sip of coffee. "Tell me about her."

Sawyer took a breath and let it go. "Well, let's see…she teaches high school history. Her classes are always full." Sawyer smiled. "She's pretty well-liked, really creative. She puts a lot of effort into her lessons and her students." She smiled again. "Won the national award for teacher of the year once—got to go to Washington D.C. and everything. She's like one of those teachers you remember at your 20th reunion. You know what I mean?"

Sage smiled warmly. "Yeah, I think I do. Sounds like she's given you good reason to be very proud."

"Yeah, she has," Sawyer said. "She's the best. They don't come any better than Amber."

Sage noticed the tightening of Sawyer's jaw. "Good, that helps. It gives me an idea of who Amber was in the workplace. Career choices and performance often say a lot about a person." She glanced at the handgun visible just inside Sawyer's jacket. Then, against her will, her eyes moved upward.

23

Sawyer caught her and their gazes locked. "Career choices do say a lot." She leaned back and stretched her arm across the back of the couch. "What do you think being a social worker says about you?" Sawyer seemed more comfortable, confident.

Sage smiled. "I think it says I care about people. It also says I can be a strong advocate for them if they need me to be."

"Okay," Sawyer said. "I'll buy that."

Sage continued. "I think it also says that I care about their feelings." Her gaze lingered longer than was typical. She felt her internal temperature rise as her pulse quickened. She recognized desire and, for a brief moment, felt afraid. Sage rubbed the back of her neck. "So, tell me about Amber as a child. What was it like to be her twin sister? To grow up together?"

Sawyer froze and began to sweat. She checked her watch, reached for her Smartphone, and squirmed in her seat. "Uh…I don't know. She was just a regular kid, that's all." She gripped the arm of the couch so hard that Sage was sure she saw the blood being squeezed from her knuckles.

Sage leaned forward. She paused to give Sawyer a moment and then continued. "How about your family? Do you have any other siblings?"

Sawyer shifted her gaze and position. "Nope, it's just us." She crossed and uncrossed her legs.

Sage tilted her head and took off her glasses. "Okay, well how about your parents? What were they like?"

Sawyer gulped a breath, stood, and began to pace. She paced, but didn't bolt.

Sage watched Sawyer become increasingly agitated with each subsequent question. It wasn't her intention, but she seemed to be forcing her to step on dangerous ground. What in the world had happened? Why couldn't she find a safe topic? She stood to look directly into Sawyer's eyes. Patient or not, she had to intervene. She gently placed her hand on Sawyer's upper arm and nudged. "Sit with me a minute. You're okay, just sit with me." Sage inhaled and exhaled, hoping Sawyer would follow her lead. She did, and Sage sat quietly next to her. No questions, just breathing. Sawyer breathed too.

After quite a while, Sawyer spoke. "You've probably already figured out that this is going to be very hard for me." She looked to Sage. "I'll try to give you what you need, but it may be more than I can do."

Sage smiled and touched Sawyer's hand. "I know you will and I'll be right here with you all the way. If you'll let me, I'll help. I really do want to help you, Sawyer."

Sawyer looked away, and then back to Sage. "I'll need you to."

Sage could see that Sawyer couldn't take much more today. "You want to see your sister for a few minutes? She's doing better. Still immersed in her psychosis, but not as fearful. A bit more communicative, too." Sage wrinkled her brow. "She's been talking a lot about a room under the stairs and a dog named Sadie, just bits and pieces of experience or psychosis. We're just not sure." She raised an eyebrow and shook her head. "This could take a while, but we're starting to make progress." She stood and met Sawyer's gaze. "Want to?"

"Of course I want to," Sawyer said. "Lead the way."

"Now, don't expect too much," Sage said. "Amber still has a very long way to go."

***

Amber sat in a chair beside her hospital bed studying each of her fingers with keen interest. She didn't look up when Sawyer and Sage came into her room.

"Hi Sis...it's me, SD. How ya doing, sweetie?" Sawyer's voice was kind. She sat down on the bed. "I talked to Mr. Simms. He says your students are asking about you. They want you to get well really soon...I do too."

Amber didn't respond. She just continued with her careful finger examination, that is, until Sawyer reached over and tried to touch her hand. Unfortunately, her response was in the form of a blood-curdling scream. It didn't stop until a nurse came running into the room and sedated her.

Sawyer looked like she was going to be sick. "Please help her...I'll do whatever you need me to do." Her moist eyes met Sage's. "Please help her get better."

Sage smiled. "We'll do our best. You can count on it. Amber's not well, but she's better today than she was yesterday. It just takes time and patience." Sage put her hand on Sawyer's upper arm. "How about we call it a day. I'll bet you're exhausted."

"I am," Sawyer said with an audible exhale. "I'll see you tomorrow."

Sage called to Sawyer, as she was about to turn the corner. "What's the 'D' stand for?"

Sawyer turned around, confused. "What?" Then she grinned. "Oh, it's Dane...Sawyer Dane."

"Just wondered," Sage said with a smile. "See you tomorrow."

***

Sage sought out her friend before heading home that evening. She wanted to thank her for her quick response, but hadn't had time. Cathy was a skilled psychiatric nurse. Thank God, because without her prompt assessment and intervention that morning, the situation with Amber would have rolled straight downhill. She was also one of the few people at the hospital that Sage would ever trust enough to confide in.

"Hey, thanks for coming on the run this morning," Sage said as she slid her night's reading material into her briefcase. "We were losing it pretty fast in there."

Cathy grinned. "No problem. You call, I run. That's the way it's always been, right?"

Sage chuckled. "Yeah, if you say so." She shook her head. "Perspective is everything."

"Want to grab a cup of coffee before we head out?" Cathy asked. "I'm in absolutely no hurry to get home to do the ton of laundry that's waiting for me."

Sage raised an eyebrow. "Not fixing dinner tonight?"

"Nope." Cathy's eyes twinkled. "Mike has a double shift and the kids are with their Nana. I'm as free as a bird…except for the laundry."

"Cool," Sage said. "Their loss is my gain. How about Starbucks?"

"Sounds wonderful, a hot cup of coffee and you can tell me all about whatever it is that's kept you so preoccupied." Cathy cocked her head and locked their eyes. "I know it's something interesting because it makes you blush."

***

Sage took her first sip of coffee. "Table in the corner okay?"

Cathy grinned. "Perfect, we'll have lots of privacy." She settled into a chair and immediately caught Sage's eye. "Okay, I can't stand it any longer. I know you're up to something. Come on girl, take pity on me and tell me what's going on."

Sage squirmed and looked away. "I don't know. It's just been a strange couple of days. I think I'm going through some kind of self-discovery phase or mid-life crisis or something. I can't sleep." Her eyes widened as she shook her head. "I might be going crazy."

Cathy rolled her eyes. "You're not going crazy."

Sage smiled. "I know…thanks for asking. I need to talk and I don't think I'd have mentioned this on my own." She took a breath to summon her courage. "I'm so confused, Cathy, and yet, I'm not confused at all. It's bizarre." She exhaled. "See, there's this detective…."

Cathy laughed. "Oh my! I was hoping it would be a guy." She winked. "Is he cute? I'll bet he is if he's caught your eye."

Sage sighed. "It's a she. If you ask me if she's cute, I've got an answer." Sage waited for Cathy to process what she'd just said.

Cathy inhaled an audible breath. "Well…okay then. That explains a lot…." She looked into Sage's eyes and smiled. "So, is she cute?"

Sage shut her eyes for a moment. She opened them and smiled back. "She's got the most amazing blue eyes…and body," Sage sighed. "Oh my God, what am I going to do?" She laid her forehead into her palm.

"What do you want to do?" Cathy asked.

Sage lifted her head and looked into Cathy's eyes. "I don't know, because if this isn't a mid-life crisis, then it's me discovering the real reason that I don't date." She dropped her head back into her hand and talked softly to the table. "Do you think I'm a lesbian?"

Cathy touched Sage's arm. "It's not what I think that counts, honey. It's what you think. Either way, it doesn't matter as long as you're happy."

Sage knew her friend was right. "I've never felt this way before, never even close with my ex-husband. He knew it too." She chuckled. "Thus, the reason for our divorce." She held her head again. "Now, I've got this non-stop fantasy. I can't ever remember having man fantasies." She bit her lower lip. "And certainly none that ever drove me to the point of orgasm…not until now."

Cathy raised an eyebrow. "Okay then. I think that's our biggest clue. So have you two talked about any of this?"

"Oh my God," Sage said. "Are you kidding? It's too complicated. She may not even be gay for all I know. And even if she were a lesbian, I wouldn't know where to begin this conversation. I have absolutely no point of reference for this, none whatsoever." She shook her head and looked away. "I shouldn't have said anything. I don't know what's wrong with me. I'm just so confused."

Cathy smiled and laid her hand on Sage's arm. "I'm your best friend and you can always talk to me…about anything." Her gaze was tender. "If you're meant to be with this woman, with any woman, you'll know what to do and say when the time comes. In the meantime, I think you need to relax and go for a bike ride."

Sage smiled. "Good advice. You'd make a good social worker, you know."

Chapter Four

Sawyer was always soothed by the chatter on her police radio. The same was true for close proximity to vast bodies of salt water. She made sure to absorb plenty of both each day on her way to and from work. It helped her settle her mind, usually, but not tonight. Tonight, she was wired. It had been a day full of worry about Amber and thoughts of Sage.

Sawyer's visit to the hospital had turned out to be as unsettling as she'd expected. Amber had been almost as upset as she was the morning the ambulance had brought her in. She'd thought about that all day and knew she'd have to summon the courage to help her. But she was afraid, something she rarely admitted to herself, and never to another person. Today, she'd come to the realization that if she wanted Amber back, as she was, she'd have to let Sage in on her secret. Tomorrow, she'd have to speak the unspeakable and tell her what she'd never told anyone before. Somehow, telling Sage seemed easier, but that didn't change the fact that she needed a drink to help her get through the night. She promised herself she'd have just one. It was a promise she'd made many times before, but had always broken. She set her jaw and decided tonight would be different. She parked in her usual spot and went inside.

"Hey Butch," Sawyer called out as she walked through the door. "How about one for the road."

"You got it," the bartender said. He popped the top, slipped on two slices of citrus, and handed the bottle to Sawyer.

Sawyer took a slug and sat down at the bar. "Just one and no more. I mean it, Butch."

"Okay pal, you got it."

***

Sage had cleared her morning schedule just in case Sawyer was in the mood to talk. She was in early again and suspected the detective would be too. She looked up and smiled when she heard footsteps approach her office door. "Good morning. I thought you might be here before 7:00. Come in." Sawyer's eyes looked troubled, even more than they had the day before. "Want a cup of coffee?"

Sawyer's facial muscles tightened. "No…thanks though." Her eyes held on. "My stomach's a little off this morning." She sat down, popped up, and then paced to the far wall.

Sage watched Sawyer study the framed print before her. She examined it closely and then paced some more. She fidgeted with her keys, her sunglasses, her Smartphone, and papers on Sage's desk. Sage patiently waited and hoped that she'd settle on her own. Finally, she gave up and stood to shut her office door. She sat back down and patted the seat next to her. "Come sit by me."

Sawyer paused and looked up. Her voice cracked as she spoke. "I have things to tell you this morning."

Sage smiled tenderly. "I know you do. Come sit down."

Sawyer paced a tight circle and then crossed the room. "I don't know where to begin."

"Just start," Sage whispered. "Come sit down."

Sawyer sat, stood, paced, studied the print, and sat again. She blew out a breath and began. "He said if we told he'd kill our dog. Her name was Sadie. He was mean. Our dad was a really mean man, especially when he was drunk. We knew he'd do it, knew he'd kill her, probably just blow her head off, so we did what he wanted. We always did whatever our dad told us to do."

Nausea climbed into Sage's throat, but she swallowed it down. She had suspected sexual abuse based on Sawyer's reactions to her questions the day before. Now she knew that her suspicions were about to be confirmed. She needed to focus and help her get through what would most likely be a very difficult disclosure. "You're safe with me…go on."

Sawyer took another breath. "I think we were about six the first time. The last time I know for sure. We were 16." She swallowed hard. "It was the day our mom died…just before. He made us do everything to him that day, and to each other. It made us sick, but we did it anyway. What else could we do?"

Sage took slow and steady breaths. She had to hold herself together. It was worse than she'd imagined—years of abuse. Her mind went for a moment to her own happy childhood. She pulled it back and forced it to listen to the other extreme. Normally, she wouldn't have blinked, but in this situation she did, and she knew why. "You're doing fine, just push through."

Sawyer gulped air deep into her lungs. "We were weak. No, I was weak...and worthless. It's a wonder that one of us didn't get pregnant in that smelly little room." She paused. Her lower lip and chin began to quiver. "Our dad was one sick bastard." She stood and walked to the door.

Sage held her breath, but didn't say a word. She waited.

Sawyer took a deep breath and sat back down. "We left the day they buried our mom. I don't know how we managed, but we made our way from Illinois to Florida and never went back. We stayed anywhere that Sadie could stay too. Eventually, we ended up in Sarasota with Laurie." Sawyer smiled a sweet smile and then looked away. "Sadie died that next year. We buried her in Laurie's backyard."

Sage touched Sawyer's arm.

"I'm so sorry."Sawyer's voice was filled with anguish as she continued. "Laurie put a roof over our heads and made sure we finished high school." A tender smile crossed her face. "I fell in love with her that year. She was, still is, a very beautiful woman. She was my first. We were together for five years before I left after a drunken rage." Sawyer paused as an expression of sadness and regret eclipsed her face. "It's been one long dry spell for me ever since. Amber's never really had a relationship that I know of, other than a boyfriend that she toyed with for a little while in high school." She met Sage's gaze. "He didn't suit her, you know?" Sawyer's fidgeting stopped.

"I think I do," Sage said softly.

"We've never told anyone about any of this," Sawyer said. "We made a pact to never talk about it. We couldn't, you know? We had to put it behind us." She sighed. "I just felt like I had to tell you so that you could help Amber. I feel bad, but…."

Sawyer had disclosed without a single tear. Sage knew what she needed to do to help her heal. It wouldn't be easy for either of them, but she had to. "Come sit beside me."

Sawyer walked across the room. She sucked in a breath like you might do on a crisp fall day and met Sage's gaze. "Well, that wasn't too bad," Sawyer said as she sucked in another breath and stretched. "I'm surprised too because I was sure it'd be horrible. I thought telling you about this would literally drop me to my knees. But here I am, still standing."

Sage pursed her lips. "So, how do you feel?"

Sawyer sucked in another breath and looked around. "Surprisingly good. Like I said, I didn't think I'd make it through this in one piece, but I did and I'm okay." She grinned a too-wide grin. "The things we do for a sister, huh?" She raised an eyebrow. "So what do you think? You're the social worker."

Sage's gaze remained fixed as she took a breath. "I think you're still in a lot of pain."

Sawyer sucked in air and locked her jaw, trying desperately to maintain her composure. "God Sage…no…." She swallowed back insistent tears. "Please don't do this to me… I can't."

"Yes you can," Sage said softly. She laid her hand on Sawyer's bouncing knee. "You're strong—strong enough to feel your pain. Feel it Sawyer, and then let it go." Sage opened her arms and pulled Sawyer close. She kissed the top of her head and felt Sawyer's shoulders begin to heave. "You're safe, baby. I've got you. You're safe with me."

***

Sawyer turned the corner just as Laurie stepped onto the porch. They could talk about anything now and she enjoyed the time they spent together more than ever. That hadn't always been the case, but now it was. It was good to have finally moved through the painful period that had followed their break-up. She smiled as Laurie ran out to jump in her car. She was such a beauty. Too bad Jo didn't appreciate her.

"It's hard to believe that Amber's been in the hospital for two weeks already," Sawyer said as she bit off half a taco, chewed, and swallowed. "At least now they've finally got her back to her old self again."

Laurie washed down her bite with a sip of iced tea and crinkled her brow. "So what is it that's wrong with her again?"

Sawyer swallowed the second half of her taco. "Well, they ended up diagnosing her with something called 'brief psychotic disorder'. I guess it looks a lot like schizophrenia, but doesn't last as long. If it comes back…." Sawyer cleared her throat. "Anyway, it's not very common. Usually it's triggered by a traumatic event or something." She shook her head. "That's the problem—Amber didn't have one, at least not one that we know of."

Laurie nodded. "It's good she's back on track."

"Yeah, it is." Sawyer smiled. "Mostly, I think it's because she's got a really good therapist."

Laurie looked up mid-bite. "Uh-huh…and what else?"

Sawyer shrugged. "Nothing, that's all."

Laurie raised an eyebrow. "Then why are you all flushed?" She pursed her lips and squinted her eyes. "You like her, don't you?"

Sawyer squirmed uncomfortably. "Maybe, but it's not going anywhere." She shook her head. "She's way ethical and probably not gay." She shrugged again and met Laurie's gaze. "I got a couple vibes, but I don't know." She dipped a chip deep into the salsa. "Don't worry, it's not going anywhere. You above all people know why."

"Uh-huh…sure." Laurie leaned back. "So, what's she look like?"

Sawyer's gaze drifted out the window. She felt her internal temperature rise. "She's beautiful." She bit her lower lip. "She's got shoulder-length red hair and gorgeous emerald green eyes." She looked back to Laurie. "A few years older."

"Older never used to be a problem," Laurie said. "Is it now?"

"Nope, not at all." Sawyer felt a twinge inside. "Might as well go back to your lunch because I'm done talking."

"Uh-huh," Laurie said. "I'll bet you are."

***

Sawyer was glad she hadn't made any late day appointments because lunch had extended well into the afternoon. By the time she got back to the bullpen, most of the other detectives were either out on interviews or gone for the day. She poured a cup of coffee and settled into her chair to enjoy the few moments of quiet. It wasn't long before she returned to puzzling over what had caused Amber's break from reality. Her mind just seemed to naturally go there these days.

Sawyer decided that the best thing to do might be to approach the problem as if it were a case. She pulled out her notebook and began to brainstorm a list of possibilities. Then, she embarked on the process of ruling them in or out one by one.

She picked up the phone and dialed a familiar number. "Good afternoon. Is Mr. Simms available? Thank you, I'll wait…doing much better, thanks for asking…. Hey Greg, I'm just trying to figure out if something unusual might have happened to my sister just before her breakdown…. Got a phone call? Huh…."

Sawyer hung up and dialed again. "Hello, Detective James, Sarasota…I need phone records for Tampa High School. The last 30 days will do fine, thanks. Oh, and I need phone records for Amber James too, 1616 North Lemon Street, Tampa. Yeah, the same dates. Okay, tomorrow's good…thanks."

Sawyer finished her long list of calls and called it a day. She grabbed a quick burger and ate it on her way to Tampa. She looked forward to her visits with Amber and also to the possibility that she might see Sage. Tonight, she'd gotten away late and didn't expect to be so lucky, but she was.

"I didn't expect to find you here," Sawyer said as she poked her head around the doorway. "It's pretty late."

Sage looked up from her work. "Hey there, Detective." She smiled and held her gaze. "Yep, working late. I've got a report to finish before tomorrow's staffing." She shook her head. "I don't know why I always have to wait until the last minute."

"Well, I won't keep you then," Sawyer said. "I just wanted to stop in and say hi. Amber's getting a quick visit too. Snoop and I still have to check on her apartment, water her plants, and get her mail. It's our new routine. Amber doing okay today?"

"She's doing very well," Sage said. "I know she'll be pleased to see you regardless of how long you stay." Sage cocked her head and pinched her brow. "Who's Snoop?"

"He's my dog," Sawyer said with a smile. "I'll have to introduce you two one of these days. You'll like each other."

Sage grinned. "I'm sure we will." Her gaze lingered. "I'm glad you stopped by. I got used to seeing you in the morning. It was a nice way to start my day."

"Yeah, it was," Sawyer said as she made a sweep up Sage's body with her eyes. "Evening's good too."

Sage blushed and smiled.

"Catch you next time," Sawyer said with a wink. "Don't work too hard."

The report took less time to write than Sage anticipated. She had her key in her hand ready to lock up when her desk phone rang. For a moment, she considered not answering, but the nurses knew she was working late to finish her report and wouldn't call unless there was a problem. She answered. "Mark James?" She exhaled. "He's not to go near that room. I'm on my way."

***

Sawyer scooped the mail out of the box and let herself into her sister's comfortable two-bedroom apartment. She smiled as she walked through the rooms thinking the place was totally Amber. It was quite a showplace with its mid-century décor and bright 70s colors. If Amber hadn't been a teacher, she could've easily been an interior decorator. She was so creative. Satisfied that all looked in order, Sawyer sat down at the breakfast bar and began absently sorting through her twin's gigantic stack of junk mail. How in the world could one person accumulate so much? She was glad that Amber had told her that all of her bills came electronically. It would make the decisions as to what to throw away much easier.

Sawyer pressed play on the answering machine and listened to her sister's new messages. There were a couple from friends in her bridge club, one from the parent of a student needing to retake a test, and then one that came in within minutes of her arrival. Sawyer's pulse raced as she listened to that message. Her head filled with rage. She shot straight out of her chair, flew down the stairs, and out the door. The cruiser tires squealed back and then forward. Sawyer slammed the accelerator to the floor, flipped on the lights and siren, and flew out of the parking lot. She radioed her destination, Tampa General Hospital, and requested back up. Her adrenaline pumped hard–ready for battle. "You bastard!"

Sawyer switched the lights and siren off as she cruised quietly up the ramp and into the hospital parking garage. She scanned for Illinois license plates along each and every row. As she swung around the corner onto the second level, she noticed movement in the shadows and heard a woman's echoed screams in the distance. Her blood ran cold. She slammed on the breaks and jumped out of the cruiser–weapon drawn. Snoop joined her on command. They approached low and fast on foot.

"Oh God. No…not Sage," she choked out loud. She was crying, naked on the cement floor. Her clothes, the beautiful silky cream blouse, was ripped to shreds.

Sawyer lunged forward with a wild scream as the bastard climbed on top. She grabbed Mark James by the back of his scrawny neck, lifted him high, and slammed him face down in the middle of the downward lane. His head bounced and his forehead began to spurt blood onto the pavement. Mark lay motionless. He could be dead for all she cared. Sawyer picked up his gun and hunting knife and ran to Sage.

With a groan, Mark regained consciousness. He rose up off the pavement and met Sawyer's gaze.

"Hello, Dad," Sawyer said. Her voice was stone cold.

She looked to Snoop.

He perked his ears.

Sawyer barked two commands. "Snoop! Bite. Track."

The dog snarled and sprang forward.

Sawyer watched panic creep into the bastard's wide eyes. He got to his feet and vaulted bare-assed across the parking garage–much faster than she would have expected, all things considered. Vicious, snapping canine jaws can have that effect. Sawyer listened to her dad's screams until they faded into the distance. He was being pursued by one of the best police dogs she'd ever had the pleasure of working with. She knew he'd stay right with him until he finally took him down. She hoped he'd tear him to shreds when he did.

Sawyer was just beginning to assess the extent of Sage's injuries when she noticed a significant amount of blood beginning to pool underneath her slashed leg. She scrambled to apply pressure as she choked back an urge to vomit.

Sage's eyes fluttered open. She reached up to brush Sawyer's cheek. "Hey you. Don't cry, I'll be okay."

Sawyer lay over Sage and gently kissed her forehead. "I'm so sorry, baby."

Sirens in the distance signaled that help would soon arrive. The minutes seemed like an eternity.

Sage cried out as the paramedics lifted her onto the stretcher.

"Be careful with her," Sawyer growled.

"We will, Detective," one said as he worked to start an IV. "We'll be very careful." He smiled and met Sawyer's gaze. "Just step back a little so we can get to her."

Sage reached for Sawyer's hand as she was wheeled toward the ER.

"I'm here," Sawyer said softly. "I'll be right here waiting for you."

Chapter Five

Sawyer was instructed to take a seat and promised that someone would be with her as soon as they could. Déjà vu, waiting again. She pulled out her phone and dialed the psychiatric unit to check on Amber. Thank God she was all right. She stood, paced, and then resumed her position between the mom with her squalling baby and the elderly man. The hiss of the ER door called her attention to the young Tampa officer who had just entered.

"We have your dog, Detective," he said.

Sawyer assumed the worst. Her heart raced as she met his gaze.

"Don't worry," the officer said. "He's okay. Too bad he got trapped inside the fence or he'd have had our suspect down. He's a good dog. Want us to put him in your car?"

Sawyer's heart rate and breathing slowed to normal. "Yes, thank you. Just make sure to roll the window down."

"Will do," he said. "Oh, I almost forgot." He turned around. "We'll need to get your statement…the victim's, too." He cocked his head. "Do you know her?"

Sawyer shifted her position. "I do. Her name is Sage Carson. She's a social worker here at the hospital."

Officer Crawford raised an eyebrow. "You don't happen to know the suspect too, do you?"

"Yep," Sawyer said with a thin smile. "Guess it's your lucky day. His name is Mark James. I haven't checked recently, but my guess is that he's still on parole out of Illinois from drug trafficking. Wouldn't surprise me if he had a sexual assault, too." She fixed her gaze. "Catch him for me."

The officer nodded and smiled back. "You bet, Detective."

***

The nurse called Sawyer's name after only 30 minutes. "Ms. Carson has asked to see you. They still have more to do, but she's requesting that you be in the exam room with her. If you'll follow me, I'll take you back."

Sawyer jumped up. "Thank you for coming to get me. I'll be right behind you." Her thoughts ran wild as she followed along toward the exam room. Sage was probably going to be okay, otherwise she wouldn't be going back at this point…but what if she wasn't?

The nurse indicated the room, but didn't go in. Neither did Sawyer. Instead, she stood outside the door. She needed a few minutes to settle down. Sage would notice if she was upset and she didn't want to worry her.

Sawyer peeked inside. It looked like Sage was asleep, maybe sedated. She nudged the door open and padded toward the exam table. Even battered and bruised, she was beautiful. Sawyer gently pulled the sheet up to cover Sage's exposed breast.

Sage's eyes opened and their gazes met.

"I'm so sorry this happened," Sawyer whispered. "So sorry he hurt you." Her voice was shaking.

"I'm just glad you were here," Sage said. A soft sob escaped. "I was so scared."

Sawyer closed the distance and pulled Sage into her arms.

Sage snuggled against her chest as her shoulders began to heave.

"Shh, you're okay," Sawyer said as she kissed the top of her head. "You're safe with me." She rocked her gently until she fell asleep.

Sawyer must have dozed too, because she startled when the curtain whipped open.

"How's she doing?" the nurse asked.

Sawyer furrowed her brow in confusion. She'd been waiting patiently to ask the very same question for at least an hour.

The nurse must have noticed. "I'm Cathy," she said. "We met briefly awhile back. I work upstairs with Sage." Her eyes twinkled. "I'm guessing you must be her detective. I'm also guessing that you're still waiting on an update.

Sawyer raised an eyebrow. "Correct on both counts. Sawyer James, Ma'am."

"Pleased to meet you," Cathy said. "I must say, I've heard a lot about you."

Sawyer grinned. "All good I hope."

"All very good," Cathy said with a chuckle.

Sawyer nodded toward Sage. "I just got her to sleep." She frowned. "But we could wake her if you want."

"No," Cathy said. "Let her sleep. Just tell her that I stopped by to check on her when she wakes up."

KA Moll

Sawyer nodded. "I'll tell her."

***

Sage slept until the ER doctor stepped back into the exam room. When he did, her eyes opened and looked for Sawyer. Sage reached for her hand. "Stay with me."

"I'm right here," Sawyer said. "I'm not going anywhere."

The doctor stepped closer. "You're going to be fine. Your x-rays didn't show any sign of fracture and we've stitched up the laceration on your leg. As expected, we also saw no sign of vaginal or anal tearing."

Sawyer began to crack her knuckles.

Sage reached out to squeeze Sawyer's hand.

The doctor paused, but then continued. "You did hit your head pretty hard. Although we saw no sign of concussion, you do need someone to be with you for at least the next 24 hours. You can go home tonight if you can meet that requirement."

Sawyer looked to Sage and then to the doctor. "She can. Either I'll stay with her or she can stay with me."

The doctor smiled. "Sounds like a good plan. I'll have the discharge paperwork drawn up and brought in for your signature." He looked to Sage. "I want you to call if you have any of the symptoms that we discussed."

Sage nodded. "I will, Doc." She smiled a half-hearted smile. "Thanks."

The doctor left and Sage swung her legs over the side of the bed. "I need you to go up to my office and get me a change of clothes." She picked up the pile of her shredded clothing. "These certainly aren't fit to wear. My duffle bag is in the bottom drawer of the cabinet by the door. The keys are in my purse."

***

Sage dressed in her biking clothes. They were the only extras she kept at the office. The nurse went over the discharge paperwork, Sage signed, and was ready to be on her way. She could have walked, but the nurse insisted on wheeling her to the door. Hospital policy. Sawyer had retrieved the cruiser from the garage and was waiting outside. Sage got in with minimal assistance.

"Wow," Sage said. "I've never been in one of these before." She smiled and caught Sawyer's eye. "That's a good thing, right?"

Sawyer grinned. "It is...unless you're me." She shook her head. "I can't imagine not being in one of these every single day of my life."

Sage held Sawyer's gaze. "Thanks for doing this. You don't have to, you know. I could still go to my parents'."

"Are you kidding? It's the least I can do." Sawyer smiled. "Plus, it's my pleasure."

A wet nose poked through. "Well hello there," Sage said. "You must be Snoop." She rubbed the big dog's head. "I've heard a lot about you. You were a good boy tonight."

Sawyer looked over and met her dog's eye. He wagged his tail. "You were a good boy, weren't you buddy?" Her attention returned to her driving.

Sage gave Sawyer directions to her apartment. As they made their way across town, she noticed her grip tightening on the steering wheel. Sage was sure she knew what was going on. "If you grip that wheel any tighter," Sage said, "your fingers are going to fall off. Do you want to talk about it?"

"No, I'm good," Sawyer said through a clenched jaw.

Sage took a breath. She knew what Sawyer needed to hear. "He didn't rape me." Silence. "Did you hear me, Sawyer? Your dad didn't rape me. He didn't because you showed up. I don't know how you knew to be there, but you did. You probably saved my life." She reached over to touch Sawyer's hand. Sage felt Sawyer's muscles tighten and heard her suck in a breath. She stroked lightly with her fingertips and continued. "He touched me, but he didn't penetrate me." She caught back a sob as she leaned forward to look into Sawyer's eyes. "I'm okay, sweetheart. I probably wouldn't have even gotten the cut on my leg if I hadn't been kicking."

Sawyer slammed her palm against the wheel. "Son of a bitch! Out of all his fucking choices, why the hell did he have to pick you?"

Sage took another breath. "Maybe because I realized who he was earlier this evening and prevented him from seeing Amber. He probably waited until I packed up to leave and then followed me out."

Sawyer's face reddened. "He'll pay dearly for this." Her eyes filled with angry tears. "He'll pay the ultimate price for hurting you."

Sage rubbed her leg. "I'm okay, just a cut and a couple bruises." She needed to help Sawyer put the incident out of mind. "Let's talk about something else, okay?"

Sawyer nodded but didn't say anything.

"I'll bet this thing's fun with the lights and siren," Sage said hoping that Sawyer would take the bait and relax.

Sawyer turned to meet her gaze. "It is." She smiled playfully and flipped switches to demonstrate. The lights flashed and the siren wailed. She pressed the accelerator to the floor and the cruiser shot forward at an incredible speed.

They laughed. Sawyer was more relaxed, but Sage was still a bundle of nerves. It was no wonder. She had just survived a violent attack. But then there was also that little matter of spending the night alone with Sawyer, the woman who now played the leading role in her increasingly sexualized dreams. Yeah, that could make a person nervous, especially if that person had never had a sexual experience with another woman.

Sawyer parked in the space nearest the front door of Sage's apartment building. She looked around. "Nice place. I love the palms…and the pool."

Sage smiled. "Thanks, I like it." She nodded across the parking lot. "You can park in my carport if you want. It's right over there."

"Thanks, but I think I'd better keep the cruiser a bit closer to the door. You sure you're okay with Snoop staying the night? I could run him home."

Sage shook her head and made a face. "Of course I'm okay. After tonight, I wouldn't boot him out if my life depended on it."

Sawyer nodded. "Okay then, he stays. Don't worry, he's better behaved than most kids."

Snoop crouched low and barked.

"Come on, big guy," Sawyer said. "Let's get Sage settled in."

***

Sage unlocked the door and the trio stepped inside. "Sorry to leave you on your own, but I've just got to have a shower." She limped a little as she headed toward the bathroom. "Make yourself at home."

"Okay, I will. How about I fix us something to drink?"

"Perfect," Sage said. "Iced tea for me."

Sawyer located the kitchen with no trouble. The glasses were easy to find too. A quick search of the refrigerator and she poured the tea. She'd just set the drinks on the coffee table when she heard Sage call out her name. Sawyer was afraid Sage had a problem and ran to see. She skidded to a halt just inside the bathroom door. Sage was perfectly fine, naked and dripping in the shower. Sawyer sucked in her breath.

"Would you hand me a towel?" Sage asked in what could easily have been interpreted as a seductive tone.

Sawyer exhaled. She yanked a towel off the rack, tossed it into the shower, and stomped into the living room. She was still seething when Sage joined her. They sat without words for what seemed like an eternity.

"So, do you want to tell me what just happened in there?" Sage asked softly. She clearly didn't have a clue.

Sawyer glared. "You tell me. What did just happen?"

"I don't understand what you're so angry about," Sage said. "Are you going to tell me?"

Sawyer looked away, then turned and glared. Sage calling her into the bathroom had been intentional and it'd had nothing to do with the need for a towel. It might be irrational, but she was furious. "Do you even know what you're doing?" She clenched and unclenched her fists. "I don't think you do."

"Why are you acting this way, being so mean?" Sage asked as her eyes filled with tears. She got up, marched to her bedroom, and slammed the door.

A framed print fell to the floor with a thump. Sawyer got up to return it to its place on the dining room wall and sat back down. She needed a drink worse than ever.

*****

Sage cried until she finally fell asleep. It's funny how sleeping on a problem can help you gain perspective. When she awoke around 2:00, she saw the situation much more clearly. She got up, slipped on her robe, and headed for the living room. She found Sawyer lying on her back, wide awake, staring at the ceiling.

Sage dropped down beside her and looked her in the eyes. "You're absolutely right, I don't know what I'm doing. I just know I have feelings that I've never had before. I'm shaking inside and I don't know what to do. Never in my life have I ever noticed a woman the way I notice you." She paused to wipe a tear as it trickled down her cheek. "You're right, I don't know what I'm doing, but I do know what I want. I want you."

Sawyer's eyes brimmed with tears. Her body trembled and she looked away. "You're playing with fire. You're smart enough to know that, right?"

Sage could see Sawyer struggling with her emotion and laid her hand on her arm. "What's going on?"

Sawyer didn't respond, not with words anyway. She swallowed hard and swallowed again.

"I read people pretty well," Sage said. "I think you're interested in me, too."

Sawyer gripped the couch cushion. "I'm interested."

"Good," Sage said with a smile. "Now we're getting somewhere." Her eyes held onto Sawyer's. "I think you're afraid, maybe because you'd be my first, or maybe because you think you'll hurt me somehow."

Sawyer looked away. "Both."

"Alright," Sage said. "What else?"

Sawyer's eyes were angry again. "If we do this thing, it's not going to be just a fast fuck on the couch." She choked, but continued. "And it's not going to be on the same night that my bastard dad put his hands all over you." She shook her head and curled her lip in disgust. "I don't get how you could even think about this after what happened to you tonight."

"I get that," Sage said as tears streamed down both of her cheeks. "I'm sorry I pushed you." She stood, walked slowly back to her bedroom, and quietly shut the door.

"You've got to give me some time," Sawyer called out. "I just need time."

Sage didn't respond. She also didn't sleep another wink. When she got up, just three hours later, an unsettling chill was in the air. She regretted the way she'd left things with Sawyer last night. She knew better. She also knew they should talk. She was just still too angry to carry the weight of the conversation. "I'm going to my parent's today," she said as Sawyer clipped on Snoop's leash. "Would you mind dropping me off on your way to work?"

"No problem," Sawyer said. "I've arranged security for you and Amber so don't be surprised if you see a patrol."

Sage picked up her bag and headed for the car. "Whatever…"

Chapter Six

Sawyer slumped over her desk, still upset over last night's angry words. She wondered if Sage was too. Determined to be productive in spite of it, she picked up her serial rapist file for the umpteenth review. Sawyer had the feeling that something significant was right in front of her. She just couldn't see it, couldn't seem to anticipate his next move. Sawyer struggled to concentrate as she read the file again, but the details of Sage's attack kept invading. Then, as if a light bulb had gone on in her head, she knew why. That's the way it always happened for her, but this time was different. This time it was personal. Sawyer picked up the phone and dialed Tampa P.D., knowing now that their case was intimately connected.

Sawyer ended up feeling good about the day, mostly because she was pretty sure she made a breakthrough on her case and Tampa's. It was good, and yet at the same time it made her skin crawl. She turned the corner onto Sea Breeze and slowed. It was her second pass by the well maintained home. She peered through the arched windows again hoping to catch a glimpse of Sage. She wanted to stop, wanted to apologize for how she'd acted, wanted to take back the hurtful things she'd said, but she didn't. Instead, she just drove on. Her condo was only three blocks away.

***

Sawyer stopped to let Snoop out. Within 15 minutes, she'd changed clothes and was back in the car. She needed a drink. She also needed to talk to someone. She wasn't sure which she needed worse. She dialed the number she knew by heart. "You and Jo want to meet me at Butch's? Okay…then how about just you? I'll be inside." Sawyer had finished her third when her ex stepped through the door.

Laurie stretched up and slid onto the bar stool next to Sawyer. "Hi baby." She leaned over and gave Sawyer a squeeze around her shoulders. "Rough day?"

"Yeah, you could say that," Sawyer mumbled. "Iced tea?"

Laurie smiled. "Yep, the usual. Want to move to a booth?"

"Yeah, okay." Sawyer picked up both drinks and moved them to the more secluded location. "Thanks for coming." She shook her head. "I'm a mess. Bet you wonder if I'm ever gonna grow up and cut the umbilical cord."

Laurie laid her hand on Sawyer's. "I'll always be here for you. Always."

Sawyer told Laurie everything that night, even the things she'd never told her before. Sage had gotten her started, and now she couldn't shut up. After her fifth, she looked into Laurie's eyes. "What am I going to do? I'm not fit for anyone, and Sage is so special. She wants me, but I can't be her first." She fell quiet and blinked away insistent tears. "I can't be her anything."

Laurie sat for a moment, reflecting on what Sawyer had shared. Sawyer was in as much pain as when she'd first come to her. In the 20 years they'd known each other, she'd never seen a public tear fall from Sawyer's eyes. Her tears spoke volumes. Laurie nodded to the bottle, looked over, and pinned Sawyer with her eyes. "That's your last one. You're done. I mean it."

"Yeah, okay," Sawyer said. "I was done anyway."

Laurie's gaze softened. "Don't say you're not fit, because you are. I wouldn't change a thing about you and I never would have left." She pursed her lips and sighed. "But your drinking is a serious problem and you need to get a handle on it. Sage could probably help you…if you'd let her." She brushed Sawyer's cheek with the back of her hand. "You can be gentle, you know, when you're not drinking." She looked away. "You used to be such a gentle lover. If you're not drunk, you won't hurt her."

Sawyer brushed a tear from Laurie's cheek with her thumb and looked into her eyes.

"We made love when you were sober," Laurie said softly. "Remember? You can do it again. If you want her, you need to get a handle on your drinking."

"I always loved you, you know," Sawyer said quietly, "and I never meant to hurt you."

Laurie smiled a sad smile. "I know, baby, I know."

***

Sawyer walked out of the bar that night having made a decision not to go back. She didn't either, not that week nor the two that followed. She was on a roll. Unfortunately, she'd been on that roll before. The path between drunk and sober was a familiar one. Three weeks was a long time for her though and it gave her hope. Maybe this time she'd stay on the wagon. She knew Laurie was right. She had to if she wanted Sage and she wanted her more than anything in the world.

Sawyer had managed to stay sober in spite of the fact she was consumed by worry. Soon Amber would be ready to go home. Once that occurred, she knew there'd be no more intentionally-accidental encounters at the hospital. She had to get things straightened out with Sage before it was too late. Why hadn't she just had the courage to talk to her? She knew Sage was giving her time. She knew it was her move. The pain that gnarled in the pit of her stomach told her that it was now or never, and she picked up the phone.

***

Sawyer wasn't the only one who was worried. Sage was too, and it was beginning to negatively impact the quality of her work. People, including Cathy, were beginning to notice.

"So what do you really think?" Sage asked for the second time. "Should I call her?"

Cathy sighed and answered again. This time, she was more blunt. "I think you care about her and I know she cares about you. I saw it in the way she held you that night in the ER. I think you're both being too stubborn for your own good. Better get your act together before Sawyer's sister gets discharged. Once that happens, she's gone.

"I know," Sage said. "I know…."

Cathy stood. "Okay, I can't sit here any longer. I've got work to do." She left Sage sitting at the break room table where she'd found her.

***

Sawyer pulled into the Carson driveway at 7:00 sharp. If she'd known it would be this easy, she'd have called Sage much sooner. She sat with the engine off and tried to decide whether she should walk up to the door or wait for Sage to come out. She opted to go to the door. It seemed proper. She climbed the steps and rang the doorbell. An older, but equally beautiful version of Sage answered.

Sawyer straightened her jacket. "Good evening. Sawyer James, Ma'am. Uh, I'm here to pick Sage up for dinner. We're...uh, friends."

Jenny held open the door and smiled. "I know who you are, Detective. Come in. Sage should be here in a minute. Can I offer you something to drink while you wait?"

Sawyer shifted from one foot to the other. "No, thank you, Ma'am. I'm fine."

"My daughter missed you." Jenny's gaze was piercing. "I'm glad you two finally resolved your issues."

"Uh...yes, Ma'am. Me too." She dabbed a bead of sweat from her brow, just as Sage came around the corner in a snug pair of designer jeans and a silky black blouse. It was unbuttoned way down. Sawyer swallowed hard.

Sage met Sawyer's wandering gaze with a blush.

"You two have a good time tonight," Jenny said. She looked to Sage. "Will you have time to stop by in the morning?"

Sage smiled and kissed her mom's cheek. "I should. Who knows, maybe I'll just stay all weekend." She stepped onto the porch.

Sawyer followed. "Your mom knows…uh…she knows this is a date?"

Sage made a face and then winked. "Of course she knows. I tell her everything."

***

The parking lot of The Old Salty Dog was full. Sawyer was glad she'd called ahead for a reservation. She'd chosen this place for its food and atmosphere. It was rustic, romantic, and had a five-star rating. Plus, its blackened grouper was amazing. She parked the cruiser and walked around to open the door for Sage. "God, you're beautiful." She chuckled. "I thought I was going to have a heart attack when you came out in that outfit."

"You look pretty good yourself," Sage said. "I don't think I've ever seen a jacket fit quite like that one." Her gaze lingered. She raised up to put her arms around Sawyer's neck, tilting her head as she kissed her on her lips. "God, I've wanted to do that for the longest time. I don't know what made me pick a parking lot to do it, though."

Sawyer did. It was the first time she'd really let down her defenses. Sage was a perceptive person. She'd sensed it. Sawyer pulled Sage close and kissed her again, deeper this time. She felt familiar panic well inside her, closed her eyes, and willed it back down. Sage had somehow given her the courage to try again.

Sage moaned and arched intimately into Sawyer's embrace. "Wow. I've never been kissed like that before."

Sawyer pushed away. "Come on." She smiled and tucked her arm around Sage's waist. "Let's go have dinner."

***

They stood inside the doorway behind two other couples. Sawyer scanned the restaurant as they waited their turn to be seated. Most of the tables were already occupied and she was once again pleased that she'd remembered to call ahead for a reservation. Tourist season wasn't even in full swing. The place was already hopping. Her gaze fell on a favorite table by the water. "I don't believe it." She shook her head and sighed. "I'm so sorry."

Sage furrowed her brow. "About what?"

"A huge mistake. I told Laurie where I planned to take you to dinner," Sawyer said with another sigh. She pointed with a nod. "There they are, right over there, waving at us. God, I'm so sorry."

A grin crept across Sage's face. "Laurie, as in your ex-girlfriend and first, that Laurie?"

"Yep, the one and only, and her partner, Jo." Sawyer shook her head, pursed her lips, and sighed. "We'll just say hello and then move on to another table."

Sage's eyes widened. "Are you kidding? We most certainly will not. We'll be joining them for dinner, that is, if we're invited." Her grin widened. "This should be quite interesting."

Sawyer groaned. "Oh, we'll be invited alright. I'm sure that was all part of Laurie's plan. She was determined to meet you. Now, she'll not only get to meet you, she'll get to spend the evening watching us together and visiting."

They walked over to the table and Sawyer locked eyes with Laurie. "So, exactly when did you two decide to eat here? I'm guessing around 4:00." She cocked her head and squinted one eye. "Am I close?"

"Well, let me see," Laurie said with a smile. "That sounds about right." She turned on her puppy eyes. "I had to. You would have taken forever to introduce Sage on your own."

Sawyer's eyes tacked Laurie to her seat. "We're not done with this conversation." She made introductions and they sat down.

Jo stood a moment later. "I'm on my way to the bar to get a beer." She looked to Sawyer. "Want one?"

Laurie glared, first at Jo and then at Sawyer.

"No thanks. You go ahead," Sawyer said. "I think we'll stick with iced tea this evening."

***

Although Sawyer hadn't planned on a double date, she had to admit the evening had turned out to be fun. She was surprised by how much she enjoyed seeing the two women in her life together. It was interesting how very different they were. In fact the only obvious similarity was body type. Everything was good until her Samsung rang and ruined everything.

Sawyer slid back in her chair. "Excuse me, I need to take this call." She swiped her phone. "Detective

James…uh-huh…God, no." She sighed. "Not again. On Tamiami near University—got it. Be there by—" She checked her watch. "2130."

Laurie shook her head and glanced across to Sage. "Might as well get prepared. I believe your evening is about to be cut short. It happens all the time."

Sawyer was shaking her head when she ended the call. "Bastard rapist. The son of a bitch just got another one." She pressed her lips together, then sighed. "God, it's a homicide this time." She looked to Sage. "Sorry, but I have to go. Would you mind if these guys took you home?"

Sage smiled and reached up to brush a lock of hair from Sawyer's eyes. "That's fine. Whatever you need to do is always good…as long as I get a rain check. I know being a detective has to come first right now. It's fine."

"You bet you'll get a rain check," Sawyer said as she leaned down to kiss Sage on the lips and across to kiss Laurie on the cheek. "Thanks." She shook Jo's hand, spun, and jogged toward the door.

***

Sage had been waiting for an opportunity to talk with Laurie without Jo being present. Finally, when Jo stood and headed back to the bar Sage leaned across the table. Her voice was low. "So, I'm dying to know what that glare was all about? You know, the one when we first got here."

Laurie pursed her lips. "Has Sawyer talked with you about anything? Recently, I mean?"

"No…I don't think so," Sage said.

Laurie sighed. "I can't say anything. It's not my place." She shook her head. "God, I want to, but I can't." Their eyes met. "You need to ask Sawyer. I'm sure she'll tell you if you ask her. Actually, it might help her begin a conversation that you two need to have anyway."

"I get that," Sage said with a nod. "I totally respect keeping someone's confidence. I'll talk to her." She smiled. "But I'm not done asking questions. How often does a person get alone time with an ex? It's like a golden opportunity. I can't waste it."

"Oh girl," Laurie said with a wide grin. "I like your style."

"You might not after you hear my questions." Sage looked directly into her eyes. "You still love Sawyer, don't you?"

Laurie inhaled, then exhaled slowly. "Well now, you don't mince words, do you?"

"No, not usually." Sage smiled. "I am a social worker, you know."

"Yeah," Laurie said, "I love her. I probably always will, but I'm no threat to you. Sawyer hasn't looked my way in 15 years and she's not gonna start now." She smiled tenderly. "She's only got eyes for you. I've never seen her look at anyone else that way, including me, not in 20 years." Her eyes moistened with tears. "I remember aching so bad after she left me. Thought about just ending it all, but then I got my head screwed on straight again and moved on. I found a way to survive without her. Jo isn't Sawyer, but she's better than nothing, and she's who I've got now."

Sage met Laurie's gaze. "I'm so sorry."

"It's okay…now," Laurie said. "We moved on." She dabbed the corner of her eye with a tissue. "Sawyer's a treasure. Love her well."

Sage reached across to hold Laurie's hand. "I will. And I don't feel threatened, even knowing how important you are to Sawyer and how important she is to you."

"I was her first," Laurie said. "A first always holds a special place in your heart. Sawyer's never been anyone's first before, but I know she'll be perfect. Just wait, you'll see."

Jo re-appeared. "What'd I miss?" she slurred as she sat down and took a slug of her beer.

Laurie looked disgusted. "That's your last. You hear me? You've had enough."

"Yeah, yeah, yeah...sure," Jo said as she tipped the bottle back and gulped the rest of the golden liquid down her throat.

"And I'm driving us home," Laurie added.

Jo curled her lip. "Yeah, sure you are."

Chapter Seven

Mark James crouched down in the thicket, far enough away so as to not be spotted but close enough to see everything clearly. He knew working a crime scene like he knew the back of his own hand. Mark trained his binoculars on the action. He watched as he looked forward to seeing her again. *Ah, there you are.*

The white cruiser squealed around the corner, coming to a stop alongside at least a half-dozen other police and emergency vehicles. Mark smiled with pride as he watched the tall muscular woman, with dark brown hair the color of his own, jump from her car and jog to join her brothers in blue. He fantasized that his daughter felt him near, as she stood over his latest bled-out victim. Sawyer had always been his favorite, his strongest child. She was the one most like him. He smiled again as he thought about her early years. Sawyer had been a little cop since the day she was born. And look at her now, in command of a bloody crime scene.

***

The familiar yellow tape marked the parameter of the gruesome scene. Sawyer scanned to assure the area had been properly secured before seeking out her briefing.

"Evening, Detective," the young patrol called out. "Sorry to interrupt your dinner. We called you instead of Jones even though he was on call. I hope that's okay. This one just seemed to fit your serial rapist's profile, except of course that this victim's dead."

"It was a good decision," Sawyer said. "What've we got?"

"Thirty-six year old female, throat slashed, clothes sliced off, left naked. Looks like it all occurred right over there in the marsh." He pointed. "Just beyond the jogging path. Looks like she'd been out for an evening run. The slash across her throat and down her thigh was the only obvious injuries."

Sawyer shook her head in disgust. "I'll take a look then you guys can start bagging the evidence." She made her way slowly toward the bastard's sixth victim. She pulled back the plastic and an image of the stitches that ran down Sage's thigh filled her mind. She sucked in a breath, nauseous. Then she did what any good cop would do. She swallowed it down and pushed through. Once she got her legs back under her, she called to arrange for increased surveillance on Sage, Amber, and her own condo. All she could do now was do what she could to protect them.

***

Sage knew something was up when the second unmarked patrol made a slow pass and then backed into a secluded location in good view of the residence. It was just before midnight. She peered out the window and could see the officer's gaze trained on their front door. Her thoughts flashed back to her own assault and she jumped up to be sure all of the door and window locks were secure. She'd always been an independent woman, perfectly capable of taking care of herself, but tonight she felt afraid and wanted Sawyer.

Finally, just before sunrise, the familiar white cruiser pulled into the driveway. Sage breathed a sigh of relief. She'd been sitting by the front window all night. She watched Sawyer get out and stumble toward the door. Sawyer looked exhausted. Sage ran to her before she could pull off her jacket.

"Oh honey," Sawyer said. "I'm really dirty. I don't think you want to get that close."

Sage nuzzled into her chest. "I think I do. She tightened her hold and pulled even closer. "Close is exactly where I want to be." She looked up and found Sawyer's eyes. "I know something happened." Sage began to cry. "I saw the extra patrol. I know it's worse than I was."

***

Sawyer held Sage and she told her all she knew. She hated to frighten her, but knew that the information could save her life. "This is a dangerous situation and I don't want you out without an officer until I tell you different." Sawyer was dead serious. "Do you hear me? I can't risk you being hurt again." She brushed a red curl behind Sage's ear. "I need you to promise that you won't leave without a police escort. I have to be able to focus and I can't if I'm worried about you."

"I promise," Sage said. "I'll stay right here until you return."

"Good," Sawyer said. "Now, I've got to go home and take a shower. Maybe if I'm lucky, I can catch a little sleep before I have to go in." She kissed Sage on her lips. "You gonna be okay?"

Sage raised an eyebrow. "Will you come back for dinner tonight?"

Sawyer smiled. "Sure I will."

Sage smiled back. "Then I'll be okay."

***

Jenny Carson stepped around the corner the moment the front door clicked shut.

Sage shook her head. "Tell me you weren't eavesdropping."

Jenny pursed her lips. "Maybe a little." She met her daughter's eye. "Sawyer's really worried. She's worried that guy will go after you again, isn't she?"

"Yeah mom, she is. But don't worry. Sawyer is really good at what she does. She's got patrols posted. We just need to stay inside. We're safe."

Jenny looked uncertain.

"Don't worry, Mama. She'll catch him." Sage hoped that what she'd just said was true. The muscles in her mom's face relaxed and Sage could tell that she believed her. Now, if she could only convince herself.

"She really cares about you," Jenny said softly. "I can tell."

"I know," Sage said. "I care about her too."

"Have you two…." Jenny paused and met Sage's gaze.

"Oh my God," Sage exclaimed. "I can't believe you'd ask me that." She felt herself blush. "I'm almost 40 and you were just about to ask me for details about my sex life." Her eyes widened. "You were, weren't you?"

Jenny chuckled. "Now sweetie, don't get your panties in a twist. I just didn't think you'd ever…well…leaned that way before. I just wondered. That's all." Jenny looked into her only child's eyes. "And I wanted to be sure you knew that you could talk to your old mom about it if you wanted to, even if you are almost 40." She paused "And…I wanted you to know that I was with a girl once, back when I was still in college." She smiled. "Well before your daddy stole my heart." She raised an eyebrow. "I'm here if you ever feel like you need to talk."

Sage stood with her mouth gaping wide. She was speechless. It was one of those times when she'd been given far more information than she wanted. Now she'd have to try to get that image out of her mind.

***

Sawyer drug-in well after 8:00. She was hungry and looked dead tired. Sage met her at the door and led her to her place at the table. A minute later, Jenny set a mouth-watering plate of food before her. Sawyer ate like she hadn't eaten in days, like she was starved.

"I'm sorry I was so late for dinner," Sawyer said. She shook her head. "Sometimes it's just hard to get away." She shoveled in her last bite of meatloaf and moaned. "Especially with a case like the one we're working now." Sawyer wiped up the gravy on her plate with bread as she met Jenny's eye. "The meal was wonderful. Thank you."

Jenny beamed with pleasure. "I'm glad you enjoyed it. My meatloaf was always one of Bob's favorites." She looked away. "I'm not sure he remembers that now."

"Well, now it's mine," Sawyer said with a wide grin.

Jenny picked up Sawyer's almost clean plate and headed for the kitchen. "I'll remember that you like it."

Sage followed to see if she could help.

"You go on now," Jenny said. "Go back in and spend time with Sawyer. I've got these." She smiled as she caught Sage's eye. "And Sage, I thawed an extra cinnamon roll. Just in case."

Sage shook her head. "She won't stay, Mama. She has to go home to let Snoop out."

"You're not very observant tonight," Jenny said. "I believe the dog is sitting in the passenger seat of her car. Go on, you tell her she can bring him in. They're both welcome to stay the night, if you want."

Sage went in to join Sawyer on the couch. "Snoop can come in if you want. He doesn't have to stay out in the car. In fact, my mom just made a point to tell me that you could both stay the night." Sage winked and smiled. "Want to?"

Sawyer flipped off the TV. She turned so that she could look Sage squarely in the eye. "There are some things I need to tell you. I guess tonight's as good a time as any." She got up to go get Snoop. "I'll be right back."

***

Sawyer sat back down on the couch. Sage scooted close and laid her head on her shoulder. The closeness felt good. They sat in silence as Sawyer struggled to find her words.

Sage waited for a while and then she spoke. "That was some stare Laurie gave you last night."

Sawyer nodded. "Yeah, she knows me pretty well."

Sage raised an eyebrow. "Uh-huh…"

Sawyer looked into Sage's eyes. "That's part of what we need to talk about." She squeezed the cushion and let it go. "Laurie didn't want me to have a beer because she knows I wouldn't stop. I have a problem." She swallowed the lump that had formed in her throat. "I drink too much and when I do, I can be violent."

"Okay," Sage said. "That happens to some people."

Sawyer felt the urge to run, but didn't. "Yeah, but I get really violent. Just ask Laurie." Her jaw clenched tight. "And the kicker…I haven't had sex in 15 years because of it. The panic attacks started, then I became a drunk." Sawyer looked away. She was afraid to tell Sage the rest of the story. Once she knew the truth that'd be it, but she had to tell her. She sucked in another breath and continued.

"The last time was with Laurie. We'd been out to the bar. As usual, I was wasted. She didn't want to that night. She knew I was drunk and I'd get too rough. I wanted to anyway. I wanted to because I knew I could. I always could, if I was drunk enough." Sawyer hung her head. Tears welled up in her eyes. "We argued all the way home. I wanted it. She didn't. I exploded the minute we got inside the door. I beat her bad and then I raped her." Sawyer caught back a soft sob. "I didn't know how bad she was hurt until the next morning. I was sick and so disgusted with myself. I left her that day, for her own good."

Sawyer looked into Sage's eyes. "I promised myself that I'd never get into a situation where anything like that could ever happen again, and I haven't. Until now. That's why I reacted like I did the other night. It scared me that you wanted more. I knew I could hurt you." She held Sage's gaze. "I was so afraid I'd hurt you, Sage."

Sage's voice was tender. "I'm not afraid you'll hurt me." She kissed Sawyer gently on her lips. "I want us to try."

"Me too," Sawyer said as tears streamed down her face. "I haven't had a drink in three weeks. I don't know how long this'll last, but for me three weeks is a pretty good start. I'm sober."

Chapter Eight

Sage couldn't believe she was in the same situation again. Being objective and therapeutic with someone you're falling in love with is virtually impossible. She'd proven that beyond a doubt the day Sawyer disclosed in her office. So how in the world could she possibly be in the same situation again? How could she not see a better option? It was a good question, but one for which she had no good answer.

"I'm sober," Sawyer said. "But if I'm sober, I can't have sex. I know I can't because I've tried. Before I even get started, a panic attack will swallow me whole." She touched Sage's cheek. "You deserve so much better than me."

Sage did the thing she did at least 20 times during every therapy session. She took off her glasses and rocked them between her forefinger and thumb. "So what happened just before everything changed?" She put the glasses back on. "I assume you had a normal sex life with Laurie up to that point. Am I right?"

Sawyer pinched her brow. "Yeah, I guess so. I don't know what happened. It all just changed in a split-second."

"How about counseling?" Sage asked. "Did you try that?"

Sawyer shook her head insistently. "No way." Her expression was pitiful. "I couldn't do that. I just couldn't."

Sage sat forward. She turned to look Sawyer squarely in the eye. "I know therapy scares you to death. I know that. But we got past your fear and made good progress not so long ago. Do you remember? You could handle it and you know it's what I think you need to do." She took a breath and couldn't believe she continued. "But for now, let's see if I can help." The glasses came off again. "So, not even one serious attempt since the last time with Laurie. Huh…."

Sawyer shook her head. "Nope, not one."

Sage nodded. "Fifteen years is a long time. People change in the course of a lifetime. You might just surprise yourself."

Sawyer cocked her head and raised both eyebrows. "You're the therapist, but I don't know…."

Sage slipped her glasses back on. "That's right, I am." Her eyes met Sawyer's. "Okay we'll try, but you need to know that our sex life is not going to be one big therapy session. I won't have it." Sage heard her words but couldn't believe she'd said them. They'd just fallen out her mouth without any warning. Never before had she been concerned about having a sex life at all. Sex was just something you had, when you felt too guilty not to. "And before we begin, I need you to agree that you'll go to counseling if what we try isn't effective." She watched Sawyer's quick intake of breath and responded. "Don't worry, you won't have to go alone. We'll go together, deal?"

"You drive a hard bargain," Sawyer said.

Sage smiled. "So I've been told."

Sawyer met her gaze. "You've got a deal, and you can be sure I'm gonna give this a valiant effort. No way do I want to go to counseling."

Sage patted Sawyer on the leg. "I expected no less." She paused until she had Sawyer's full attention. "You know, research has shown that drinking doesn't ease panic attacks. It actually triggers them."

Sawyer cocked her head. "Then wh—"

Sage held up her finger and stopped her question in mid-air. "Your initial panic attack was probably triggered by something quite random in your environment. Maybe it was a sound or a movement, something that was present during your victimization. You assumed that having sex had triggered the panic attack based on timing. I think your panic attacks may have actually continued simply because you expected them to. I also think it's possible that you worked yourself into one, each and every time you became aroused."

Sawyer leaned against the back of the couch. "So what do we do to fix me?"

Sage leaned back as well, confident. "I'll teach you a cognitive approach that will hopefully knock the wind right out of a panic attack. If you put in the effort you say you will to learn this technique, you might just fix yourself. You've got homework. I want you to have intense sexual fantasies over the next few days. You can fantasize about anyone you want to as long as you can convince your body that you're about to have sex. If, or rather when, you start to feel the initial symptoms of a panic attack, I want you to consciously refocus your thoughts to the worst possible outcome. Think about it, what's the worst thing that could possibly happen? Maybe you or your partner won't orgasm?"

"That's it?" Sawyer asked.

"That's it," Sage said. "Thus ends our therapeutic relationship. If you need more for us to have a sex life, then we go to counseling." She looked into Sawyer's apprehensive blue eyes and smiled. "Don't worry, it'll be okay. I'm good at this. You need to trust me...and do your homework."

Sawyer kissed Sage's forehead. "I do trust you and I will do my homework."

Sage stroked Sawyer's cheek and decided that this was as good a time as any to say what she needed to say as well. "You know, before you came into my life the possibility that I might be attracted to another woman had never crossed my mind." She shook her head. "Can you believe that? I'm almost 40 and it had literally never occurred to me that I might be a lesbian. It should have, I guess, because heaven knows I never felt sexual desire for a man, but it didn't." She looked away. "I remember feeling such relief when my divorce was finalized. It wasn't that we didn't get along, it was just that I grew so tired of having to come up with excuses to not have sex. It got old and I was relieved when it was over. I think he was, too." Sage took a deep breath and released it. "Everything's different with you. I feel desire and I want us to have a fulfilling sex life. I want it, but I can wait." She nestled against Sawyer's chest. "I just want you to know, that when you're ready, I'm ready. There'll be no excuses."

***

One street over and two houses down, a head poked above the mangroves. Mark settled into a comfortable position. The curtain was open and he could see inside. He raised his binoculars and watched his daughter kiss the pretty redhead. *Enjoy her while you can, SD. Soon, she'll be mine.*

***

Snoop crouched low and ran his nose along the bottom edge of the door. He snarled under his breath and then headed for the bedroom to wake Sawyer.

Sawyer was disoriented at first. She remembered going into Sage's bedroom to snuggle before heading home. They must have fallen asleep. She shook her head to sharpen her senses. Snoop would only wake her if there were a problem. She retrieved her arm from underneath Sage's head and sat up. "What is it boy?"

Snoop growled.

Sawyer gently lifted her handgun off the nightstand. "Hold on."

Sage sat up. Her brow was furrowed with concern. "What's wrong?"

Sawyer slid the Glock into her holster. "He thinks he heard something. I'll be back in a minute."

Sage's eyes widened and her mouth fell slightly open. "You're going out at this hour... alone?"

Sawyer couldn't help but chuckle. "Well, yeah." She raised an eyebrow. "It's kind of my job you know, to serve and protect." She smiled and kissed Sage on her forehead. "Don't worry, I'll be fine. Go back to sleep."

"Yeah, right," Sage said. "Fat chance of that happening."

"I know, but try anyway." Sawyer clipped the leash on Snoop's collar and gave it a tug. "Come on, big guy. Let's go take a look around."

Sawyer stepped onto the porch. All looked quiet, but she knew that looks could be deceiving. She nodded to the patrol and he nodded back. Her palm instinctively rested on the butt of her Glock as she walked the parameter of the property. It was a good 30 minutes before she came back inside.

"Nothing out of the ordinary," Sawyer said as she bent over to kiss Sage goodnight. "All quiet. I think I'll be on my way." She took Sage's head between her hands and gave her another quick kiss, this time on her forehead.

"Please be careful," Sage said softly. She read people better than some read the newspaper. She knew something was wrong.

Sawyer smiled. "Don't worry, I will. Just stay inside." She kissed her again. "I'll talk to you in the morning."

Sawyer hadn't been able to shake the uneasy feeling that someone had been watching her. She'd finally convinced herself that it must have been the patrol and came back inside. She'd take another look around on her way home.

***

Sawyer backed out of the driveway and crept up the street. She nodded as she passed the officer on duty and he nodded back. She parked just down from the Carson residence and released her seatbelt. Comfortable wasn't easy in a cruiser, but she'd try. She sensed the bastard was nearby. He was so close that she could almost smell him. She knew she'd be there for the long haul. There was no way she could leave Sage's safety in the hands of someone else.

After an hour or so, Sawyer figured she might as well make good use of her time and decided to do her homework. She willed her thoughts to drift back 15 years, prior to the last time she'd made love to Laurie— sober.

It had been a wild night. God, Laurie had been a fantastic lover. Sawyer remembered collapsing after coming three times in a row. Laurie had rolled off and reached across to the nightstand. She needed her drink and her after-the-love-making cigarette. After that, everything was a blur. All Sawyer remembered clearly was going crazy. She remembered Laurie jumping up, scared half to death. Laurie couldn't understand what had happened. She couldn't figure out why Sawyer had gotten so upset, why she was so panicked and furious. Sawyer remembered bolting. She'd been naked, but it didn't matter. She didn't know what was wrong with her, just that she had to get out of there. Sawyer was standing in the front yard when she finally came to her senses. Laurie was standing next her, crying hysterically. She'd been so afraid. Her eyes… God, those eyes.

Sawyer loved Laurie, but she'd known that night that nothing would ever be the same between them. She sensed somewhere deep inside that she'd never be able to return to their bed—not sober, anyway. She'd wished every single day that she wouldn't have ever tried. If she hadn't tried, she never would've have hurt her. The end of their relationship wasn't too far down the road. The suffocating sadness still lingered in Laurie's eyes after all these years. The sparkle that had once been there was gone most of the time. It broke her heart.

Sawyer cringed at the memories. She felt the squeeze in her throat, felt her heart race in her chest, and felt her body shake with tremors. She'd gulped down the nausea and struggled to do as Sage had instructed. She yanked herself back into the present. Her heartbeat slowed and she stopped hyperventilating. It worked.

Chapter Nine

Jenny was already up preparing breakfast when her daughter padded into the kitchen. "I see Sawyer didn't stay," she said as she stirred cheddar cheese into the scrambled eggs. "I thought maybe she would." She popped the cinnamon rolls into the oven.

"It's too soon," Sage said unconvincingly. "We're just getting to know each other." She'd suspected the topic would be pre-breakfast conversation and had practiced her response. It hadn't come off as well as she'd hoped. Maybe she'd get lucky and her mom wouldn't push for more.

Jenny looked over her glasses. "I saw the way she looked at you the other night. If you ask me, she knew you pretty darn well before you got out the door."

Sage blushed. "Mom, please...."

Jenny raised an eyebrow at her daughter and cracked a smile. "You're not getting any younger, you know."

Sage shook her head. "Oh yeah, that's how to make a girl feel better about her big upcoming birthday."

Jenny laughed. "Okay, I give up. You'll throw me a crumb when you're ready." She took a peek into the oven.

Sage caught a whiff of the cinnamon rolls. They reminded her of her childhood. "Mmm, smells good."

"Go on," Jenny said. "They're almost ready. Go call your daddy for breakfast." She met Sage's gaze. "But stay with him. He won't be able to find the kitchen on his own."

Sage had already noticed her dad had been especially confused that morning. She knew her parents needed her now more than ever. "You need help with him? I could stay a bit longer."

"You sure you don't mind?" Jenny asked.

Sage pinched her brow and then smiled. "Come to think of it, I've got plenty of vacation time. Maybe I'll just take a few days off. Can you stand me for a week or so?"

Jenny threw her arms around Sage's neck. "You're such a wonderful daughter. We've been so blessed." She buttered a piece of whole-wheat toast. "Maybe you can help me arrange for some respite." Her eyes brimmed with tears. "I was hoping things wouldn't progress this quickly, but…."

Sage kissed her mom's cheek. "I know you weren't." She wiped away a tear. "It's hard, but we'll get through it together."

***

Sawyer headed home just before dawn. All-nighters weren't as easy as they used to be when she was younger. She dropped into bed with a groan and managed to doze for a couple hours. It'd be a long day on little sleep. Her thoughts went immediately to Sage. She couldn't shake the feeling of foreboding. The damn sixth sense that made her an excellent cop was a curse as well as a blessing. She rolled over, picked up her Smartphone, and dialed. Sage answered on the first ring. She'd obviously been waiting for a call.

"I'll be back as soon as I can," Sawyer said. "Remember, no going anywhere without your police escort."

Sawyer had figured that Sage would be heading back to Tampa that morning and was pleased to learn that she wasn't. Too bad it had to be because her dad wasn't doing well. She didn't tell Sage how relieved she was that she'd be staying close that week. There was no use worrying her any more than she already was.

Sawyer's intention was to visit Amber later that afternoon. She'd hoped to talk Sage into riding along, but knew she probably wouldn't. If Bob was so confused that she'd taken the week off, she knew Sage would want to stick close to her mom. Sawyer didn't want to leave town without her, but had to. Amber was scheduled for discharge on Wednesday and they'd yet to agree on an aftercare plan. Amber would have to stay with someone for two weeks at a minimum—maybe Laurie. She didn't work outside the home. Whatever, they needed to make the plan in short order because Sawyer needed to get back home.

***

It turned out to be an even busier day at the Carson residence than Sage had anticipated. Bob was more confused than ever, certainly more than she'd ever seen him. Even worse, he hadn't been still for more than a minute the entire day. Her dad probably needed an anti-anxiety medication too. Tomorrow, they'd call the doctor.

Sage was exhausted. How in the world had her mom managed to do this for so long alone?

"I'll watch him," Sage said. "You take a break. Why don't you go relax in the bathtub a while?"

"Mmm," Jenny said. "That sounds wonderful. Are you sure?"

Sage smiled. "Yeah, I'm sure." She raised an eyebrow. "You doubt my ability to handle daddy for 30 minutes on my own?"

Jenny's gaze lingered. "Of course not. Just yell if you need me. I'll hurry."

Sage released an exaggerated sigh. "You don't have to hurry, Mama. Take your time. I've got this." She smiled when she heard the bathwater running.

"Come on, Daddy," Sage begged. "How about you sit down for a minute and work on your puzzle? You like puzzles."

Bob sat, thank God, and began to study the pieces that Jenny had already arranged by color. Sage sat down beside him in the comfy chair. She must have nodded off for a minute because when she looked up, he was gone. She searched every single inch of the house at a runners pace—every inch except the bathroom. Her dad was nowhere to be found. Her heart raced in her chest. She had to find him. It was too dangerous for him to be outside alone. For the moment, she forgot her promise to Sawyer and reacted without thinking. Her dad was missing and she had to find him. She ran to the garage, jumped on her old bike, and rode right past the officer who'd been charged with her safety. He was totally captivated by his donut and didn't even notice her. Sage peddled hard. Her mom had trusted her to care for her dad for 30 short minutes and she'd let him slip out the door.

***

  Sawyer rolled down the interstate 10, mostly 15, miles above the speed limit. She wasn't in a huge hurry, she was just getting back later than she'd hoped. She was 20 to 30 minutes outside of Sarasota when her cell phone rang. Sage's photo flashed onto the screen of her Smartphone. She answered, expecting to hear her voice. Instead, she heard only the alarm in Sage's mother's. "What problem? What do you mean Sage and Bob are gone? Son of a–I'm on my way."
  Sawyer ended the call and slammed her palm into the steering wheel. *Please God, let her be okay.* If only she hadn't left town. She jammed the accelerator into the floor, flipped on her siren and lights, and dialed the patrol assigned to protect Sage. When he answered, she verbally ripped his head off his shoulders.

***

  Mark James watched the old man skitter out of the house and down the street. Minutes later, his daughter's redhead peddled out of the garage after him. Mark had always been partial to redheads. Obviously, Sawyer was too. Yet another thing he and his oldest had in common. A deranged laugh erupted from his mind and then his throat. "Well, how about that," he muttered to no one in particular.
  Mark quickly packed up his gear, then darted quickly between the houses. He knew if he hurried, he'd

cross Sage's path and have his way with her tonight. He crouched low behind a parked car to wait. Before he knew it, there she was. As the redhead's front tire spun past, he jumped into her path—expecting her to swerve, lose control, and crash. Instead, the crazy bitch sped up and headed right for him. She hit his groin with a thud, jumped, and ran. Damn bitch screamed loud enough to be heard for miles. He hurt like hell, but Mark managed to quickly untangle himself from the twisted pile of bicycle parts and hobble away. He needed to get out of the neighborhood before it was crawling with cops. Next time, the bitch would pay.

***

Sawyer made a slow pass through the neighborhood. She was systematically searching every nook and cranny for Sage and her dad. She had just rounded the corner when she heard a woman's terrified screams in the distance. Sawyer radioed for back up, slowed to a crawl, and directed her floodlight between the houses. Finally, her beam fell on Sage. She choked with relief, drew her weapon, and jumped from the car—terrified, furious, and out of control.

Sawyer grabbed Sage by her arm and forcefully led her toward the cruiser. "Do you have a death wish? Were you fucking trying to get yourself killed?" She could feel the veins in her neck bulge. "Get your ass in this fucking car! I'm taking you home."

Sage hiccupped sobs as she got in. Her door had barely shut when the cruiser spun and then lunged forward. She cried even harder as it bounced into her parent's driveway.

"Get out," Sawyer screamed.

"Sawyer, please listen," Sage whimpered.

Sawyer reached across to shove the passenger door open. "I said get out." She was angry, but she cared and watched until Sage was safely inside. Bob was standing in front of the window. She was glad he was home safe and sound. She backed out, turned on her lights and siren, and flew forward.

Sawyer orchestrated a massive search of the area where Sage had almost been attacked. She came up without much to show for it. The only thing she really had in terms of evidence was what was left of Sage's bicycle. She took another look at it as it was loaded into the SPD van. She was sure that the bloodstain on the front tire would confirm her suspicion that the serial rapist, now murderer, was her father. She beat down a wave of nausea as she thought about how close she'd come to losing Sage. She was ashamed about the way she'd treated her. It was the wee hours of the morning before she stumbled back to her cruiser. Having a drink was almost all she could think about.

***

Sage ran right past her parents and directly into her bedroom. She was crying hysterically and slammed the door. Her heaving sobs went on for well over an hour before Jenny knocked. When Sage didn't respond, she went in anyway. She'd never seen her daughter like she was right now. It was heartbreaking. She sat down on the bed, pulled her into her arms, and rocked her gently.

"Aw, sweetie," Jenny said as she stroked and soothed. "What happened, honey?"

Sage sobbed softly and told her mom everything. "Sawyer was so angry. I've never seen anyone that angry before. I was scared." Her sobs grew louder. "I just went out to look for daddy."

"I know honey," Jenny said softly. "But I think Sawyer was afraid she'd lost you. I've never heard fear in someone's voice like I did in hers when I told her you were gone." She pulled Sage tight against her breast. "She loves you, honey. You haven't lost her. Now lay back and try to get some sleep." She kissed the top of her daughter's head. "It'll look brighter in the morning."

Chapter Ten

Three days passed without any contact with Sawyer. Sage had tried to call, but she wouldn't answer her phone. She broke down each time she looked out the front window at the patrols. Sage was sure she'd cried more in the past three days than she'd cried in who knows how long. She didn't know what to do. All she knew for sure was that she couldn't let Sawyer go.

"Is there someone who you could talk to?" Jenny asked. "Maybe someone who knows her fairly well?"

God, what a good idea…why didn't she think of it herself? She looked up and smiled. "There is. Thanks, Mama." She stepped out on the porch to make the call. Sage was choking back sobs by the time Laurie answered.

"Honey, are you crying?" Laurie asked. "What's wrong? Did something happen to Sawyer?"

"No," Sage sniffled. "At least, I don't think so." Another wave of sobs took hold. "I need help with her, though."

"I'll be right over," Laurie said. In 15 minutes she was knocking on the front door.

Jenny answered. "Sage will be right with you. She's in the bathroom."

***

Sage splashed cold water on her face. She dried off and checked the mirror once more. Her eyes looked like giant red puffballs. They met Laurie's as she came around the corner.

"Hi," Sage said. "Thanks for coming. I didn't know who else to call." She poured two glasses of tea and they sat down at the kitchen table. Eventually, she told it all. Laurie was so kind. She was a special person and Sage could see why Sawyer loved her.

"She won't answer my calls," Sage choked, "not even at night. I'm afraid I've lost her and I don't know what to do to make things right." Her shoulders heaved with sobs. "How in the world did I let myself get into this situation?"

Laurie stepped behind Sage's chair to massage her neck and shoulders. Her touch was nice and Sage quieted.

"It'll be okay," Laurie said. "You haven't lost Sawyer. She's just acting the fool like she does from time to time, especially when she's scared. Don't worry, Sawyer loves you. She wouldn't be acting this way if she didn't."

"So what do I do?" Sage asked.

Laurie pursed her lips. "Has she talked with you yet? I mean about…."

Sage nodded. "Yeah, we talked. She told me about the…sexual issues." She looked Laurie squarely in the eye. "Sometime, I'd like you to tell me about what happened between you two." As much as she didn't want to hear the details, she knew she had to if she was going to help Sawyer. She needed to know more about the last time Laurie made love with Sawyer. "You know, just before her first panic attack."

Laurie took a deep breath and looked out the kitchen window. "God…I'll have to mentally prepare for that conversation." Sadness immediately filled her eyes. "Her drinking is the problem, you know. She won't admit it, but it is. It has been, ever since that night." She sucked in another deep breath and exhaled slowly. "We'd made love just like we always did." She smiled. "She used to be the sweetest lover." She shook her head. "I don't know what happened. Obviously, something did." She dabbed tears that had begun to fall. "After I opened my soda, she went nuts. It was never the same again." She looked up. "That's it. That's all I know."

Sage twirled her glasses. "Nothing different? Nothing at all?"

"Not really," Laurie said. "You're going to try to help her, aren't you?"

Sage looked away. "I'm not sure if I can, but if she'll let me, then yes. I'm going to try."

A smile crossed Laurie's face. "Help her. I promise she'll be worth your effort."

"You still love her," Sage said. "I know you'd take her back." She shook her head. "I don't understand why you're helping me."

"I do love her, but she doesn't love me…not like she loves you. She never did love me that way. I love her enough to want her to be happy. I want her to find the one who makes her whole."

"You think that's me?" Sage asked.

"Yeah, I do." Laurie smiled and touched Sage's cheek. "Come on, sweetie, let's go get Sawyer." She stood and her expression became serious. "I think you can help her, but you need to be very careful. If she's drunk, she can hurt you."

Sage bit her lip. "Yeah, she told me. I know."

***

Mark James shifted weight off of his sore knee as he watched the two women walk out and get into the Mustang. *Hot women in a hot car.* He reached inside his pants. They drove off with a patrol on their tail. He wondered where they'd gone. Sawyer's new girlfriend was with her old one. His hand whipped as he fantasized about what he'd make them do to each other.

***

Sawyer sat slouched over the bar, drunk. Eight Miller Lite empties were lined up in a not-so-neat row. She'd managed to stay sober for three weeks, but sobriety was gone again. It was the story of her life. "Give me another, Butch."

The bartender shook his head as he popped the cap off of number nine. He set the bottle down in front of her. "If you need to talk…."

"Nope, I'm good," Sawyer slurred. She picked up the new arrival and swallowed it in one gulp. It numbed all the way down.

The bell on the front door jingled, but only Butch looked up. Sawyer was too far gone. He nudged her and moved to the far end of the bar. "You've got company. Heads up."

Laurie headed straight for Sawyer.

Sawyer looked up and met the familiar glare. "What?"

"You think you need that many?" Laurie asked. "Nine fucking beers? Pretty soon you won't even have a liver."

Sawyer clenched her fist and then her jaw. "Maybe I don't care."

Sage stepped back.

"Had to drown your sorrows in a bottle, didn't you baby?" Laurie shook her head. "I'm so disappointed in you."

Fury swirled behind Sawyer's eyes. Her insides were burning and she yanked at her collar. She glared. "Who made what I do your business? You and I are nothing. We are ab–so–lutely nothing."

Laurie didn't blink. "Why, Sage did sweetheart. She made it my business." Her glare held on. "How much are you gonna hurt her before you get brave enough to deal with your shit?"

Sawyer's eyes moistened. Her gaze fell into her beer. Bile rose up in her throat and she felt sick. "It's me. I'm a piece of shit. You know I'm no good for Sage." She locked eyes with her ex. They talked as if Sage wasn't standing right there. "You more than anyone should know she can do better than me."

Sage shifted her stance. She stepped forward, then back, then forward again. In those moments she realized what Sawyer needed and knew what she had to do. She stepped closer.

Laurie stepped back.

Sage found Sawyer's eyes. "I've missed you." A soft sob escaped her throat and she struggled to hold herself together. "I made a mistake. I'm sorry."

Sawyer felt like her heart was being ripped from her chest. "I missed you too. And it's me who's sorry." She looked into Sage's swollen eyes. "I'm such a jerk."

Sage ran her fingers through a lock of Sawyer's hair. "That you are, but you're a jerk that I've fallen in love with."

Sawyer shoved away from the bar. "That's it, I'm done." She tried to stand. The room swirled around her head and she sat back down. She looked to Sage. "Take me home?"

"Let's go," Sage said. She helped Sawyer off the stool and with Laurie's assistance managed to get her out the door and to the car. Before they could get her safely in the seat, she pulled away, determined to drop into it on her own. Too bad she missed by almost a foot and landed hard between the car and the curb.

"Fuck," Sawyer slurred at the top of her lungs. "Ouch."

Sage scowled, but helped her up. Sawyer was relieved. She couldn't have untangled her legs on her own. Sage buckled her in without uttering a single word. The silence continued all the way back to drop Laurie off at her car. Sage said good night to Laurie, but resumed her silence as they made their way to the condo. God, she was mad. Sawyer was hoping she wasn't too furious to help her inside. She didn't think she could make it in on her own.

Sage helped her. In fact, she stayed by her side all the way back to the master bedroom. "You need to take a shower. You smell like a drunk." She glared. "That's not who you are, Sawyer."

Sawyer swallowed. "I know."

Sage left Sawyer to take a shower on her own. God, she was mad.

By the time Sawyer stumbled barefoot back into the living room she was beginning to sober up. She adjusted her jeans and sat down next to Sage on the couch. They held eye contact until Sage spoke.

"Don't think we're going to have this discussion while you're still intoxicated," Sage said. "Go to bed and sleep it off. I'll be right here when you wake up."

***

That next morning was when Sawyer first noticed the change in her relationship with Sage. She could feel it in her heart. It was good, even though Sage was still angry as hell, so angry that Sawyer wondered if she'd ever cool off.

Sage met her gaze. "What?" Her tone left little doubt how furious she was.

"Uh, nothing," Sawyer said, "just a little headache." Actually, it was mind-numbing, but no way was she ever going to admit that out loud.

"Uh-huh, I'll bet!" Sage scowled over her glasses. "No sympathy here."

Sawyer rubbed her temple as she unscrewed the cap on the bottle. She popped three Tylenol and swallowed without water. "Want to go with me to pick up Amber?"

Sage pursed her lips and glared again. "Yeah, I'll ride along."

Sawyer exhaled. "Good." Her gaze lingered as long as Sage would allow. "I hoped you would."

Chapter Eleven

Amber was waiting on the edge of the bed when Sawyer and Sage arrived. She felt rested and was more than ready to go home, even if home for the next two weeks would be Laurie's trailer. She hated Jo, but had made the decision to deal with it. She'd just stay in her room.

"I'll ride in the back," Amber said. "I don't mind the cage."

"No," Sage said. "You sit up front with Sawyer. I'm good back here. I don't mind it either."

"You both might mind when you see how hard the seat is," Sawyer said. "It's not meant to be comfortable."

Sage glared. "I haven't been comfortable for days."

Amber looked from Sawyer to Sage and back again. Clearly, she'd landed in the middle of one hell of an argument. She looked to Sawyer. "So, the last time we talked, you thought my therapist was hot, but you guys weren't an item. Now, I'm thinking the situation may have changed."

Sawyer didn't respond. Her lack of response spoke volumes.

Sage leaned forward against the cage. "Would such a relationship be difficult for you?"

Amber raised an eyebrow as she turned in her seat to meet her therapist's gaze. "Are you kidding? I think you're hot too. My sister always did have great taste in women." She winked and flashed a grin. "Just kidding." But Amber wasn't really kidding. Sawyer had been with the most amazing woman in the world. She just hadn't had enough sense to treat her right—to keep her.

Sage tried to contain it, but a smile broke free of its restraint. "Okay then. I guess I won't worry about it." She leaned back.

Sawyer broke into laughter.

It was contagious.

***

Sawyer rubbed Snoop's head as she came through the door. "Hey big guy, look who I brought home." She held Sage's hand for him to sniff. As he did, she said "Sage," then told him to go lay down. She wanted the dog to pair Sage's name with her unique scent.

"Well…that was different," Sage said in a less angry tone.

Sawyer didn't respond, just continued her conversation with Snoop. "I'll take you out in a minute, after I give Sage an update on my homework. That is, if she's not too angry to be interested." She looked in Sage's direction. "I'd hate for her to forgive me before she's ready."

Sage felt Sawyer's gaze fall onto her breasts. Sawyer's desire made her gasp. Her thoughts raced with her blood to sensitive places and her breathing quickened. She felt a little afraid, but mainly excited. She swallowed. "I'm ready…."

Sawyer smiled. "That's good, because I wanted to tell you about the fantasy I've been working on." Her voice dropped low and sexy. "See, in the fantasy, I let Snoop out...kind of like I'm gonna do in a minute."

Sage closed her eyes as she bit her lower lip. She re-opened them.

Sawyer stood a couple feet from Sage as she unbuttoned the second button of her shirt. "And while I'm outside, you're in here thinking about how much you want me on top of you." Her eyes were like lasers. "You want me inside you—want me to taste you."

Sage hissed in another breath. "God...."

"So anyway," Sawyer said softly, "Snoop and I go for a walk. We give you plenty of time to do whatever you need to do to get ready. You slip out of everything—even your panties." She licked her lips.

Sage licked hers in response and thought about Sawyer making love to her. "God...."

Sawyer smiled. "You're damp from your shower. You look down and notice your nipples—hard. You slip into my bed."

Sage moved toward Sawyer.

Sawyer stepped back. "Not yet. The chill of the sheets makes them harder and you can't wait for me to get back. You touch yourself. I open the bedroom door—" She took a deep breath and picked up Snoop's leash. "I'll tell you the rest when I get back inside. Come on big guy, let's go for a walk."

Sage stood motionless for what felt like several minutes after the door shut. Her knees wobbled as she made her way into the bathroom. She undressed and turned on the shower. She'd have to be careful or the beads of warm water would trigger an orgasm.

***

Sawyer nudged the bedroom door open. Sage was exactly where she expected to find her–in her bed. She unstrapped her holster and gently laid it on the dresser. Sage watched as she unbuttoned her shirt. She turned to give Sage a better view as she undressed, got into bed, and pulled her close.

"I think what you taught me might have worked," Sawyer said with a proud smile. She kissed Sage's forehead and held her. Sawyer thought she looked a little afraid. "We'll know in just a little while. You ready?"

"Oh yeah," Sage murmured as she tipped her lips toward Sawyer.

Sawyer kissed her, then rolled to top and kissed her again, this time with tongue. She kissed down her neck and across smooth breasts, larger than her own.

Sage moaned as Sawyer suckled each nipple— beautiful and so aroused.

Unfortunately, Sawyer became nauseous in a matter of seconds. Her heart thumped wildly and she trembled all over. Sweat poured off her brow. "God…no…" She rolled off and onto her back.

Sage propped up and met her gaze. "It's okay. This'll happen a couple times—just re-focus your thoughts. What's the worst thing that can happen here? We'll stop and try again, that's all. Now slow your breathing and regain control."

Sage ran her fingers through Sawyer's damp hair. "That's right…" She kissed her temple. "There you go, you've got it. Good girl." She stroked her fingertips across Sawyer's breasts and abdomen, kissed and tongued her navel.

Sawyer's breathing quickened, but this time not from panic. "Mmm, you're good at this."

Sage kissed lower. "Maybe I'm a natural."

Sawyer flipped her onto her back. "Maybe you are."

Sage began to tremble.

Sawyer rose up to brush a curl from her eyes. "You okay, baby?"

She smiled through quivering lips. "Yeah, it just took me a little off guard. It's been so long since I felt this way. Actually, I'm not sure I've ever felt this way before." Her moist eyes met Sawyer's. "Make love to me."

Sawyer surged with passion. It had been so long. Her mouth lowered onto one nipple and then the other.

Sage writhed beneath her. She panted and moaned.

Sawyer ran her tongue down Sage's taut abdomen and kissed the swelling below. Then, her passion faded as quickly as it'd come. She gasped for air and her struggle to survive took hold. "Oh God…not again. No—" She rolled to her back—again.

Sage shut her eyes for a moment, exhaled, and pulled her close. Her tone was gentle, yet firm. "Shh, you're okay. Now focus, come on now—slow your breathing. The worst thing that can happen here is we won't finish, that's all. Come on now…you can do this…"

The pain in Sawyer's chest lessened. She felt her pulse and heart rate slow.

"That's right," Sage whispered, "deep, slow breaths. Good girl." She stroked and kissed her neck, her ears, and her breasts. "Come on. Take me, sweetheart…"

Sawyer's passion returned from nowhere. She rolled on top and filled Sage's mouth with tongue. Again her heart began to race, but this time she slowed it down on her own.

"Feels so good," Sage moaned. "Oh God, I'm close already. You're gonna make me come," she gasped and pressed into Sawyer's mouth.

Sawyer sucked harder and dipped inside with tongue. "Mmm, you taste so good." Strong contractions gripped her fingers.

Sage screamed in pleasure. "Wow…that was beyond anything I could've imagined," she moaned. "Yep, I'm a lesbian."

Sawyer couldn't help but smile. "Yeah, I think maybe you are." She kissed her forehead. "Sorry your first time had to be packed full of therapy."

Sage locked her gaze. "You have absolutely nothing to be sorry about."

***

Sage wanted to make love to Sawyer more than anything. Nothing had ever felt so right, and yet…. She laid there trying to figure out what she was afraid of. Normally, new didn't faze her at all, but this time it did.

Sawyer rolled to face her. She looked into her eyes. "What are you scared of?"

"I don't know," Sage said softly. Their lips met in the softest kiss. "Maybe that I'll choke. Or maybe that I won't be able to do what you like."

Sawyer threw off the sheet. "You'll do fine."

Sage looked into her eyes and then lower. Sawyer was beautiful—so perfect and so strong. God, she wanted her.

"Come on," Sawyer whispered. "Make love to me."

Sage sighed and moved into her arms. She felt her passion rise. It must've been stored for a lifetime. She touched Sawyer's small firm breasts and suckled each of her nipples. It felt so right. She kissed and ran her tongue lower until she lay between her legs. She spread her and lowered her mouth.

Sawyer thrust upward and moaned. "That's it baby. Suck hard." She reached down to hold Sage tight against her. "Ahh, right there…"

Sage sucked harder and then slipped her fingers inside.

Sawyer jerked and cried out.

Sage felt spasms squeeze her fingers. It was like nothing she'd ever felt before. It felt so good, so right.

Sawyer groaned. Her body stiffened. She collapsed, but Sage kept on. "Easy, sweetie," Sawyer panted. "Let me rest a minute."

Sage lifted up and looked in her eyes. "God, that was good." She noticed the sweetest taste on her lips and again she wanted more.

Sawyer smiled and stroked her hair. "Yeah, it was. I told you that you'd know what to do." Her smile widened to a grin. "And did you notice? No panic attack that time."

Sage smiled. "Yeah baby, I noticed." She kissed her lover on the lips. "I'm proud."

"I love you," Sawyer murmured.

Sage curled up against her back. "I love you too."

Chapter Twelve

Sawyer awoke before sunrise. She'd been lying quietly watching Sage sleep. Sage was everything she'd ever wanted in a woman—strong, smart, beautiful, and so feminine. The fact that they seemed to have perfect sexual chemistry was just an added bonus. She shivered at the thought of how close she'd come to losing her and rolled over to pull her close. Sawyer needed to feel the warmth of Sage's body pressed against her own.

Sage's eyelids fluttered open. She stretched and rolled to her back. "Good morning, handsome."

Sawyer extended her arm and Sage shifted to her shoulder. "Good morning, beautiful lady." She pulled her even closer. "You doing okay?"

Sage crinkled her brow like she was puzzled for a moment. Then she smiled. "Yeah, I'm good." She kissed Sawyer's lips. "Last night was amazing. I never dreamed sex could be that good."

Sawyer brushed a stray curl out of Sage's eyes. "Yeah, it was good wasn't it?" She ran her fingertips up Sage's inner thigh. "But I'm not sure I got quite enough."

"Mmm," Sage purred. "Too bad. I guess we'll just have to see what we can do about that." Sage spread her legs. "Those fingers were absolutely unbelievable last night." She bit her lower lip. "Let's see what they can do this morning."

Sawyer rolled to top her. "Okay, let's see."

***

It was a workday, but Sawyer had all the time in the world. She'd taken one of her many accumulated vacation days so that she'd be available in case Sage needed to talk. She didn't usually take days off, but priorities were priorities. It wasn't that she'd expected Sage to have a problem. It was just that Sage had never been with a woman before. Sawyer wanted to be sure she was there if she needed her. She'd been beyond pleased when Sage woke up feeling good, wanting her. How perfect that they had plenty of time to make love before their play day started.

Sage slid her purse onto her shoulder and put her sunglasses on. "Are we ready?"

"All ready," Sawyer said as she put on her own dark shades. "I wouldn't mind swinging by to check on Amber if that's okay by you?"

"Sure," Sage said. "Maybe we can run by to see my parents for a minute, then head on out." She slipped her arms around Sawyer's neck. "Just one more kiss before we go?"

Sawyer leaned in and ran her palm along the swell of Sage's breast. "Mmm, my pleasure."

***

Jenny was standing near the front window when the white cruiser turned into her driveway. She studied her daughter. There was something different about her this morning. Jenny stepped onto her front porch. "Good morning you two."

"Morning Mama," Sage chirped. "You look chipper this morning. I hope that means daddy's doing well."

Jenny smiled. "He is. We actually had an almost normal breakfast conversation this morning. I think the new meds are helping him." She savored Bob's good times. They were becoming less frequent and she feared one day, too soon, he'd be gone.

Sage kissed her mom's cheek and stepped inside. "That's good. Maybe we'll hold him steady for a little while."

Jenny nodded. "I hope so." But her tone was full of uncertainty.

Sawyer said hello and headed off in search of Bob. They'd become pals in short order. Jenny was glad that Bob had a new friend as well as the opportunity to talk with Sage alone. "So, it looks like you two are getting along well this morning." She raised an eyebrow. "Big night last night?"

Sage's eyes widened and she chuckled. "It's like you have radar or something. Yeah, you could say that."

"Good," Jenny said, "that makes me happy." She'd grown to like Sawyer a lot and was rooting for her daughter's budding relationship with her. Sawyer was a complex person with a really big heart. Any less and she knew Sage wouldn't have been interested. She nodded to the puzzle table and smiled. "She's a sweetie."

Sage looked over just as Sawyer helped her dad put a piece into his puzzle. "Yeah, she is. She's perfect, Mama." Sage looked up with teary eyes. "I'd given up ever having this with someone." She shook her head. "You know I never had it with John."

Jenny opened her arms and pulled her daughter close. "I know. I'm so glad you have it now with Sawyer."

***

Mark James felt as at home on his belly with a gun as anywhere. Maybe it was because he'd spent so many hours in that position. Those years in uniform were the best of his life, but they were gone and had been for a very long time. He holstered his Beretta 9mm and raised his binoculars. The front door opened. He watched the couple step outside. It was handy that his daughter's condo and Sage's parents were only three blocks apart. He could easily move between them on foot. *Mmm, she's all cozied up to you this morning. I'll bet you got some last night.*

***

Sawyer felt a chill run up her spine as she walked down the steps toward the cruiser. She tightened her grip on Sage and pulled her close. She could smell the bastard in their immediate vicinity. God, she had to catch him before he hurt someone else. Snoop snarled under his breath. He smelled him too. She opened the door for Sage, got in, and they were off. Sawyer tried her best to keep their conversation light-hearted, until….

"Code 3," the dispatcher announced. "All available units proceed to 111 Sea Breeze Lane. You have a 10-71 shooting and possible rape. 10-45D—dead. Proceed with caution. The coroner is responding."

Sawyer flipped on her lights and siren. She immediately recognized the address and prayed that it wasn't Bob or Jenny. The cruiser spun in the direction of oncoming traffic as she looked to Sage. "Sit tight, sweetie. We're gonna fly."

Sage had already begun to cry. "Oh God, not Mama."

Sawyer words were gentle, but she was all business. She had to be a cop right now. "You are not to get out of this cruiser. Do you hear me, Sage? Under no circumstance do you get out of this car."

Sage nodded and sobbed harder.

Sawyer looked over her shoulder to Snoop. The dog recognized the signals and stood at the ready. "Watch Sage. Stay in the car." She hung a sharp right and bounced into the driveway as she squeezed Sage's hand. "Just sit tight and let me see what's going on." She drew her weapon and was gone.

Sawyer yanked and the screen door opened. Thank God both Jenny and Bob were alive.

Jenny burst into tears the moment she saw her.

Sawyer opened her arms. "Come here, sweetie."

"Thank God you're here," Jenny whimpered. She looked around. "Where's Sage?"

Sawyer smiled and gave her an extra squeeze. "She's safe in my car—where you're going to be in just a minute."

***

Sawyer had never felt sick as often as she had since transferring from narcotics to special victims. She knew the work would turn her stomach, but she couldn't turn the job down. You could say that catching sexual perverts was a calling. She did it for the victims. She did it for herself. Roughing them up before throwing them into a cell was just an added bonus. It's funny how a person is drawn to situations that force them to deal with their issues, at least that's the way it was for Sawyer. She rubbed the back of her neck at the smell of the stench of death, dried blood, and semen. She gagged as she gulped down the lump in her throat. "I'll get you, you sick bastard."

The choppy sea in Sawyer's stomach had just begun to settle when her old friend approached. She nodded hello. "We've gotta stop meeting like this," she said with a grin. "People are gonna talk."

Detective Lin Yang laughed. "Just let 'em."

Sawyer and Lin had been good friends since the academy. They worked well together. She was someone Sawyer could totally trust. "Thanks for coming out on this."

Detective Yang smiled. "No problem. I thought you were off today."

Sawyer sighed, "I was." She shook her head and then nodded toward the house. "My girlfriend's parents."

Lin met her gaze. "Ugliness too close to home."

"Yep," Sawyer said, "but it is what it is." She returned to the business at hand. "What've you got?"

Detective Yang's eyes widened. "It gets worse. I think you need to see this for yourself."

Sawyer snapped on her gloves. "I'm right behind ya."

The victim laid as the bastard had left her– stiffening in a pool of her own congealing blood. The slashing and the bullet in her head were gruesome. The area reeked of death. Sawyer studied the victim. Her long wavy hair reminded her of Sage. She stepped back and turned toward the tree. She was fighting the urge to gag.

Officer Yang squatted down to further examine the details of the crime. She pointed to the crumpled piece of paper that was jammed between the victim's thumb and her index finger. "This time he left us a note."

Once department procedure had been followed they removed the paper to take a closer look. It was printed in flawless calligraphy using the victim's own blood. The bastard had taken his own sweet time to write the only letter he'd ever written to his daughter. Sawyer folded her arms and rocked in place—unprofessional or not, she couldn't stop her tears. Lin pulled her aside until she regained composure.

In a couple moments, Sawyer was barking orders into her phone. "I want 24-hour monitoring of his cell phone, credit card, everything we have. If he turns on that phone for even a split second I want to know about it." She hung up and looked to Lin. "He's gonna strike again. It's personal. I've gotta get him."

Chapter Thirteen

Several hours passed before Sawyer walked back around the house. When she did, her demeanor was so unsettling that Sage had the urge to hold her. She leaned against the cruiser for a minute before opening the door. Sage recognized that Sawyer was struggling to pull herself together. She was a tough cop. It was hard for her to let anyone see her cry.

"Sorry I had to leave you guys sitting here so long," Sawyer said. "It took a while to get this one wrapped up."

"It was fine," Sage said softly. "Mama and I had a nice chat and Daddy enjoyed Snoop." She met Sawyer's eye. "Really bad, huh?"

Sawyer sighed and kissed her lips. "Yeah, really bad—the worst I've seen in a very long time," she exhaled. "Now come on, let's get you guys inside." She forced a smile. "That is, if you can still stand up."

"We can stand," Sage said. "You just watch us." No more had she said the words than she watched her mom struggle to pull herself up and out of the car. She was struck by how much her mom had aged during the past year. Caring for her dad as he deteriorated had been really hard on her. Memories of her strong, confident mom filled her mind. Both of her parents were literally wearing out before her eyes. It made her sad, and for an instant, she felt alone.

Sage put her arm around her mom as they stepped through the door. She gave her a gentle nudge toward the living room. "You go sit with Daddy and Sawyer. Help them finish that puzzle they've been working on." Her voice was stern. "Go on now, I'll fix dinner."

Jenny resisted. She wanted to help.

Sage raised an eyebrow. "You want me to have a chance to cook for Sawyer, don't you?"

Jenny smiled. "Of course I do, but judging from the way she looks at you, I don't really believe she cares how well you do in the kitchen." Jenny met her daughter's eye. "Thank you, honey. I am a bit tired."

***

Sawyer shoveled a monster bite of chicken pot pie into her mouth. "Oh my God you are such a good cook. You made all this from scratch?"

Sage grinned with pride. "Sure did, even the crust."

"Mmm, you make crust from scratch in addition to all your other talents. I think I just might keep you around."

Jenny watched the interaction with amusement and chuckled out loud.

"Just for that, Ms. Smarty Pants, you can help me do the dishes."

Sawyer laughed. "What? What'd I do?" She gathered the plates, set them on the counter, and picked up a dampened dish towel. She gave Sage a good swat. "Huh? What'd I do?"

Sage looked up. "Ouch!"

Sawyer swatted again, but Sage stepped to the left. She missed that time.

Sage grabbed hold of the towel and pulled Sawyer close. "You know what you did." She slipped her arms around her neck and nibbled an ear.

"Mmm," Sawyer moaned. "And now my behavior's reinforced."

Sage slid her hand underneath Sawyer's shirt. "Uh-huh, I'm sure it is."

Sawyer tugged them into the corner just as fingertips brushed her nipple. "Easy, your parent's are in the next room."

Sage slid her palm down Sawyer's abdomen. "Don't worry. Mama won't come in…."

***

Sage stepped onto the front porch just as Sawyer ended the call. They met each other's gaze.

"Jo screwed around with some woman at the bar. Laurie found out. Now they're in one hell of a cat fight," Sawyer said. "I'm glad Amber had the sense to call."

"You're worried," Sage said.

Sawyer sighed. "Yeah, Amber said Jo hit Laurie in the face. Jo can be a bitch when she's drunk. Amber's gonna get in the middle of it, I just know it."

Sage rubbed Sawyer's tense shoulders. "You've got a patrol in front of the trailer. Can't she intervene?"

Sawyer shook her head. "No, not if Laurie doesn't want help…and she won't." She twisted her watch around her wrist. "Unless she's hurt."

113

Sage leaned in for a kiss. "Come on, let's take a ride out that way to make sure everything's okay."

Sawyer nodded. "Might be a good idea." Her gaze fell on the cruiser parked two houses down. She nodded to the officer. "Your mom and dad should be fine while we're gone."

"They will be," Sage said. "I'll go get my purse and tell Mama where we're going." She came back out to find Sawyer already in the car with the engine running. Sage had no more than buckled her seatbelt when the radio blared.

"Son of a–" Sawyer said as she slammed her palm into the steering wheel. "I knew it." She keyed the microphone. "Detective James, go ahead."

Sage settled back into her seat and held on. She could tell from Sawyer's end of the radio conversation that they were going to rip toward Laurie's in a matter of seconds. She'd learned to be prepared.

"No one moves in unless the situation escalates," Sawyer barked. "ETA, 1830." She looked to Sage. "Hang on."

Sage smiled. "I know—because we're gonna fly."

***

At 1825 the crushed shells crackled under the weight of the cruiser as it skidded to a halt. Sawyer turned to Sage. "Sorry, but you'll need to stay in the car again, at least until I'm sure we've got things under control." Domestics were some of the most dangerous situations for a police officer. People get crazy-violent when it comes to their families. She didn't want Sage to get hurt.

"That's okay," Sage said. "Just be careful."

Sawyer kissed her. "I will. I love you."

Sage smiled. "I love you too."

***

The young officer jogged alongside Sawyer as she came across the front yard. Jo and Laurie continued to scream at each other, oblivious to the fact that police were there.

Sawyer scanned the area. Neighbors were leaning over their porch rails to watch, but she didn't see Amber. "Where's my sister?"

The officer nodded toward the nearby cruiser. "Safe, with my partner."

Sawyer nodded. "Good, keep her there and stay back. Let's see if I can talk 'em down." She slowed her pace. "I'll signal if I need back-up."

The officer dropped back too. "Yes, Ma'am."

"Hey there," Sawyer called out in as friendly a tone as she could muster. "What's going on?" She scanned the area and caught sight of the hunting knife in Jo's right hand. Sawyer's adrenaline pumped as her finger automatically located the trigger of her weapon. "Drop the knife, Jo!"

Jo looked over and glared. "Get out of here, SD! This isn't your business."

Sawyer's focus was laser-sharp. "Hey now buddy, it is my business. You know I'm a police officer. Come on now, you don't want to hurt anybody. Drop the knife."

Sawyer continued to assess the situation. Laurie looked okay with the exception of the left side of her face. Sawyer caught her eye. "Stop screaming at Jo and step away!"

Laurie stepped back, but not enough.

Jo's lip curled into a snarl. "Oh yeah, you always do whatever SD wants, don't ya baby?"

Laurie stepped toward Jo. "At least I'm not fucking everything that moves, like you do."

Jo hurled spit in Laurie's face. "No, you just fuck her in your fantasies. You wouldn't spread for anyone real."

"Laurie," Sawyer shouted, "I said step away. Now!"

Again Laurie stepped back.

Jo lunged for Laurie with the knife.

Sawyer took Jo down with the efficiency of a predator. She rapid-fire slugged her gut and jaw until she dropped motionless to the ground. Jo was laid out before she knew what hit her.

"That was for Laurie," Sawyer snapped. She bared her teeth as she slapped on handcuffs and bagged the knife. "You have the right to–anything you say can and will be used against you–right to an attorney–watch your head." She slammed the rear door of the patrol car and leaned inside the front window. "Lock her up."

Sawyer immediately walked back toward the cruiser. She smiled as she caught Sage's eye. "You guys can get out now."

"Man," Sage said, "I thought that only happened in the movies. She looked into Sawyer's eyes. "I was scared, but so proud." She leaned up to kiss her lips. "Is everyone okay?"

"Yeah, they're fine," Sawyer said. "Laurie has a few facial bruises." She grinned. "I think Jo might be noticing a couple cracked ribs by now."

***

"Now hold still," Amber said as she dabbed on the disinfectant. "I can't work on a moving target." She couldn't stand to see Laurie hurt, never could. That's why she hated Jo. That's why she'd stayed angry with Sawyer for the longest time. She'd just started to tend to Laurie's black eye when Sawyer and Sage stepped through the door. Laurie disregarded her instruction and jumped out of her chair. Sawyer opened her arms and Laurie ran right for her. Laurie nuzzled and kissed Sawyer's neck as if they were lovers. Who knows, maybe they still were from time to time. Amber pounded her fist into her thigh. She glanced at Sage who looked like she was about to cry. When was her sister going to think of someone other than herself? The phone rang. Laurie ran to answer. Amber thanked God.

***

Sage would never have considered herself to be a jealous person, not until this moment. John could have had an affair and she probably would've barely noticed. Heck, she probably would've been relieved that he'd provided her with an indisputable excuse to not sleep with him. Her breathing quickened as she struggled to stop insistent tears. She was enraged and couldn't hold her tongue. Had Sawyer been paying a lick of attention, she'd have seen it coming. Instead, Sawyer just sat there, dumbfounded.

Sage looked her dead in the eye. "I can't compete with that and I won't try. You two were lovers and you've got history. I get that. What I don't get is why you feel the need to let your ex slobber all over you 15 fucking years after you say you broke up." Sage felt her face flush and blew out a series of short breaths as she tried to regain control. "If you want her, Laurie's all yours. I know damn well she still wants you. She made that perfectly clear tonight, even with an audience." She shoved back her chair with enough force that it teetered and almost tipped over. "I'm really glad I could help you two get through your dry spell." She glared at Sawyer and marched out. The door slammed shut behind her. Sage ran toward the road, still trying her best not to cry. No way was she going to let Sawyer see her crumble— not tonight.

***

Sawyer looked up as Amber stormed out of the room. She heard the bedroom door slam behind her. "Shit! Now you're both pissed at me? That's just fucking great!" She slammed her fist into the kitchen counter and stared out the front window. Sage was standing by the car. She almost went out to talk with her, but then as an afterthought, sat back down. It might be better to give her a few minutes to cool off. The next time she looked out the window, Sage was getting into a cab. Sawyer ran to the front yard, but the cab drove off. She'd realized the gravity of her error a minute too late. She went back inside and laid her head down on the kitchen table.

"Fuck," Sawyer muttered to herself.

Laurie strolled back into the room without a clue. "What in the world? Amber's in her room, throwing things and cussing up a storm. You're out here rubbing bruised knuckles and looking like the world ended while I was on the phone." She looked around and out the door. "Where's Sage?"

Sawyer's facial muscles tightened into a scowl. "She left, hurt and angry. I need to go after her, but I waited. I wanted to talk to you first."

Laurie took a breath, concerned. "Okay...."

"You know I care about you...and seeing you beaten today," Sawyer shook her head, "like I beat you...well, it broke my heart. But you and I both know that friendship is all we have. We're not lovers. We were, but we're never going to be again." Her eyes met Laurie's. "Sage used to believe that, but now, after watching us this evening, she doesn't." Sawyer fought back tears. "Sage is my lover now and my behavior tonight hurt her. This can never happen again." She stood and headed for the door. "Tell Amber I'm sorry. I'll call her later."

***

Laurie watched the cruiser back out of her driveway. "Goodbye, Sawyer," she whispered as tears trickled down her cheeks. Laurie felt strong arms come around her from behind. She arched into the warmth of the embrace.

Amber pressed her body against Laurie's back and held her close. "I don't know why you throw yourself at women who either don't love you the way you love them, or worse, throw yourself at ones who beat you. You do that, and all the while look past the ones who'd treasure you for a lifetime." Amber choked. "It's not like you'd ever have to just settle. You're a beautiful woman and you don't deserve to be treated like a piece of shit."

Laurie's lower lip began to quiver. "You're so sweet." She brushed Amber's cheek with the palm of her hand. "But I don't think that I'm the type that someone's ever going to treasure."

"Ah," Amber said with a lingering gaze, "but you're so wrong about that."

***

Mark James crouched behind the hedgerow as he waited for his prey. The morning's hunt had been exhilarating, but as often was the case, he wanted to do it again. His mind drifted back to all his past victims. It was such a shame to have settled for rape all these years. The killing afterward was so much more satisfying and dead victims solved so many problems. He smiled as he thought back to his most recent kill. He licked his lips. She had an exquisite look of terror in her eyes when she saw the knife. He wished he hadn't had to put a bullet in her pretty little head. It'd been the only way to shut her up. The woman simply would not die. He wondered if Sawyer knew that her daddy had chosen the red-haired neighbor as a present to remind her of her girlfriend. *Mmm, I'll bet your girlfriend's a screamer too.* It was becoming harder to keep his focus. His mind drifted again. He thought about his daughters. Amber used to be a screamer. He grinned. All of his meth-rotted teeth showed and the sound of his own deranged laughter flooded his conscious mind.

***

Sage sobbed softly in the backseat of the cab as it headed toward her parents' home. She always cried when she was angry. Tonight was worse than ever. She tried to ignore her phone as it buzzed in her purse. She knew who it was, but was too angry to talk. It stopped buzzing and she dug it out. She was angry, but not so angry that she couldn't listen to Sawyer's voicemail.

Sage had never felt this way before, not even during the breakup of her marriage. The pain that ripped through her center felt unbearable. She couldn't blame Laurie for what happened tonight. She'd just seized an opportunity. Of course she wanted to be close to the woman she loved, especially tonight. She'd been hurt and was probably scared. No, Sage wasn't mad at Laurie, but she was furious with Sawyer—so furious that she'd barely recognized herself.

The cab rounded the corner and turned into the subdivision as Sage frantically rummaged through her purse. The quicker she paid the driver, the less he'd see of her swollen eyes. She noted that the house was dark when they came to a stop in the driveway. Her mom and dad must have gone to bed early. She looked at her watch. It was 10:55 p.m. Nope, she was just home really late. She handed the driver a 20 and got out of the cab. He drove off as she sniffled her way up the sidewalk toward the front door. She was thinking about Sawyer and not paying one bit of attention to her surroundings.

Mark James crawled behind the hedge. He was on his belly, inching ever closer to the front door. He noticed that Sage was crying. She was coming home alone and he guessed the tears were because of Sawyer. It was like she'd been handed to him on a platter. She was preoccupied. It was dark. Best of all, the officer assigned to her wasn't paying any attention at all. It was time for shift change. Mark grinned his hungry grin. His eyes widened with anticipation. Sage stepped onto the porch. Sawyer should've known better. Mark reached through the hedge and pulled her off her feet. She'd been fiddling around trying to insert her key into the front door. In a blink, Sage was down at his level. Quick as a snake, he slapped a piece of duct tape over her mouth. It prevented her from getting off her second scream. He lay on top of her until he was certain that his attack had gone unnoticed.

Chapter Fourteen

Sage screamed, but her cries were hushed. She gasped, but her lungs didn't fill. The tape that affixed her lips was smothering her hope for survival. She struggled, but couldn't break free. Her body was held tightly against the ground by the oppressive weight of the sickening, vile man.

Mark pressed himself into her. She felt his hardness and cringed.

"Like it?" he asked. "I'll bet you do." He spread his lips to show his rotten teeth. "I'll show it to you later." He licked them.

Sage caught a disgusting whiff of his decomposing mouth. She turned her head and tried to turn her body. Bile slithered up the back of her throat. She wanted to throw up, but it would've choked her. She whimpered instead.

Mark reached roughly underneath Sage's blouse and squeezed her left breast. "Come on, let's go finish what we started." He waved his gun. "I said get up! On your feet or I knock you out. I'll carry you if I have to. Either way, you're going."

Tears streamed down Sage's cheeks. Her hands were tied. She had to let them fall.

Mark pointed toward the inlet behind the Carson residence with the barrel of his gun. "I said move!"

123

When Sage didn't immediately comply, he pistol-whipped the left side of her face. She sobbed without a sound and stumbled down the hill. The water felt slimy. Funny, she'd never noticed that as a child. She felt a trickle run down her left cheek and paused. The red dripped onto her blouse. Sage felt the hard barrel press into her back and trudged forward, wishing her last words with Sawyer hadn't been said in anger.

***

Sawyer continued to ring Sage's cell, but she didn't answer. She'd left voicemails, but Sage hadn't called. In a way, she wasn't surprised. She was really angry and Sawyer knew she deserved every bit of her wrath. If only she could convince herself that it was just that, and not a more serious problem. She had a feeling in the pit of her stomach, the kind of feeling a seasoned cop gets when there's danger or when something has gone terribly wrong. Another shiver traversed her body. She jammed down the accelerator, this time all the way to the floor. It was dark and she was in a quiet residential neighborhood, but priorities were priorities. She spotted an old model pick-up truck about a half-mile up the road and drove past the entrance to the subdivision to check it out. It had an Illinois license plate. "Oh God, no…."

Sawyer dialed the patrol parked outside the Carson residence. "I want an immediate welfare check." She rolled past the truck again, nice and slow. She didn't want to draw attention to herself. Sawyer keyed her microphone. "Code 2–urgent—no lights—no siren–10-49–all available units respond." Her cell phone rang and she checked the screen hopefully. "Detective James, go ahead."

"The Carson's are safe in their residence. However, there's indication of a struggle just outside the front door." The officer hesitated and then continued. "According to the mother, Sage Carson was due home by now."

Sawyer's mind screamed. She couldn't think. The radio frequency remained open while she tried to gather her thoughts. "I want a GPS lock on Sage Carson's cell." It was unlikely that Sage still had it with her, but it was worth a try.

The dispatcher chimed in. "You've got it, Detective."

Sawyer made another slow pass by the truck as she struggled to push images of her dad's previous victims from her mind. She would've once considered him to be a more than worthy opponent. Unless he'd deteriorated a hell of a lot, she'd have to sharpen her focus if she was going to save Sage. She considered where she was in relation to the Carson residence. It was half to three-quarters of a mile. The shortest route would be through the marshy inlet. Sawyer turned around, made another slow pass, parked, and then exited the car. Snoop jumped out and she clipped on his lead. She rubbed his nose into Sage's jacket to remind him of her scent. Thank God she'd left it in the car. "Track. Find Sage." Snoop's nose hit the ground at a run.

That feeling, the one that made Sawyer sick in the depths of her stomach, continued to grow stronger with each step. It was something that only a cop would understand. She knew the bastard was in close proximity.

She felt his presence. Sawyer smelled him and she knew without a doubt that he had Sage. She'd kill him if he hurt her. Maybe she'd kill him even if he didn't. Either way, he deserved whatever he got.

They hadn't gone far before Sawyer was certain that Snoop had Sage's scent. She drew her weapon and followed his lead along the water. It was barely an eighth of a mile before they stopped dead in their tracks. Snoop cocked his head and perked his ears to listen. Sawyer listened too. They both heard it—steady slurps of boots in water moving in their direction. She dropped to her belly and crawled. A few more yards and she'd be in a perfect position to get off a lethal shot. She released the clip on Snoop's lead. He stepped close. They waited and watched.

He was such a cocky bastard, sloshing as if he didn't have a care in the world. Who would dare to interfere with the great Mark James? Sawyer sighted a target between his eyes as his head bobbed just above the mangroves. He had Sage by her hair. Sawyer saw the blood on her face as she released the lock on her Glock 9mm. She held steady and waited for a clear shot. Regrettably, she didn't get one off before he saw her. Shots exploded from two directions. Sawyer choked out her final words as she crumpled down. "Snoop. Watch Sage."

***

Everything changed in the fraction of a second, of a splash and a thud. Sage had mentally prepared herself for the worst. She'd expected to be raped, tortured, and then murdered. That's what had happened to the other victims and that's what she believed would most likely happen to her. Her dread became hope the moment she spotted Sawyer. Their gazes locked. Their eyes spoke the words they'd left unsaid–I love you–I'm so sorry–stay alive.

Sage had not had much experience with guns and startled when the shots rang out. She hadn't realized a gunshot would be so loud. Brain matter splattered all over her face. It was crazy, but for an instant she appreciated that the duct tape had prevented it from getting into her mouth. In a matter of minutes, a herd of officers thundered toward them. She assumed that Sawyer had alerted them of her location before she'd gone down. Thank God. In a blink, blue was everywhere.

A young female officer came directly to Sage. "It's okay. You're safe now." She removed the duct tape from her mouth.

Sage screamed—sobbed—screamed again. "Please help Sawyer. God, please help her."

The officer released the clip and freed Sage from her attacker. She helped her make her way out of the water. She was kind and gentle. "I see blood on your face, Ma'am." She moved in for a closer look. "Are you hurt anywhere else?"

"No," Sage cried. "Sawyer's the one who needs help." She screamed hysterically. "God, please help her."

"She's being taken care of, Ma'am," the officer said as she slipped the rope off of Sage's ankle. The radio squawked and she looked down, most likely to slip it off her belt.

Sage bolted in that instant. She clawed her way up and out.

Sawyer's eyes found Sage's the moment her head popped above the mangroves. Sage was still crying hysterically as she ran to her side. Snoop, right beside her.

"Good boy," Sawyer said.

"Oh my God," Sage whimpered. "You're alive." She dropped to her knees beside Sawyer. Her shoulders heaved in gut-wrenching sobs.

Sawyer tried to reach for her, then lay back down. "I'm so sorry, baby. I didn't mean to hurt you." She shifted her position to try to ease the pain. "I don't want Laurie—God, it hurts—just you."

Sage kissed Sawyer's lips. "Don't worry. Everything's gonna be okay."

Pain shot through Sawyer's shoulder and down her arm. "Oh God," she murmured through gritted teeth. It was a through-and-through to the right shoulder. The paramedic was gentle, but it hurt like hell.

Sage glared at the first responder. "Can't you give her something?"

The woman shook her head. "No Ma'am, I'm sorry I can't. They'll give her something when she gets to the ER."

"Then get her there already," Sage ordered.

Sawyer rose up to look around. "Where's Snoop?"

"He's fine, sweetheart. I called my mom to pick him up." Sage pointed toward the road. "See, they're right over there." She kissed Sawyer's forehead. "I'm afraid he'll have a taste for meatloaf, mashed potatoes, and gravy when he comes back home."

Sawyer looked into Sage's eyes. "Did I get him?"

"You did, baby," Sage said softly. "You got him before he could hurt someone else." Her smile was tender. "Now lay back down. We'll be at the hospital before you know it."

***

Sage gained a new perspective as she waited for updates on Sawyer's condition. Forever passed between each and every one of them. In the meantime, she tried to clean up a little in the restroom and made calls. Her first was to Amber, and of course, Laurie. They came immediately. She was glad for the company, but most of all, she was glad to get clean clothes.

Amber voice trembled when she spoke. "So she's gonna be okay, right?"

Sage hugged Amber. "No one has suggested that she's not." She smiled the best she could. "She's tough. I'm sure she'll be fine."

Sage said the words, but inside she was scared. She'd seen patients deal with debilitating complications after a shoulder injury and prayed that wouldn't be the case for Sawyer. Hopefully, the bullet missed everything important–the huge blood vessels, the delicate nerves, and the ball-and-socket joint. She stood to pace some more. "You'd think they'd have more consideration." Sage looked at her mud-splattered watch. "It's been almost an hour since anyone's come out."

Laurie touched Sage's arm as she passed by. "Come on, sweetie. Sit down."

Sage didn't mean to, but she glared. Jealousy can be ugly.

"I'm sorry," Laurie said softly. "I didn't mean—"

"Let's worry about Sawyer right now," Sage said. "She's really my only concern."

"Yeah, okay," Laurie said. "But I'm a little concerned about you." She looked into Sage's eyes. "Think maybe you should have 'em look after that nasty cut?"

Sage softened. "Yeah, maybe I should."

***

The nurse swooshed through the double doors and headed directly for Sage. She probably knew who she was by her smell–fish and whatever. Or maybe it was her butterfly stitches. "Detective James is asking for you. If you'll follow me, I'll take you to her." The nurse looked to Amber and Laurie. "I'm sorry, but we can only allow just the one visitor."

Sage put her hand on Amber's shoulder. "Go on back home. I'll call you as soon as I know something."

Sage turned to follow the nurse down the hall, breathing slow and steady, holding back tears. It was a lost cause once her eyes met Sawyer's. She'd been so scared. "God, I thought I'd lost you."

Sawyer extended her good arm. "I'm so sorry. I didn't mean for any of this to happen."

Sage nestled gently and let Sawyer hold her close. "I know."

Sawyer kissed the top of her head. "It wouldn't have happened if I hadn't been such a jerk."

"We got out alive," Sage said. "That's all that matters." She didn't want to think about Laurie in Sawyer's arms or how much of a jerk Sawyer was–not right now. She just wanted to feel good. After all, they'd survived against the odds and they were together. Discussion of what had brought them to this point could wait until Sawyer was better..

Sawyer swallowed hard. "He didn't...." She rubbed her neck and tugged at her hair. "He didn't, did he?"

Tears welled up in both their eyes.

"No baby," Sage said softly, "he didn't." She didn't want to think about how close she'd come to being raped, or worse. She changed the subject. "What are they saying about your shoulder?"

"It's all good. They say it went clear through without too much damage—that is, unless you count the size of the hole." She looked into Sage's eyes. "I got lucky."

A couple day stay in the hospital and IV antibiotics was the best Sawyer could've possibly hoped for. Taking a few weeks off work was another matter, but she wasn't worried. She'd find a way to get around the mandatory time-off.

"I'm so relieved," Sage said. "I was afraid with you being right-handed it would be a problem."

"Nope. Maybe some rehab, but that's all." Her gaze lingered. "I can tell you're still mad."

Sage nodded. "I am, but it's nothing you need to worry about. I love you." She kissed Sawyer on the lips. "I really love you. We're okay."

A nurse's aid popped her head through the curtain. "Ready to head up to your room?"

Sawyer nodded. "You bet." She looked to Sage. "Please come with me."

Sage gave her the look and smiled. "Absolutely, I wouldn't be anywhere else." She winked. "Man, I hope your room has a shower."

Sawyer winked back. "I'm sure it does."

Sage made a point to chat with the nurse as they walked to the elevator. "So, I assume she'll be followed by a hospital physician?"

"Yes, she will," the nurse said. "One of our hospitalists will assume responsibility for her care once she's up on the floor. He'll most likely stop by sometime in the morning."

Sage fell quiet. She was afraid to ask who had been assigned.

Chapter Fifteen

Sawyer had managed to eat almost half of her scrambled eggs before the soft knock on the door interrupted her breakfast. "Come in," she called out in the loudest voice she could muster.

A tall blond-haired doctor with the most engaging blue eyes stepped into the room. He flashed a perfect smile and shook Sawyer's left hand. "Good morning, I'm Dr. Pierson. I'll be following your care while you're in the hospital." He glanced to the other side of the bed and raised an interested eyebrow. Then his attention snapped squarely back to Sawyer. "So, how are you feeling this morning? I'd expect a little sore."

Sawyer had noticed the doctor's distraction, but hadn't figured out what to make of it. "Yeah, a little sore, but much better than last night." She smiled. "You guys have some really good drugs in here." Doctor Pierson didn't seem amused by her comment. He was too busy making eyes at Sage. Sawyer's smile faded. The mutual gazes were too familiar.

"Hello John," Sage said softly. Her ease made Sawyer's skin crawl.

The doctor met her gaze and smiled. "It's good to see you again."

"Good to see you too," Sage said as she glanced to Sawyer.

Sawyer recognized the serious expression. Her stomach turned and knotted.

Sage held her gaze, and then nodded toward the handsome doctor. "My ex-husband, John."

Sawyer's blood ran cold in her veins.

***

Sage had known last night in the ER that there was a good chance this might happen. Why hadn't she had a conversation, then? It wouldn't have been pleasant, but at least Sawyer wouldn't have been blindsided. Now it was too late and they'd have to deal with the fallout.

Sawyer's eyes flashed with anger. "Well, now this is awkward."

Dr. Pierson cocked his head and pinched his brow. "Awkward? How so?"

Sage met the gaze of her ex-husband. "John, Sawyer and I are lovers." She glanced quickly to Sawyer and then back to her ex. "You being here—well, let's just say it's caught Sawyer by surprise."

John looked away for an instant. When his eyes returned, his attention was fully on his patient. "Sage, could you step out for a minute while I give Ms. James a quick exam."

"She can stay," Sawyer said through her clenched jaw. "I want her here."

John nodded. "That's fine, whatever makes you feel most comfortable."

Sage's smile was loving. She moved close and tried to help by untying Sawyer's gown. She took one look and clamped her hand over her mouth. "Oh my

God...." The bandage covered most of Sawyer's chest and virtually all of her right shoulder.

Sawyer reached up to stroke Sage's cheek. "I'm okay, baby. It's just a tiny little hole. It'll heal in no time." She demonstrated how small with her thumb and index finger. "It's all bandage. You stand right here and look for yourself...I'm just fine."

Sage cringed at having broken down in front of John and tried to steady herself in Sawyer's eyes. "Go ahead John, do the exam. I'm fine." When he was finished, she re-tied Sawyer's gown.

"Your wound looks good," John said "There's no sign of infection and we want to keep it that way." He jotted a couple notes into the chart. "We'll change dressings in here for a couple days, administer another round of antibiotics, and then let you go home. How's that sound?"

"It sounds good," Sawyer said. "The sooner the better."

"I'll stop by to check on you later on," John said as he took a couple steps toward the door. "Try to get some rest." He turned around and looked to Sage. "Could I speak with you for a minute in the hall?"

Sawyer's jaw locked. Her good hand clenched tightly around the bar on her hospital bed.

Sage met her gaze. She stepped close and swept a lock of hair from her eyes. "Everything's okay, baby. I'll be right back." She looked to John. "Sure, but just for a minute. I don't want to leave Sawyer alone too long."

***

Sawyer watched them step into the hall. She gasped as an unexpected, but all too familiar surge of panic gripped her throat and squeezed. Her heart raced and her brain froze. She tried to get out of bed, but the tubing held her down. Trapped and irrationally scared, she laid back and struggled to breathe. Feeling vulnerable could always push her to her limit in no time. She rammed her thumb into the buzzer. "My IV bag's empty," she barked. "With what I'll end up paying you people, could you at least take care of it without me having to tell you? Would you please get the fuck down here and turn off this incessant beep?" She heard the quiver in the young nurse's voice and for a fleeting moment felt bad.

"Yes Ma'am," the nurse said. "I'll be right there."

***

Sage had positioned herself just outside the doorway. Unfortunately, both she and John had heard Sawyer's rant. Sawyer was so sweet unless she was scared or intoxicated. "Sawyer's having a tough time. I need to get back in there." Sage turned to leave. "She'll act much better if I'm not out here in the hall with you."

John reached out to delay her departure. "Sounds insecure to me."

"Not usually," Sage said as she moved her arm to free herself from his grasp. "Now, if you'll excuse me."

"Wait—are you satisfied?" he asked softly. "I mean, with her? With a woman?"

Sage paused and met his gaze. "I am. More than I ever dreamed. I'm just sorry I didn't know this about myself...before. You know?"

John's gaze was tender. "I'm not sorry. I have no regrets that we were *us*. I love that you were once my wife."

He looked sad. Sage touched his cheek. "I don't regret us either," she said, "but you and I both know it was never going to work in the long run."

***

Sage loved Sawyer's distinctive mix of strength and vulnerability. She loved how in an instant she could swing from one extreme to the other. Today was a perfect example. Sawyer was so strong and fiercely protective, and yet at this moment, as Sage watched her from the door, she looked as terrified as a baby rabbit snared in a trap. Sage took a breath and tried to settle herself before walking back into the room. She knew that Sawyer would be enraged and didn't want to make matters worse.

"Anything I need to know?" Sawyer spat before Sage had fully made it through the door.

Sage took a quiet breath and responded softly. "Is there anything you want to know?"

Sawyer turned away and shut her eyes. "Just forget I said anything."

Sage stepped next to the bed and nudged her chin. Their eyes met for an instant. "You don't get to do that. You don't get to spew that attitude all over me and then just say forget it. That's not how it's gonna work with us." She laid her hand on Sawyer's thigh. "I saw your reaction to John and I think there are things that we need to talk about."

Sawyer flipped so fast that it had to hurt. If it did, she didn't let on. "You want me to talk, I'll talk." She almost snarled. "It looked to me like you two still have a thing for each other." She glared. "Did you forget to tell me that part?"

Sage shook her head. "There's nothing going on between us." She sat down and scooted close. "I haven't even seen him in almost five years."

"Whatever," Sawyer hissed. "I saw what I saw."

"I'm not going to engage in an argument with you over whether or not John and I are involved. I told you we're not. If you saw anything, it was a remnant from years of being married. We're not involved." Sage shook her head. "For goodness sakes, we were barely involved when we were married."

"Whatever," Sawyer said. "Whatever…."

Sage exhaled loudly. "That's it. I'm going home. You call me when you're ready to act civilized again." She bent over to kiss Sawyer goodbye, but Sawyer turned her head away. "Sometimes," Sage shook her head, "you are absolutely unbelievable."

***

Sawyer crashed and burned the moment Sage walked out the door. She had no doubt that Sage was headed straight for John. Who wouldn't, given the choice? She tried to convince herself that she was being irrational, but she couldn't stop the images from flashing through her mind. Her fear that she was losing Sage, irrational or not, had yanked her off solid ground. Sawyer ripped out her IV, got dressed, and slipped out the door.

A cruiser, much like her own, pulled into the circle drive shortly after she got downstairs. She'd been watching for it. Sawyer walked out and slid gingerly into the passenger seat. "Thanks for the lift, Sir. I appreciate you taking time to do this."

The Captain shook his head. "No problem. Are you sure you're ready to leave?" He raised an eyebrow. "You don't look so ready to me."

"I'm ready, Sir," Sawyer said as she shifted her position. She faked a smile. "You watch, I'll be back to work in no time."

The Captain reached across and patted Sawyer's good arm. "I have no doubt, Detective." He smiled. "You did a good job out there. It'll put you at the head of the line for promotion."

Sawyer nodded. "Thank you, Sir. I hope so."

***

Jenny dried her hands and picked up the phone. "Hello...well my goodness, John. It's good to hear your voice. " She called out for Sage to join her. "I hear you've been taking care of our Sawyer."

Sage shook her head as Jenny handed her the phone. She answered with irritation. "John...you can't start calling me. Sawyer's already pissed enough...what? Oh, no." She sighed. "You've got to be kidding." She looked to her mom. "Sawyer pulled out her friggin IV and left the hospital. God, she's unbelievable!" Sage sat down, rubbed her temple, and then returned her attention to the phone. "No, she's not here, but I have a pretty good idea where to find her. I'm sorry about this. It was partly my fault. I shouldn't have left her. That'll teach me for trying to shape bad behavior when I'm emotionally exhausted." Another sigh. "God, what am I gonna do? I'll never get her to check herself back into the hospital." She hung up and went to change her clothes.

Sage had little doubt where she'd find Sawyer. She loved her, but sometimes the woman could be such a pain in the ass. She declined her mom's offer to ride along, went out, and got in her car. This was something she had to do on her own. Minutes later, the bell jingled and the bartender looked up as she walked through the door. She watched him lean over to alert Sawyer of her arrival and shook her head.

"Don't look now," Butch said, "but your lady's here, and does she ever look pissed."

Sage heard the comment and watched the bartender scurry to the far end of the bar. It struck her as funny, but she didn't smile. Sawyer didn't look up when she stepped beside her. Thank God she only had time to empty one bottle. "Look, I'm exhausted," Sage said softly, "and in no mood to mess around." She leaned in for solid eye contact. "Please, go get in the car."

Sawyer didn't move for several seconds and Sage was afraid she'd miscalculated her approach. Then, Sawyer slowly shoved away the bottle she'd been working on. She hung her head, and then looked up. Her eyes were red and swollen. "I'm sorry."

"You'll be staying with us tonight," Sage said. "If you want, we can stop by your condo to pick up some clothes."

Sawyer nodded and they walked toward the car. She dropped into the passenger seat. "Sage...I'm so sorry."

Sage walked around and slid behind the wheel. She started the engine and glanced over to Sawyer. "I know you are." Sage slammed the Mustang gearshift into drive and left a trail of rubber. "We're going to have a serious conversation, but not now."

***

Sage unloaded the luggage as Sawyer made her way up the walk. Sawyer didn't like having her do it, but knew she was already in too much trouble to object. She'd caved in the interest of self-preservation. If there was one thing being a cop had taught her, it was to choose her battles wisely.

Jenny met Sawyer at the door with a big hug and a kiss on the cheek. "Thank goodness you're okay." Her eyes were as kind as her daughter's. "And thank you for all you did for our Sage. I don't know what we'd have done if we'd lost her."

"Me neither," Sawyer said. "But I may have done just that." She met Jenny's gaze. "God…she's so mad at me. I don't know if I'll ever get back in her good graces."

"She'll get over it," Jenny said. "You have nothing to worry about."

They stepped to one side as Sage plowed through the door with an armload. She looked directly at Sawyer as she went by. "Come on, let's get you changed into some loose fitting clothes."

Sawyer caught Jenny's eye as she followed along. "I hope you're right."

Jenny smiled. "Don't worry, I am."

***

The doorbell rang shortly after Sawyer got settled in on the couch. The remote was in her hand and Snoop was on the floor beside her. She was as comfortable as she was going to get for the moment.

Sage paused beside her on her way to answer the door. "I had to make some arrangements since you went crazy and yanked out your IV." She scowled. "Who does that, anyway?"

Sawyer looked up to meet Sage's angry gaze. She started to answer, but Sage continued on.

"Whatever you have to deal with," Sage said firmly, "you'd better behave."

Again Sawyer started to say something, but Sage was gone.

***

Sage was embarrassed that she had to ask for a favor from John. She just hadn't seen any other option. When her mom agreed that it was a good idea, she'd called him. "I really appreciate you doing this for us," Sage said as she opened the door. "Come in."

John kissed her cheek and stepped inside.

Sage turned her head to avoid being kissed on the mouth.

John held up his medical bag. "It's no problem. I had it with me anyway." He raised an eyebrow. "Plus, as you know, you're on my way home."

Sage smiled, and for a moment her gaze lingered. The years since they were married seemed like an eternity ago and yet…. "Yeah, I remember."

John grinned. "So, your mom's really gonna dust off her white cap?"

"Yeah, she is," Sage said. "She's excited. I don't think she was really ready to retire, but daddy got sick…you know."

"I heard," John said. "That's too bad." His gaze felt too familiar and Sage looked away. "So, where's my patient?"

"On the couch," Sage said, "and she'll be surprised to see you. I'm sorry about that too." Why hadn't she just told Sawyer that she'd called John?

John raised his eyebrow. "Don't worry, I'm sure she'll be on her best behavior."

Sage chuckled. "Yeah, right. I guess we'll see, won't we. Come on."

***

Sawyer's gaze darted between John and Sage. "What's going on?"

Sage sat down beside her. "I'm sorry I didn't check with you about this first." She reached for Sawyer's hand. "But I was afraid you'd say no."

"Okay," Sawyer said with a frown. "So tell me now."

Sage did. When she finished, Sawyer was almost sorry she'd asked. But she had to admit, the plan wasn't half bad, except for the part that included John. All in all, it was better than being cooped up in the hospital. She pursed her lips. "Whatever you want. It's fine."

Sage threw her arms around her neck and kissed her. "I love you."

Sawyer smiled. "Uh-huh, that's why you decided to torture me."

John began to fidget and finally stood. "So how about we get your exam done and change your dressing. I've got a couple more stops to make on my way home." He looked to Jenny. "You can insert the port when she's due for her next dose of antibiotic."

Jenny nodded.

Sawyer held John's gaze. This would be hard, but she was determined to act as if it wasn't. "I'm sorry to cause you extra trouble."

John smiled that friendly smile that made Sawyer sick to her stomach. "It's no problem. You've had a rough couple of days. You deserve to be cut some slack." He slipped his arm around Jenny as he looked to Sage. "Besides, stopping by gave me a chance to see the Carson's again."

Sawyer exhaled.

Sage squeezed Sawyer's hand, trying to lighten the mood. "Come on, sweetie. Let's go get you naked for the doctor."

Sawyer groaned. "God, Sage…"

<u>Chapter</u> Sixteen

Amber shook her head as the terrifying fog moved in and took control of her thoughts. She shook it again and again and again. Something wasn't right, but she couldn't put her finger on what it was. Somewhere in the recesses of her memory, she knew she'd dealt with it before. If she could just remember.... Amber's fear ramped up as she tried to escape her mind.

Laurie looked up from her newspaper. "What's wrong, honey?" She pinched her brow. "Are you alright?"

"Shh, he'll hear you," Amber snapped.

"Who will hear me?" Laurie asked. "She got up and joined Amber at the kitchen table. "We're alone. It's just us."

Amber ducked low and hid behind her chair. "Daddy will. Shh, you have to be quiet."

"He's not gonna hear us," Laurie said softly. "He's gone. You remember...."

"Sawyer just thought she killed him," Amber whispered, "but he fooled her." She popped into Laurie's space.

Laurie startled.

"He's really smart," Amber said. "Now stop talking. You have to be quiet."

"Easy. I will." Laurie leaned back and slyly slipped her cell phone from the table to her pocket.

***

Sage walked John to the door before joining her mom in the kitchen. Jenny had just turned off the faucet and was drying her hands. A beautiful crust lay rolled out on the counter. "Mmm, you're making pie."

Jenny smiled. "I am. It's for Sawyer. I felt bad for her. She was so embarrassed."

Sage actually felt bad too. She knew how hard it must've been for Sawyer to get naked for the guy that Sage used to sleep with. But no way was she going to admit it out loud. "Sawyer wouldn't have had a problem if it had been just us." Sage chuckled. "Sometimes, consequences can be a bitch.

"Well, I feel bad anyway," Jenny said, "and I'm baking her an apple pie. In fact, she gets all her favorites for dinner tonight."

Sage chuckled again. "I love her too, Mama."

Sage heard her cell phone. She ran to get it from her purse and answered. It was Laurie. "What do you mean something's off with Amber? No, I can't leave right now. Can you bring her by? Bring her pill box with you."

***

Sawyer remained in the bedroom after John left. She was no longer in the mood for TV and decided to try to take a nap. Unfortunately, sleep wouldn't come. Her mind was busy and her pain meds had almost worn off.

She hoped the soft knock on the door would be Sage, but it wasn't. It was Jenny. She was glad to see her too.

"Okay," Jenny said, "let's see your left arm."

Sawyer had known it was coming. She stuck it out for Jenny to swab on the alcohol.

"A little pinch," Jenny said as she inserted the needle. "And it's all over." She smiled and bent down to kiss Sawyer's cheek. "Good job, sweetie."

Sawyer lay back as the antibiotic and pain meds began to flow through her IV. The next thing she knew, Sage was climbing into bed beside her. Sawyer stretched and met her gaze. "Guess I must've finally fallen asleep."

"You did. I'm sorry I woke you," Sage said. "I came in to see how you were and then couldn't resist." She kissed Sawyer's lips. "How's the shoulder feel?"

Sawyer adjusted her position. It hurt, but only a little. "It's better with plenty of pain meds." For a few moments, neither spoke a word. "Sometimes, I can be such a jerk."

Sage nodded. "I know, but only sometimes." She scooted a little closer. "You know I'm still upset."

"I know." Sawyer knew the serious conversation was coming. It was just a matter of time. She kissed Sage's forehead. "You want to talk?"

Sage shook her head. "Not yet—later." She sat up. "Laurie called while you were asleep. She's concerned that Amber may have had another psychotic episode. I asked them to come over. I thought maybe we'd invite them to stay for dinner, but I wanted to check with you first."

"Yeah, that'd be nice," Sawyer said, "as long as your mom's okay with it too."

Sage smiled. "She will be." She got up, but paused at the door. "You need help getting dressed?"

"No, I'm good," Sawyer said. "I'll be out in a few minutes."

***

Sage couldn't take her eyes off of Amber from the moment she arrived. With her new haircut, she looked exactly like Sawyer. It was unsettling–definitely something that would require getting used to. Sage hoped her gawking hadn't been too obvious. She just couldn't stop herself. The problem resolved when Sawyer padded barefoot into the room. She was wearing jeans and the black shirt that Sage found so sexy.

Sawyer raised an eyebrow and smiled. She stepped behind Sage's chair and leaned in close. Her warm breath trailed across the back of Sage's neck as she whispered in her ear. "I want you too."

Sage shivered. "I'm glad." Where had this insatiable sex drive come from? It was like she had a wild animal trapped inside. Even angry, she wanted this woman.

Sawyer kissed Sage and continued on in search of Bob.

Sage watched her sexy backside.

***

"Dinner's ready," Sawyer said as she picked up a piece and placed it into the puzzle. "How 'bout you and I get our hands washed and head for the table?"

Bob looked up with the biggest smile. "I think I might be hungry."

Sawyer laughed. "Well then, I think dinner's right on time."

"She's really something," Sage said as she watched Sawyer interact with her dad.

Laurie looked that way and nodded. "Yeah, she is. She loves you, you know—more than she's ever loved anyone."

"Yeah, I know." Sage pursed her lips, got up, and headed for the dinner table.

***

Sage continued to observe Amber throughout the evening. She hadn't noticed anything out of the ordinary. What she needed was an opportunity to talk with Laurie alone. She had to be sure she wasn't missing something.

Sawyer looked up from the puzzle as she approached.

"Would you mind keeping Amber busy for a little while?" Sage asked. "Laurie and I need to spend some time together. I thought maybe we'd step outside, take a walk."

Sawyer's eyes widened. "Sure, I guess."

Sage touched her cheek and leaned down for a kiss. "You don't need to worry. I just want to talk with her about Amber." She pinched her brow. "I haven't seen any of the behaviors that she described." Then she shook her head. "I don't know if she had an episode that's resolved or if I'm missing something."

"Good," Sawyer exhaled. "Yeah, she can help us with our puzzle. Right, Bob?"

Bob smiled an absent smile.

Sawyer picked up a piece. It fit. "Hey Sis, come over here. We need your expert eye."

***

Sage waited a few minutes before she approached Laurie. She gave her a nudge and they stepped aside. "Come on, let's take a walk."

Laurie looked uneasy.

Sage couldn't help but chuckle in her mind. "Don't worry, I just want you to tell me what you observed today with Amber. It's a beautiful evening. I thought we'd talk outside."

Laurie exhaled. She raised an eyebrow and released a nervous laugh. "I wasn't sure after the other night" Their gazes locked. "I'm really sorry."

"I know—and to a certain extent, I understand," Sage said. "I really do, but I won't tolerate that behavior again."

"You won't have to," Laurie said. "Actually, Sawyer told me the very same thing before she left the other night."

"Good," Sage said with a thin smile. "I'm glad we're all on the same page. What's done is done. We're good." She nodded. "Now, tell me about Amber."

Laurie talked and Sage listened. They walked under the streetlights for almost an hour.

"Huh," Sage said as she bit her lower lip. "So, what was Amber doing just before the episode?"

Laurie's eyes widened with insight. "Oh my God. She'd been on the phone for at least two hours making burial arrangements for their dad." Mark James was to be interred in the family plot in Danville, Illinois. "She said that since Sawyer was good enough to kill him, disposing of his body was the least she could do." Laurie's expression was a mix of pity and disbelief. "I can't imagine feeling that way about your own father. Anyway, she seemed to handle it just fine, but I guess not, because it wasn't long before she was talking crazy and acting wild."

Sage nodded and smiled. "Ah—now it all makes sense." She wasn't nearly as concerned as she had been. Even on medication, that level of emotional stress could trigger a reoccurrence. The fact that it was extremely brief was a very good sign. She noticed Laurie was especially interested in her opinion with regard to Amber's prognosis.

"Okay," Laurie said, "I'll make sure Amber gets connected with a local therapist. I should have done that anyway."

"I'm glad it worked out for her to stay with you," Sage said. "It's really too soon for her to stay alone."

Laurie smiled. "I think we've been good for each other. She's so easy to have around."

***

The company had barely gotten out the front door before Sawyer headed for bed. Being upright for so long had put extra strain on her shoulder. She stripped to her boxers and climbed in, hoping that Sage would join her. Before that, she knew she'd be seeing Sage's mom.

Sage popped her head in the door. "I'll go tell Mama you're ready."

Before she could, Jenny side-stepped around her in the door. She winked at Sawyer as she hung her next dose.

Sage stepped out the door and was gone. Maybe she'd return once Jenny was done.

Sawyer smiled. "Thanks for all the trouble with the meal and everything. I know Amber and Laurie had a good time."

"It was no trouble," Jenny said. "I had fun cooking for you." Her expression became nurse-like. "Okay now, no more stalling. Let's get your wound dressing changed and your IV going. At least there won't be a stick this time." She winked. "That's better, right?"

Sawyer grinned. "Yeah, lots better." She peeled off her shirt. "This is too. At least you're not John."

Jenny's gaze was tender. "I felt bad. You looked so miserable. I'm glad it's better now. Heaven knows we'll have quite a few of these to do over the next several days." She carefully examined the wound for infection. It looked good. She changed the dressing and was done. "I couldn't get over how much you and your sister look alike. I'll never be able to tell you two apart on my own."

Sawyer chuckled as she pulled on her shirt. "That didn't used to be a problem, but now with Amber's new haircut, I may not be able to tell us apart on my own."

Sage slipped back in and climbed onto the bed beside Sawyer. "Don't worry, Mama. You'll be able to tell 'em apart." Her gaze caught Sawyer's. "They have very different personalities."

"You're probably right," Jenny said with a chuckle. "Our Sawyer is one of a kind." She kissed Sawyer's cheek. "Aren't ya, sweetie?" She paused at the door. "I'll listen for the beep."

"Jenny," Sawyer called out before the bedroom door shut, "I really do appreciate everything."

Jenny turned around. "I told you, it's no problem." She smiled the warmest smile. "I'm glad you're in our lives."

***

Sage laid her head gently on Sawyer's left breast. "Feel like talking?"

Sawyer took a breath and exhaled slowly. "Yeah, I think it's time."

Sage had been thinking about what she'd say for the last couple days. The conversation they were about to have was very important. She needed Sawyer to understand who she was and what she needed. It was the only way they were ever going to make it as a couple, and she wanted that more than anything in the world. She took a deep breath and began. "My mom and dad were always everything to each other. They still are. I'm afraid that when one goes, the other won't survive long." She dabbed a tear from the corner of her eye.

Sawyer propped herself up so that she could look directly into her eyes. She was surprised at the direction the conversation had taken.

Sage smiled tenderly. "Their love has always been the center of their universe and that's the way they wanted it. They were—no, they are completely satisfied with each other. Never, not even once, has either strayed. They've always looked only to the other for intimacy and comfort." Her swollen eyes locked with Sawyer's. "That's the kind of relationship I've always wanted, but I settled for much less with John." She reached up and brushed a lock of hair from Sawyer's eyes. "As much as I love you, I can't settle for less again." Her lower lip began to quiver and she tried to catch a sob. "I won't share you with another woman and I won't share you with a bottle. What happened the other night can never happen again, not if you want to be with me." Her gaze locked on. "Before we go any further, I need you to consider whether you want to be with a woman who'll expect so much of you. If you don't, I'll understand." Sage didn't say another word as she got up and left the bed. The door shut softly behind her.

***

Sage was trying to regain her composure as she stepped into the kitchen. She'd hoped she could slip through to the lanai without being noticed. Fat chance of that. Her mom was equipped with radar.

Jenny's arm slipped around her from out of nowhere. "What's the matter, baby?"

Sage hiccupped a couple soft sobs. "Nothing. I'm okay." She looked away. "Sawyer needs you to unhook her IV."

"Okay, I will," Jenny said as she tipped Sage's chin up to look into her eyes. "You've been crying."

"Yeah, I have." Sage choked back another and ran for the lanai.

Chapter Seventeen

Sawyer's machine beeped. She waited. Jenny would probably be in to take care of it in a moment. If not, she'd have to do it herself, even if doing it would get her into a ton of trouble. It wasn't like she had a choice. Sage was upset and she had to be sure she was okay. Priorities were priorities. Her jaw relaxed when she heard the soft knock on the bedroom door. "Come in," Sawyer said. "Is Sage alright?"

Jenny smiled, but Sawyer could tell she knew something was wrong. "She's crying on the lanai." Jenny unhooked the tube and shut the machine off for the night. "Did something happen between you two?"

Sawyer looked out the window. "I fail her every time I turn around." Sawyer could never seem to measure up. She'd always known she wasn't relationship material. She wished she was, but wishing didn't make it so. "Sage wants a partner who'll be to her like you and Bob are to each other." Sawyer dabbed a tear before it had a chance to fall. "She deserves a whole lot better than what I have to offer." Sawyer bit her lower lip to stifle a sob. "Maybe I should just let her go."

Jenny sat down on the edge of the bed. "Aw, sweetie. Come here." She gripped the back of Sawyer's neck and pulled her close.

It felt good to be held and, of course, Sawyer broke down. She hadn't had that problem before Sage. The woman had destroyed her defenses. She rubbed her eyes, embarrassed. "I'm sorry."

Jenny stroked her back in circles. It felt good. "For what?" She kissed the top of her head. "For showing me you have feelings?" A tender smile crossed her face. "Honey, I already knew."

Sawyer looked up and met her gaze. It'd been so long since she'd had a mom. That felt good too.

"You know," Jenny said softly, "figuring out how you fit with someone else is kind of like putting a jigsaw puzzle together. Sometimes you have to turn a piece over and look at it from a different angle to see that it's the one you were looking for all along." She squeezed Sawyer as she straightened and sat up. "It's really simple, honey. You just have to let Sage in. You have to let her know you like no one else knows you. Trust her with your feelings and let her be the one who meets your needs." She gave Sawyer a pat on her thigh. "The very fact that we're having this conversation right now tells me that you're everything my daughter's looking for in a partner. Go to her. She's waiting." Jenny stood and stepped out into the hallway.

Sawyer listened to Jenny coax Bob from his puzzle to their bed. They had what she wanted with Sage. She pulled on her jeans and considered what Jenny had said. Her words were like pearls of wisdom that were enough to carry a relationship through a lifetime. All Sawyer needed to do was apply them. She stood in the doorway of the lanai as her eyes adjusted to the darkness, inhaling the salty breeze. The sounds of the night—sobbing and wind chimes—were all that she heard. It was in that moment that Sawyer vowed to love Sage as she deserved to be loved and to raise her own expectations for herself. She stepped in quietly and straddled the chaise lounge. "Come here, baby." She patted the seat between her legs. "Come here and let me hold you."

After a couple minutes, Sage got up. "I don't want to hurt your shoulder."

Sawyer shook her head. "You're not gonna hurt my shoulder. I'm on pain meds."

Sage sat and gently leaned back, careful not to put pressure on the shoulder.

Sawyer held her, nuzzled, and stroked.

Sage wept for a little while, but then she began to moan.

Sawyer nibbled her neck and whispered in her ear. "I want this woman. She doesn't expect too much of me at all." Her hand moved up to cup Sage's breast.

Sage's breathing quickened and she arched under Sawyer's touch. "Feels good."

Sawyer nibbled some more. "It's just you that I want, now and forever. From now on, I'll never turn to the bottle or someone else. I promise." Her hand slipped underneath Sage's blouse. "Come to bed."

Sage met her gaze. "Mmm, but what about your shoulder?"

"What shoulder?" Sawyer asked with a grin. "Other parts of my anatomy are in charge right now."

"We can't," Sage said. "You'll re-injure yourself. You have to be careful."

Sawyer kissed her with tongue. "Then I'll be very careful. Come on…please."

Sage shook her head. "Promise to take it easy?"

Sawyer grinned. "Oh yeah."

In the bedroom, she watched Sage remove each item of her clothing. Sawyer caught her breath when Sage laid naked on the edge of the bed. God, she was a beautiful woman.

"Now be careful," Sage said. "I don't want you to hurt yourself."

Sawyer just looked at her. "Stop worrying." She dropped to her knees between Sage's legs. "It's gonna be all mouth."

Sawyer let on like there wasn't a problem even though Sage had sensed that there was. Sometimes, Sage knew her better than she knew herself, but not this time. Tonight, they both knew she wasn't yet well. Her shoulder pain had been worsening over the last couple of hours. Another dose of pain meds probably would've helped, but to ask for it would've meant giving up sex. The only way they were going to make love tonight was if Sawyer denied she was in pain, so she did. She denied because tonight she needed Sage more than ever. After she'd made love to her, she kissed her lips and apologized. "Next time I'll do better."

Sage kissed her and reached underneath her shirt. "You did just fine."

Sawyer gasped as Sage raked her fingernails across her nipple. She closed her eyes and tried to focus on pleasure instead of pain. No way were they not gonna finish what she'd started. She was just thankful that her T-shirt provided extra shoulder protection. She began to pant, her hair dampened, and she gasped.

Sage stopped mid-suckle. The gasp hadn't sounded quite right. She sat up and knew immediately that something was wrong. "Aw, baby."

Sage took a deep breath and tried to rein in her arousal. She gathered Sawyer into her arms. By that time, Sawyer was sobbing hysterically. She stroked her and ran her fingers through her hair as she tried to determine what was wrong. Sawyer wasn't talking, so Sage just held her and rocked her gently in her arms. The sobs seemed uncontrollable. They went on and on and on.

Sage drew on her experience as a therapist. She knew what to do to help. Nothing worked. She simply couldn't settle Sawyer down. Sage panicked and the fact that she'd panicked made her panic even more. She took a deep breath and tried to center herself. Her voice was unsteady, but firm. "Come on, you need to get yourself under control. You're too worked up. Come on, breathe with me— slow and steady."

A knock sounded on the bedroom door. It was Jenny. "Sage…Sawyer…is everything alright in there?"

Sage's voice trembled. "Yeah, we're okay."

Jenny knew her daughter well. Her voice wouldn't be shaking unless there was a problem. "I'm coming in, sweetie." The door opened and she stepped inside. "I need to see for myself."

Sawyer didn't even notice that they had a visitor.

Sage was propped up against the white headboard of her queen-sized bed. She was naked, holding a half-naked and sobbing Sawyer. She met her mom's worried gaze. "Sorry, I didn't have enough notice to get dressed."

"You have nothing to be sorry about," Jenny said. "What can I do to help?"

Sage looked down at Sawyer. Her breathing had slowed and she was less agitated.

"She's okay now," Sage said. She shook her head. "But I didn't think I was ever gonna get her to quiet."

Jenny wrinkled her brow.

"We're okay. You don't need to worry," Sage said. "Really. It's not about us, at least I don't think it is." She continued to stroke Sawyer's temples. "She's not really saying much yet. It might take us a while." She looked up and forced a smile. "Don't worry, I know what I'm doing." She motioned toward the door with her head. "Now go on. Go back to bed. We're fine."

Jenny leaned down to kiss her daughter. "I'll leave our door open just in case you change your mind."

"Okay," Sage said, "but we're fine."

***

Once the flood of tears had stopped, Sawyer nuzzled in against Sage's breast. She listened to the rhythm of her heartbeat. It soothed her in her depths.

"Want to tell me what happened?" Sage asked softly.

Sawyer looked up into her eyes. "I don't cry–not when the bastard raped us, not when he forced me to have sex with my sister, and not even when my mom died." She choked a little, but continued on. "Not when I raped and beat Laurie, not when I shot the bastard, not when he died—I don't cry. At least I didn't until you came into my life."

Sage looked into Sawyer's troubled eyes. "You feel safe with me." She ran her fingers through her hair. "I'm glad."

Sawyer turned her gaze toward the window. "Tonight wasn't a panic attack."

"I know," Sage said softly. "Want to tell me what it was?"

Sawyer looked back to Sage. "It just hit me. I watched you make love to me. It felt so right. It felt good. I felt safe." Their gazes locked. "I haven't felt safe very many times in my life. It just hit me–the sexual abuse, Amber, the death of my parents, almost losing you. It all just hit me and I lost it."

Sage leaned down and their lips met in the softest kiss. "I'm so proud of you, Sawyer." Her eyes were teary, but she smiled. "You found the courage to feel your pain. Your wounds are beginning to heal."

Sawyer shook her head. "Maybe. But God, why do I have to keep dragging my problems to bed with us? I'm so sorry."

Sage pulled her close. "Whatever you need, wherever you need it. It's fine."

***

Laurie heard the old porch swing squeak. It wasn't a surprise. It was where Amber liked to have her morning coffee. She poured one for herself and joined her. "What time did you get up?" She shook her head. "I know it was ungodly early."

Amber rolled her eyes. "Yep, it was. My sleep schedule's all screwed up." She shook her head. "I know it's gotta be all the stupid meds they have me on."

Laurie raised an eyebrow. "Or maybe it's all you've had to deal with lately."

Amber took a sip and looked into her eyes. "You're the one whose had a lot to deal with. You got beat up. You had to deal with a ton of crap to get a protective order. Oh yeah, and then there was all the crap with Sawyer."

They swung in silence for several minutes before Laurie spoke again. Her voice was soft. "I've been thinking about what you said the other night, about settling for women who don't treat me right and looking past the ones who'd treasure me."

The old swing squeaked a few more times before Amber responded. "Good, I hoped that you would." She looked over to Laurie, then back to the porch rail. The swing squeaked some more.

"I never knew you felt that way," Laurie said softly. "God, I never knew." A few more squeaks and their eyes met. "You never told me."

"There was no reason to tell you." Amber's gaze was like a laser. "You were with other people." Her eyes were glued to the post in front of her. "Plus, I knew you didn't want me anyway."

"I'm 55," Laurie said. "Twenty years older than you."

Amber whipped her head and locked her eyes. "And you were 20 years older than Sawyer. We're the same age. Remember?" The swing came to a dead halt. Amber jumped up, ran down the steps, and across the yard.

Laurie felt a twinge in the pit of her stomach as she watched Amber go. She waited on the porch until she returned a couple hours later. They went on as if nothing had happened—but it had.

***

Sawyer watched Sage pack her suitcase. She'd known what was coming when it was moved from the closet shelf, but she hadn't said a word. She'd been alone

162

most of her adult life. Now, she couldn't stand the thought of it. Regardless, there was no reason she had to act like a baby.

Sage looked up. How did the woman always seem to know what she was thinking? "Honey, I hate it too, but I have to go back to work."

"I know," Sawyer said softly. "I'm just gonna miss you."

Sage came over and put her arms around Sawyer's neck. "I'll miss you too." She cocked her head and smiled a little. "But I'm only going to be an hour away. We'll figure this thing out."

Sawyer forced a smile. "I know we will." She pulled Sage close. Their lips met and their tongues dueled. "I'm just being a baby. Go on, finish up."

Sage gathered her socks and zipped them into the pocket of her luggage. "You know it's kind of funny, I never used to mind sleeping alone. In fact, when I was married I seized every opportunity. If there was an overnight conference, I was first in line to go." She chuckled. "Boy did I love it when John and I worked different shifts at the hospital." She bent down to kiss Sawyer. "But now, I simply abhor sleeping alone."

Sawyer smiled an unconvincing smile. "Yeah, me too."

Sage reached down and roughed the fur between Snoop's ears. She'd never had a dog before this one. "You guys headed back to the condo?"

"Yeah, probably. But I have no doubt we'll be frequent visitors over here." She smiled. "See, it isn't just you who I've fallen in love with. I've fallen in love with your parents too."

Sage laughed. "And they have certainly fallen in love with you."

Chapter Eighteen

Amber washed. Laurie dried and put away. That was their routine since the dishwasher died. This evening was no exception. They were almost finished. Soon, they'd be popping popcorn and watching the new episode of Grey's Anatomy. Amber rinsed the last saucer and held it out. Laurie didn't take it. Instead, she took Amber's hand. Their eyes met and Amber forgot all about their previous plans.

"Kiss me," Laurie said softly. "I want you to kiss me."

Amber swallowed the lump in her throat. "Okay, I will." She leaned in and their lips met. Laurie's were softer than she'd ever imagined. "I'd treasure you for a lifetime if you'd let me."

Laurie dried the saucer and put it away in the cabinet. Her voice was filled with emotion. "I don't think I'd know how to act."

Amber smiled and stepped closer. "They tell me I'm a pretty good teacher." She nibbled Laurie's earlobe. "I think you'd learn in no time at all." She leaned in to nuzzle her long blond hair. "God, you smell so good." She kissed down the back of her neck. "You were always the one you know." Her hands slid down to Laurie's hips and she snugged Laurie's bottom tight against her crotch. Her dream was about to become reality. She could feel it.

She trailed her fingertips across Laurie's taut abdomen and unsnapped her shorts.

Laurie's breathing quickened. "God," she panted, "your touch is so gentle."

Amber unzipped the shorts and slipped inside. "Oh man…." She closed her eyes. "You want me too."

"Yeah," Laurie said, "I do." She tilted her head back for another kiss. "I just didn't think the first time we made love it would be on the kitchen counter."

Amber pressed closer. "Then maybe we need to relocate to your bedroom."

***

Sage whipped into her parking space with only minutes to spare. She usually wasn't late, but this morning was different. The job had literally ripped her out of her lover's arms. She hurriedly slipped her purse strap over her shoulder, slid out of the car, and headed for the door. She was still moving at a fairly good clip when she got up to her office.

"Hey girl," Cathy called out as she slipped her key into the slot. "Did you get the respite for your dad all squared away?"

"No," Sage sighed, "meant to, but didn't." She shook her head. "You wouldn't believe what my last couple weeks have been like. I feel like I've been riding a friggin' roller coaster. The highs unbelievable and the lows petrifying."

"Sounds like you had some interesting time off," Cathy said. "I think we need to do lunch. Noon?"

Sage smiled. "Yeah, that'll work. No doubt I'll still be digging out from under this mound of paper." She gave her friend a hug. "Lunch with you sounds absolutely wonderful."

***

Sawyer was packed and ready to head home by the time Sage backed out of her parent's driveway. She stood on the porch and watched her go. It would've been easier if she could've just gone to work herself. Since that hadn't been an option, she'd hung around to work on the jigsaw puzzle with Bob. It was way better than going home to her empty condo. It's funny how she'd never noticed it being empty before. When she did finally leave, Jenny and Bob walked her to the door.

"I could install door locks later this afternoon if you want," Sawyer offered. She met Jenny's gaze. "I know you'd rest better if you knew Bob couldn't get out."

"You're always so kind to us," Jenny said. She put her arms around Sawyer's neck and kissed her cheek. "Maybe afterward you'd like to stay for dinner."

Sawyer grinned. "If it wouldn't be too much trouble."

***

Sage pushed her tray past the desserts and paused in front of the salads. She slid the glass door open and removed the one that looked the most edible—chicken walnut. She spotted Cathy in a booth in the corner. Cathy spotted her too and smiled.

"Hey there girlfriend. It feels like forever since we talked." Cathy chuckled. "Judging from the preview this morning, I think I missed several chapters in the novel of your life."

Sage laughed as she freed her utensils from their wrapper. "For me to tell you everything, we'd have to do lunch tomorrow as well. You go first. What's new in your world?"

"Nothing—husband, kids, and laundry galore." She raised her eyebrow. "Now talk girl, the suspense is killing me."

Sage forked a piece of chicken off her salad. "God, where do I start?" The beginning seemed like a good place and she went forward. After she finished her story, she paused.

For a moment, Cathy sat speechless. Eventually, she spoke. "Wow…." Her eyes narrowed and her head tilted slightly. "So you slept with her and almost got killed. That's not so impressive."

They chuckled.

Sage held her friend's gaze. "Yeah, I slept with her."

"Good grief girl," Cathy said. "I can feel the heat all the way across the table." She laughed. "I don't even have to ask if you had a good time."

Sage's face reddened. "Sorry, that obvious, huh?"

"Oh yeah, that obvious." Cathy leaned back. "And you've fallen in love with her. I can tell."

Sage's eyes moistened as she looked up. "Yeah…."

Cathy seemed perplexed. "So what does that mean, exactly?" She pinched her brow. "No, I didn't ask that right."

"I get what you mean," Sage said. She thought for a moment before she spoke. "Times are changing, my friend. I guess I'd marry her if she asked."

"Wow," Cathy said as her mouth curved into a smile. "So you think you want to be a cop's wife, huh?"

Sage laughed. "Oh yeah, I always wanted to be just like you when I grew up."

***

Sawyer had spent much of the last 15 years alone. Whether at home, work, or at the bar, alone was most comfortable. Well, times had changed. It wasn't that way anymore. It'd been less than three hours since she'd left the Carson's and already she was at loose ends. The solitude was deafening. There was no Sage, no Bob, no Jenny, and no work. For God's sake, there wasn't even a jigsaw puzzle—just Snoop. She checked her watch for the umpteenth time, 2:35 pm. Sawyer furrowed her brow and smiled. They wouldn't mind if she showed up early. After all, it had become her second home. She pulled on her navy cargo shorts and a faded T-shirt. She grabbed her toolbox as she headed out the door. "Come on, Snoop."

Jenny opened the door on the first ring of the bell. "Well look who's here." She smiled.

Sawyer kissed Sage's mom hello. "Too early?"

Jenny shook her head. "Never."

Sawyer held up her toolbox. "I'll get the locks on," she said. "Then, you can point me to any project you want." She bowed. "At your service, Ma'am."

"Maybe your first one should be the jigsaw puzzle," Jenny said with a chuckle. "Bob's been wandering around like a lost soul ever since you left this morning."

***

Sage checked her watch for the fifth time since getting back from lunch—3:30 p.m. There was just another hour and a half to go. She loved what she did for a living, but man, this workday was going slowly. She lowered her head onto her folded arms and let her thoughts drift to Sawyer.

"Oh my," Cathy said as she peeked in the door. "Now, that just doesn't look good at all."

Sage raised her head. "It's been a long day."

"Uh-huh," Cathy said. "And you're just realizing how far you are from Sarasota."

"You got it," Sage said. "I don't know what I'm gonna do about it either." She met Cathy's gaze. "What would you do if you were me?"

Cathy sat down on the sofa. "Well I don't know. I'd have to think about it. Right off the top of my head, I can only see four—no, three options."

Sage perked up with a raised eyebrow. "And they are?"

"Well, behind door number one," Cathy said, "I guess you'd change jobs and move to Sarasota; door number two, Sawyer would change jobs and move here; now—door number three. Well, that has one of you commuting." She curled up her lip. "Not good."

Sage leaned back. "So what was gonna be behind door number four?"

"You'd break up with Sawyer," Cathy said.

Sage's mouth fell open. "Well that's definitely not a choice."

Cathy smiled. "I know."

"Thanks," Sage said. "You always help me clear the bugs off my windshield."

Cathy chuckled. "You're welcome, I guess." She made a face and looked down to check her watch. "Oh look, it's 30 minutes closer to quitting time."

Sage grinned and wadded up a piece of paper. She hurled it and it bounced off Cathy's rear as she stepped out the door. Their conversation, as always, had been helpful.

***

Bob followed along like a puppy as Sawyer clipped through Jenny's honey-do-list. She wondered if he realized that what she was doing was what he used to do himself. They both loved working with tools.

Bob dug through Sawyer's toolbox and handed her a pair of pliers.

"That's right, buddy. It's the one with the pointy nose. Good job." Sawyer smiled and patted him on the back. "You've been a lot of help this afternoon. Thanks."

Bob beamed. "You're welcome." He'd accomplished a useful task on his own. Lately, that was happening less and less often.

Jenny smiled as she watched the pair from the bathroom doorway. "He used to be quite the expert at the hardware store." She stroked her husband's cheek. "He could answer any question and demonstrate all the tools." Her voice faded off. "He was really something back then, a regular mechanical genius." Her eyes twinkled as they shifted back to Sawyer. "You're a regular mechanical genius yourself." She crinkled her brow. "In fact, I think that'll be your new nickname. You'll be my mechanical genius from now on." Jenny grinned. "Now you two wash up. Dinner's almost ready."

***

Sage parked the Mustang and stumbled in her front door. Maybe tomorrow would be a better day. She'd expected the first day being away from Sawyer to be rough. What she needed to do was call her and then go for a nice long bike ride. Peddling always helped.

She dialed. "Mama?" Sage's voice raised a full octave. "What are you doing answering Sawyer's cell?" She held the phone to her ear as she kicked off her shoes and hung her dress onto a hanger. "Uh-huh, that figures. So what's for dinner?" she chuckled. "That figures too…of course, it's one of her favorites. You are so wrapped around my girlfriend's little finger." Sage chuckled again. "Of course I want to talk with her."

Their conversation was a long one. When they hung up, Sage was struck by how much it pleased her that her parents and Sawyer had each other even if she was up in Tampa alone. She rolled the blue 22-speed out the front door, flipped up the kickstand, and rode. She headed for one of her favorite spots—the bike path that ran alongside 22 miles of shore. Within minutes, her mind began to clear. She breathed in the sea breeze, listened to the waves lick the sand, and peddled.

Sage knew better than to head out for a long ride without checking the weather forecast, but her mind was elsewhere. When the thunder began to rumble, she knew she was in trouble. It was near the end of hurricane season, but strong late day storms were still a possibility. A bolt of lightning crackled its way across the sky and wind gusts began to roar. She struggled to remain upright and peddle forward. Just as a golfer is at risk of being struck by lightning on a golf course, she was at serious risk on the shore. She reached into her pants pocket for her cell phone. It wasn't there. Her heart rushed blood through her veins and she peddled hard.

***

Sawyer was feeling a little better after talking with Sage. At least she'd gotten to hear her voice. She'd only been gone since morning and already they knew the situation wouldn't be workable. This was going to be one long week. The only bright spot was that tonight's dinner had offered Sawyer an opportunity to talk with Jenny about her plans for Sage's 40th birthday. Jenny seemed pleased and was glad to help.

Sawyer dialed Sage again as she backed out of Sage's parents' driveway. No answer. She walked Snoop around the block and tried one more time. Still gone. She unlocked her door and stepped inside her condo–dark and way too quiet. She switched on the floor lamp, poured a glass of tea, and picked up the remote. Her thumb flicking paused on channel nine to catch the weather. She looked at the clock, 9:33 p.m., and dialed again.

Sage should've been back from her ride by now, but wasn't. Where in the heck was she? Sawyer checked to be sure she hadn't missed her call. By this point, she was way beyond worry. She paced in front of the picture window—dialed and re-dialed—but still, no answer.

Powerful storms had moved through the Tampa area. The radar map looked awful. She wasn't sure where Sage had planned to ride, but called Tampa PD anyway. They didn't have any reports of an accident involving a bike. It was 10:39 p.m. on a work night. God, please let her be alright.

***

It was well after 11:00 when a drenched and extremely tired Sage rolled her bike onto her living room carpet. She stumbled toward her bedroom to look for her cell. It was on the nightstand vibrating. She'd expected to be home by 8:45 p.m. and knew Sawyer would've already called. Was she ever going to be livid. Sage held her breath as she answered the phone. "Oh baby, I'm so sorry. Soaked, but that's all…I didn't mean to scare you. I would've called, but I forgot my phone. Yeah, I know, not smart. Next time I'll be more careful." After they hung up, Sage flopped back on her bed and stared at the ceiling. Sawyer had clearly been afraid, but hadn't yelled at all—fear without anger. Sage smiled.

***

Sawyer slept sporadically that night, rolling out well before dawn. She took a shower and gathered several changes of clothes. If she couldn't be at work, she might as well be where she wanted. Snoop followed her out the door and got in the car.

The cruiser slowed to a crawl as Sawyer turned into the trailer park. It was early and she didn't want the shells to crackle too loud under her tires. She parked in front of trailer number five. The shades were pulled, but Laurie was probably up. She'd always been an early riser. It surprised her when Amber answered the door with Laurie right behind her. They were giggling uncontrollably, but stopped long enough to invite her inside. What in the world could be so funny at this hour of the morning?

"I just wanted to let you know I'll be in Tampa for a few days," Sawyer said. She waited for Amber's attention to leave Laurie and come to her. "Want me to stop by to check on your apartment?"

"No," Amber said. She winked at Laurie. "I think we'll head up that way in a day or two." Their gaze lingered. "Thanks, though."

Laurie's face was full of color. She did that thing she used to always do with her eyes. That, plus the strange behavior could only mean one thing. Laurie was sleeping with Amber. Unbelievable.

"Who knows," Amber said, "we might even drive by the school. I need to talk with Greg about coming back." She grinned. "Maybe by Thanksgiving."

"Man," Sawyer exclaimed, "that's soon."

"Yeah," Amber said proudly. "My therapist cleared me. It's time."

It wasn't that Sawyer doubted Amber's readiness to return to her classroom. It wasn't that she didn't want her to return. It was more that it hadn't been that long since Sawyer had feared that the Amber she knew, the one who knew her so well, was gone. She smiled as she made her way to the car. Everything was working out just fine—better than she'd ever dreamed.

Chapter Nineteen

Sawyer leaned back against Sage's office door. She checked her watch–a little before 7:00. She'd been waiting for almost an hour. It didn't matter. The most important thing this morning was that she got to see Sage before she started her day. Finally, the sound of familiar heels came clicking around the corner. It was 7:45 a.m.

Sage grinned when Sawyer caught her eye. "Good morning, handsome." She brushed intimately against Sawyer's shoulder and unlocked her office door. "I didn't expect to see you until Friday." She kissed her lips. "What a wonderful surprise."

Sawyer smiled shyly. "I couldn't wait any longer."

They stepped inside and Sage gave the door a nudge. It shut and they pressed into each other's arms.

"Mmm, feels nice," Sage said with a soft nuzzle and kiss on Sawyer's neck. "I'm glad you stopped by."

Sawyer raised her eyebrow. "I can stay if you want."

Sage shook her head and smiled. "If I want, the woman says." She laughed. "You're such a funny girl sometimes." She pulled Sawyer down for another kiss. "Of course I want."

Sawyer's plan was to stay with Sage until she returned to work. She hoped that would give them plenty of time to figure things out. As far as she was concerned, no potential solution was off the table—not commuting and not changing jobs. She'd do whatever was needed because being with Sage was what was most important.

Sage reached up and ran her fingers through Sawyer's hair. She must have sensed her thoughts. "We'll figure this out, sweetheart." She tucked a stray lock behind her ear. "Trust me, we will."

Sawyer smiled and kissed her forehead. "I know we will." Then she made a face. "Speaking of figuring things out, your mom said if I'm gonna stay here this week I have to find a nurse to do my wound care." She sheepishly met Sage's eye. "She thought it looked a bit infected last night. She thinks I went back to the gym before I was ready."

"Uh-huh," Sage said, "I'm absolutely certain of that." Her expression became pensive. "I'm sure Cathy will help."

The door opened and they both looked up. "Well, speak of the devil," Sage said with a shake of her head. "Didn't your mama ever teach you to knock?"

"I guess not," Cathy chuckled with a nod to Sawyer. "Good to see you again, Detective." Her eyes turned to Sage. "I hope I didn't interrupt."

***

Sawyer inserted the key—her very own key to Sage's apartment—and turned the lock. With Snoop on her heel, she stepped inside and dropped her duffle bag to the floor. Sage's touch was everywhere in the cozy, two-bedroom apartment. It was her first chance to be alone in her space. She walked over to study the collection of photos displayed on the far wall—a little redhead standing proudly with what must have been her first bike, graduation and homecomings that followed, Sage as maid of honor in Cathy's wedding. She turned around to examine the row of cycling trophies. Everything important to Sage either adorned these walls or was perched proudly on a shelf. She zeroed in on what appeared to be the most recent addition and smiled. Sage had saved the article from the Sarasota paper that announced her promotion to Sergeant.

Sawyer picked up the duffle bag and carried it into the master bedroom. She flopped back on the bed, swiped the screen on her Smartphone, and dialed. Cathy answered, surprised she'd called. After all, they'd just spoken two hours prior.

"Can you keep a secret?" Sawyer asked. "Because I need your help."

Cathy assured her that she could. When they hung up, Sawyer was all smiles. Her plan for Sage's birthday was coming together. The trick was to pull it off as a surprise. She spent the rest of the afternoon making arrangements.

***

Sage was sorting mail as she came through the front door–5:35 p.m., right on time. Her homecoming tickets were in the pile and she headed for Sawyer to show her. "Want to take your girl to homecoming on Saturday?" She shifted the tickets between her fingers. "It's the long awaited SuperBull."

"How could I possibly refuse an invitation to something called a SuperBull?" Sawyer smiled. "Of course I'll take you."

"Good," Sage said. "Because I usually end up going alone and then have to put up with my social work pals giving me a rough time." She giggled. "Well, this year they can just feast their eyes."

Sawyer laughed. "I should have known that I'd be a show-and-tell item."

***

Sawyer was glad to stay in Tampa with Sage, but had to admit she'd missed being around Sage's mom and dad. When Saturday rolled around, she was more than ready to head back to Sarasota. She caught Jenny's eye as she inserted the last two pieces of blue sky into Bob's puzzle. "I sure did miss you guys."

"And we missed you," Jenny said as her gaze fell on Sawyer's right shoulder. "Did you get that taken care of while you were there?"

Sawyer pursed her lips. "Yeah, just like you told me to." She shook her head. "Cathy did it." And rolled her eyes. "Soon, everyone in your daughter's past and present will have seen me naked. I'm working my way through the list, one person at a time."

Jenny chuckled. "Poor baby—so shy." She looked up and smiled as Sage came through the door. She'd taken a call from work and hadn't made it in from the driveway. She was wearing her new green and gold USF sweatshirt.

"How cute," Jenny said. "I love the ones with Rocky the Bull."

179

"I'll have to get you one," Sage said with a big smile. "Sawyer has one just like it, too. She'll put it on after we see what you think about the infection in her shoulder. Cathy thought it looked pretty good last night."

Jenny looked over to Sawyer. "Come on, sweetie. Let's get this over with."

***

It didn't matter how early you got there, close parking was always hard to come by on the day of homecoming.

"There's one," Sage yelped. "That is, if it's not too narrow."

Sawyer puffed up with confidence, "I can fit. Just watch me." She began to maneuver back and forth. Finally, the Mustang squeezed into the slot. "See, I told ya."

"Uh-huh—smarty pants." Sage shook her head. "And my blue Mustang almost had a red stripe."

"I had plenty of room," Sawyer said. She raised an eyebrow. "In fact, I had room to spare."

"Uh-huh, sure you did." Sage shook her head and chuckled. "You can be such a man sometimes."

Sawyer pinched her brow and held back a smile. "I'm not sure that was a compliment."

Sage tiptoed up for a kiss. "It wasn't." She cocked her head as the marching band fired up in the distance. "Ahh, the Herd of Thunder. They're playing the USF Fight Song." Sage squared her shoulders, grinned with pride, and formed the bullhorn symbol with her fingers. "Go Bulls!" she yelled at the top of her lungs.

Sawyer laughed until she cried. "Alright, Little Bull. Let's go join the stampede." She took Sage by the hand and they hiked uphill in search of other social work alumni."

***

Laurie breathed a sigh of relief as her old Buick chugged into Tampa. They were close enough now to get a tow without paying a small fortune.

Within minutes, Amber pointed to a carport next to a pinkish-colored upscale building. "You can park over there." She pointed again. "And that's where we go in. The elevator is right around the corner."

"Wow," Laurie said. "This is really nice, and so close to the water."

Amber smiled. "Thanks, I like it a lot." The elevator door hissed opened and they stepped inside. "Two."

Laurie pushed the button. "I didn't know teachers could afford to live in places like this." She met Amber's gaze. "I'll bet your rent's more than five times what I pay." Laurie had been looking forward to seeing where Amber taught, where she lived, and where she slept, but she'd never dreamed it would all be this nice. Even Amber's bug was the swankiest model. "I'm really proud of you. You've done well for yourself."

"It's not so much," Amber said, "just two bedrooms and a tiny kitchen." The elevator dinged, the door opened, and they stepped off. "Wait until you see it, though." Her voice filled with pride. "I decorated it all by myself. It's totally mid-century. I did it one piece at a time." Her eyes twinkled as she unlocked the door.

Laurie stepped inside. "Oh my God, it's so…'70s." She grinned. "I love it!"

Amber grinned back ear-to-ear. "Go ahead, take a look around."

***

The University of South Florida campus buzzed with team spirit and rekindled friendships. Sage was so relaxed. Sawyer enjoyed seeing her have so much fun. After everything she'd been through, she was just beginning to act like her old self.

They'd no more than stepped into the social work alumni tent when a small chorus of women screamed Sage's name from somewhere in the crowd. She perked up to listen and scanned her surroundings. "Oh my God," she squealed. "Sally–Suzie–Karen!" She grabbed Sawyer's hand at a run.

Sawyer broke into a jog behind her. "I'm coming." She grimaced as she picked up speed. "Easy on the shoulder. I'm right behind ya."

The three screaming 30-somethings welcomed Sage with open arms. Dorm-mates in college, they had obviously remained close through the years. They hugged, kissed, and hugged again. All talking at once, their conversation was a mile-a-minute. Sawyer hung back and remained perfectly still except for the movement required to soothe her aching shoulder. Her hope was to go unnoticed—fat chance of that.

Sage reached back and gave her a tug forward. "Girls, this is Sawyer."

Sawyer felt her face flush as the three straight women made noises as they checked her out. She nodded. "Ladies."

A rapid flurry of similar encounters followed. Finally, Sage settled and they sat like normal people at the bar. Sawyer wasn't surprised that Sage had so many friends, but did they all have to come to homecoming?

"Am I wearing you out?" Sage asked with fake concern.

"No way, sweetie," Sawyer lied. "I've got miles to go before I drop."

"Uh-huh," Sage said as she leaned over to kiss her cheek. "You look like it." She smiled. "Thanks for being such a good sport, and sorry about the shoulder. I just got a little overexcited."

"You're welcome, and I'm fine," Sawyer said. A wink followed. She ordered two iced teas with lots of lemon. The drinks arrived just as Sage spotted someone else.

"Jaina," Sage screamed out at the top of her lungs.

The woman looked up—surprised.

"Oh my God," Sage squealed. "It is you!" She shot straight up and sprinted toward the attractive woman at the far end of the bar.

She was about Sage's age and had long blonde hair. A taller woman with short brown hair stood behind her. Sage and Jaina hugged and chattered on for what seemed like hours. The taller woman looked exhausted. She'd probably been put through her paces on this day of the USF SuperBull too. Sawyer lifted her glass and watched. Thank God she'd been allowed to sit, even if only for a moment.

It wasn't long before Sage made her way back to make introductions. Sawyer knew that she would. Introducing her as her girlfriend seemed to be half the fun. She nodded to Jaina and shook Zane's hand—nice folks. Actually, Sawyer liked all of Sage's friends from college.

"Jaina and I were best friends," Sage said, "roommates the last two years." She looked to Jaina. God, how long has it been since we've seen each other—11, maybe 12 years?"

Jaina nodded. "Yeah, that's about right." She shook her head. "How'd we let so much time go by?"

"Got me," Sage said. "We'll have to make up for it."

Jaina grinned. "Yes we will!"

***

Sage ran into one old college friend after another that morning. It seemed like there were more than there were last year or the year before. Maybe they were there and she just hadn't noticed. This year, she felt different and they were everywhere she looked. This year, she was happy, she felt alive, and she knew who she was. What a difference Sawyer had made in every facet of her life. Sage slipped her arm around Sawyer. "So anyway, Zane's a minister in Illinois." She gave Sawyer a squeeze. "Jaina moved there when they got married." She looked to her friend. "What, about three years ago?"

Jaina nodded. "That's right."

"They have a little girl, Bonnie Kate." Sage shook her head. "Wow, big changes in your life."

Jaina raised an eyebrow. "Not just mine. I don't remember you ever bringing hot women home when we lived in the dorm."

Sage blushed. "And you certainly would've noticed." She smiled. "Guess I just didn't know what I was missing." She grabbed hold of Jaina's hand. "We have to stay in touch this time."

"Don't worry," Jaina said, "we will."

Chapter Twenty

Amber was so happy—happy to be home and happy that Laurie had come with her. Today had been the most wonderful day—a day full of snuggling and enjoying each other's company. She chuckled as she watched Laurie try to wiggle out of their most recent snuggle location, the avocado bean-bag. She'd finally gotten her limbs untangled and was struggling to free her body. Finally, she rolled out and dropped onto the orange shag carpet. With a groan, she managed to pull herself upright and walk over to the giant picture window. Amber smiled as she watched Laurie take in the sight. Amber knew it well. By this time of day, the water was usually shimmering like blue crystal under a brilliant orange sky.

"So beautiful," Laurie said as she leaned into the glass to get a better view.

Amber escaped the chair, quietly came up behind her, and pulled her tight against her body. "You certainly are."

"Mmm, that feels nice," Laurie murmured.

"Follow me to bed." Amber's hands cupped Laurie's breasts and she nibbled an earlobe. "I'll show you really nice."

***

The shades were drawn. The waterbed shimmered under the flickering black light. Roberta Flack sang softly in the background. The song, "The First Time Ever I Saw Your Face," had been carefully selected for this night.

"You're right," Laurie purred. "Really nice."

"I have a surprise for you." Amber's voice was low and sexy. She pulled Laurie's tank top over her head. The rest of her clothes followed. "Lay on your belly." The waterbed rippled under her touch. "Right here."

Laurie's gasp was audible.

Amber's arousal skyrocketed. She popped the cap on the massage lotion and squirted a dab into her hand. Her strong fingers started high, massaging Laurie's neck, her shoulders, her arms, and then much lower. She massaged, kissed, and nibbled all the way down the backside of her body, and then squirted more lotion. "Flip over." She kissed the hollow of Laurie's back. "Time to do your front."

Laurie's breathing quickened. "Oh God," she moaned. "What'd I do to deserve this trip through ecstasy?"

Amber pressed her nakedness against Laurie. "You're learning to be treasured," she whispered. "Just relax and go with it."

Laurie rolled onto her back. Her lower lip began to quiver. "God, you're so gentle…."

Amber rose up to kiss her before her strong fingers resumed their downward journey–massaging and stroking. Her mouth followed–kissing, nibbling, and suckling. Laurie panted. Her pelvis rocked. Amber massaged her thighs and calves, working her way up to her center. Her long fingers spread and exposed her and she suckled.

Laurie's moans grew louder. "Close baby," she gasped. "So close."

Amber thrust inside, and in that instant both trembled in climax.

***

Sawyer spent much of the day reviewing reports from the previous shift—a slug of them. As luck would have it, all would require the assignment of a detective. Sometimes it worked out that way, sometimes not. She felt bad that everyone on the unit had to carry such heavy loads. Right now it was mostly due to her promotion. One less body in the bullpen could make a lot of difference in times of higher crime volume. She leaned back in her chair, took a sip of coffee, and considered assigning a couple of the new ones to herself. If she did, the lieutenant and captain would definitely not be happy, not happy at all. And, she'd have to deal with a truckload of crap as fallout. Her face crinkled into an unpleasant expression. It wouldn't be worth it. She picked up the stack of new cases and marched into the bullpen.

Sawyer did the dirty deed and headed back to her office. She shut her door and dialed. Sage should have finished her last session by now. Soon, she'd be headed for Sarasota. Sawyer knew her schedule as well as she knew her own.

"I know you're almost ready to get out of there," Sawyer said, "but I had to call." She leaned back in her chair. "This long-distance thing is killing me." Sawyer leaned forward to listen more closely. "Okay, good. We can talk about it at dinner. I'm open to anything at this point...yep, got a 7:15 reservation at The Old Salty Dog."

***

The restaurant served incredible seafood and had an easy atmosphere where patrons could enjoy each other's company. Sage asked the waitress to seat them at what had become "their" table. They leaned against the beam for a couple minutes to look across the water before sitting down. A mid-sized boat—the Sea Fox—had slowed and was preparing to dock. Sage watched Sawyer watch the boat's captain maneuver.

Sawyer inhaled a deep breath of sea air. "Wow, she's a beauty."

Sage raised her eyebrow and frowned. "The captain, or her vessel?" She shook her head. "There should be rules about that. Captains should have to wear appropriate clothing."

Sawyer smiled. "Jealously becomes you, darling." She winked. "The vessel. I'll bet it's brand new."

"Uh-huh," Sage said. "Out of all the posts she could've tied-up to, she has to pick the one right by our table."

"Must have been drawn to the 'No Fishing' sign. Or maybe she knew I wanted to check her out." Sawyer chuckled and winked again. "The boat, I mean."

"Uh-huh," Sage said with more attitude than she had intended. There was no reason to be jealous and she knew it. She met the sparkle in Sawyer's eyes and willed herself to get over it. "Sorry." She looked away and then back. "I'm turning 40 tomorrow—kind of got me in a little bit of a funk."

Sawyer reached across the table. She held Sage's cheek in the palm of her hand. "You're beautiful." She smiled such a tender smile. "You'll always be the most beautiful girl in my world."

***

Sage set her purse down on the counter next to Sawyer's car keys with a sigh. Dinner was nice, but it was better to be home with Sawyer. "I am so ready for some quality alone time." She put her arms around her neck and kissed her. "It's been too long."

Sawyer hung up her jacket and unstrapped her holster. "I hate just being able to see you on weekends. We've gotta figure this thing out."

Sage met her gaze. "That's what I want to talk to you about. I have an idea, but I'm not sure you're gonna like it."

Sawyer suspected that Sage was right. She probably wouldn't like it—not at all. Sawyer wondered what had taken her so long to bring it up. After listening to her talk about how hard it was to leave Sarasota Memorial the other evening when they had dinner with Zane and Jaina, Sawyer figured it'd be just a matter of time. Sage clearly regretted leaving and there was no doubt she wanted to go back. It was a job she'd loved, only a couple miles from her parent's home, and of course, Sawyer's condo. She'd left, not because she'd wanted to, not because she was laid off, but because working with John during those days before and after their divorce had just been too difficult. It was the place she'd met him, the place they'd courted. Co-workers were in their wedding, for goodness sake. Now, she seemed to think everything would be better, that John had moved on, but Sawyer knew different. Anxiety swirled in the pit of her stomach.

Sage saw it and raised an eyebrow. "What's going on?"

Sawyer inhaled, then exhaled slowly in the form of a sigh. There was a time in the very recent past when her answer would've been "nothing," but everything was different now. She was different. She met Sage's concerned gaze. "I needed a drink." She shook her head. "I haven't had the urge in a long time." Sawyer cracked the slightest smile. "Don't worry, it's gone now."

"I'm not worried," Sage said as she wrapped her arms around her and pulled her close. "What I want to know is what you're afraid of right now."

Sawyer looked away with another sigh. "You have to promise if I tell you, you'll still do whatever you want. I don't want to be the reason you made a choice."

Sage smiled and reached up to run her fingers through Sawyer's hair. "I love you so much." Their lips met. "I promise."

Sawyer hadn't really planned to say anything, especially not tonight. Tomorrow was Sage's special day and she wanted her to enjoy it. It figured that tonight of all nights Sage would sense a problem. And of course, Sage couldn't sense one without dealing with it. Sawyer knew she had to be honest, but it would be difficult. There was no way to say what she had to say without Sage taking it personally. All she could do was try to say the words as gently as possible and then deal with the fallout.

KA Moll

Sage listened without interrupting. Listening was something she did very well, but her brow was furrowed and Sawyer could tell that she was troubled by what she'd said. Sage sat there for a moment and then got up to turn back the spread.

"But you trust me," Sage said as emotion caught in her throat. "Right?" A tear trickled from the corner of her eye. "Because I don't think I've ever given you any reason not to trust me."

Sawyer's eyes were teary too. "Of course I trust you."

"And you believe me when I tell you that I'm not the least bit interested in John?" Sage asked, still holding Sawyer's gaze. "Because I would never lie to you."

Sawyer stepped out of her trousers. They dropped to a heap on the floor. "Of course I believe you." She took a breath and sighed. "This is exactly what I was worried about if I told you. I knew you'd get upset."

Sage slipped into her nightgown. It was the silk one–the one that Sawyer liked so well. "It doesn't matter if I get upset. Being honest, telling me how you feel, that's what's most important." She frowned. "I'm still not sure I fully understand the problem."

Sawyer sat down on the edge of the bed and looked into those beautiful green eyes. "I know you're not interested in John. I know that, but you only think he's not interested in you." She swallowed hard. "He is, you know. I see it in his eyes." She couldn't help it that her lip curled. "He looks at you the way I look at you. I'm scared that you might reconsider–scared that you might think he's got more to offer than this screwed up cop."

Sage folded into Sawyer's arms. "Aw, baby." She nuzzled into the hollow of her neck. "You're not screwed up and you have nothing to worry about." Her kisses trailed down into the V of Sawyer's sports bra. "I love you more than I've loved anyone in my life."

The phone rang. It broke what had the potential to be a really nice moment. Sawyer growled. "Can't they let me be for just one night? Just one night I'd like to not be interrupted." She snagged her phone off the nightstand and barked. "Sergeant James."

Sawyer's heart beat wildly as she hurriedly began to throw on her clothes. She motioned for Sage to do the same. By the time she hung up, she'd calmed down. "Come on, a fire at your parents'. It's not that bad, but we've gotta go now."

***

Jenny must have seen the familiar cruiser pull into her driveway because she stepped onto the porch. "I was gonna call you two in the morning. How'd you know we had a problem?"

"METCAD knows to call me if there's ever an emergency at this address." Sawyer said with a smile. "You two okay?"

"We're okay," Jenny said with a sigh. "I looked away for just a second. I think Bob was trying to take the pan off the stove. Anyway, the kitchen towel caught on fire. Before I could get to it, he'd touched it to the kitchen curtains and they caught too. I called 911, but I had it out by the time they arrived."

Sage threw her arms around her mom and then her dad. "Thank goodness you're both okay."

Sawyer kissed Sage's temple. "How about we stay here tonight?"

Sage nodded. "I'd like that a lot."

"Okay," Sawyer said. "I'm gonna run home to get Snoop and our stuff. I'll be right back."

***

Sage and Jenny had cleaned virtually all evidence of the fire by the time Sawyer returned. The once yellow, now charcoal-colored curtains had been taken down, and the cabinets had been wiped free of soot. A lemony scent hung in the air.

Sage was perched on the top rung of a small ladder. Her arms were high above her head. Sawyer stood and quietly watched her from the doorway. Hanging curtains wasn't a fun job, thus she'd always stuck with blinds. She should've offered to help, but the view was just too good. God, those jeans were tight..

Jenny looked over and caught Sawyer's eye. She smiled a knowing smile.

Caught. Sawyer blushed and moved in closer.

"Mmm," Sage said as Sawyer's arms slipped around her from behind. "Hang on. We'll just be a couple more minutes."

Sawyer's fingers trailed on the inside of her waistband.

Sage held them still. "Then we can go to bed." She looked down and smiled. "Go away, now."

"Okay, okay," Sawyer said, "I'll just go in and keep your dad company. Take your time."

Chapter Twenty-One

Sage startled awake. It was the seventh, maybe eighth time that she'd been awakened to Sawyer's screams. She was becoming concerned and couldn't help but wonder if her worries about John had something to do with her nightmares. She stroked her. "Shh...it's just a bad dream. You're okay."

Sawyer jumped up gasping and looked at the clock—just 2:00 a.m. They'd been asleep for less than an hour. "I'm sorry."

"It's okay, sweetie," Sage said as she rubbed her back. "Want to talk about it?"

"It's stupid," Sawyer growled. She flopped back down and laid her arm over her forehead so that it covered her eyes.

Sage laid next her and put her head on her chest. "Maybe I can help."

Sawyer sighed. "Aren't you sick of our bed therapy routine by now?" Her upper lip curled. "I know I am."

"Look at me," Sage said as she nudged Sawyer's arm away from her eyes. "You've come so far. Look how long it's been since you've had a panic attack. You've stopped drinking. You communicate now. You laugh and you cry. You've come so far, Sawyer." She kissed her lips. "If we need to work through a dream or two, so be it. It's no big deal."

It was stupid. Sawyer would be back in Danville, hear screaming in the distance, and wake up drenched in sweat—terrified. The same nightmare was driving her nuts, night after night after night. The aftermath was even worse. She couldn't shake the feeling that she needed to go back to Danville, the place she'd worked a lifetime to get out of her mind.

"So, who's screaming?" Sage asked.

"I don't know for sure–maybe my mom." Sawyer crinkled her brow. "The voice sounds younger though." She dropped her arm back over her eyes. "I don't know."

"Is your house still there?" Sage asked. "I mean, is it still standing today?"

Sawyer lifted her arm and propped up to look into Sage's eyes. "I'm sure it is. My grandmother would still be there. That is, unless she's in a nursing home or dead by now."

Sage pinched her brow.

"We moved in with my grandma—my dad's mom—after my grandpa died. My dad got busted for drugs and lost his job." She shook her head, disgusted. "He was a loser, even before he was a bastard. I guess we didn't have anywhere else to go. I really don't know for sure."

Sage fingered through Sawyer's hair. "How old were you?"

Sawyer's eyes narrowed and she pursed her lips. "Maybe six or so. I'm not really sure about that either."

Sage lay back down. "Huh, interesting."

***

Sage opened her eyes just as the sunshine found its way through the blinds. She squinted and stretched.

Sawyer rolled over and kissed her. "Happy birthday, sweetheart."

Sage stretched again, this time with stretching sounds. "Thanks—I sure hope you like 40-year-olds."

Sawyer nibbled her earlobe. "Oh I do, especially this one really sexy 40-year-old."

"Mmm…" Sage scooted closer. "I think someone's in the mood."

"Uh-huh, I am." Sawyer nibbled lower. "Happy birthday."

"God," Sage moaned, "what you can do with that mouth." She laid back and opened to Sawyer. It wasn't the first time someone had made love to her on her birthday, but it was a first. It was the first time the gift was actually for her, and not the other person. For years, she hadn't had the heart to tell John that his lovemaking on her birthday was a nice gesture, but one she really didn't want. Finally, she just divorced him and that settled it.

Sage lay trembling in Sawyer's arms after the lovemaking. "God that was nice."

Sawyer kissed her—soft and sweet. "That was the first of several."

Sage met her gaze. "Several? I think I might have to rest up in-between."

Sawyer laughed. "Well I thought maybe just one more like this one…tonight." She kissed her again. "Your other ones are different."

Sawyer propped up and looked toward Snoop. "Retrieve."

197

The big dog got up and lumbered to the corner where Sawyer had dropped her pants. He nosed into her pocket.

Sawyer smiled when he returned with the blue velvet in his mouth and dropped it gently into her hand. "Good boy."

Sawyer set the box into Sage's palm. "Open it."

Sage didn't initially. She knew what she'd find inside.

"Marry me," Sawyer said softly, "and open the box."

***

Amber followed Laurie from room to room in her singlewide trailer. "We'll make room, honey. I don't want you to feel like you have to get rid of something just because we're combining households. Take whatever you want."

"It's mostly junk," Laurie said. "I only have a few things that are important to me. The rest is just garage sale garbage." She turned around to look into Amber's eyes. "I don't have anything as nice as what I'll have at your place."

"It's our place," Amber said. "Bring whatever you want."

Laurie smiled and leaned in for a kiss. "How did I go all these years without...." She paused and looked away. "Seeing you?"

Amber brushed a strand of Laurie's long hair behind her ear. "The most important thing is that you see me now."

Jenny tiptoed into the kitchen. She'd just settled Bob in front of the TV and wanted to see what she could do to help. Sage set down the bowl of over-whipped eggs and turned around.

"Sage…" Jenny's brow furrowed in concern. "Have you been crying?" She moved to hold her. "Aw honey, not on your birthday."

Sage sniffled and held out her ring finger. "They're happy tears, Mama. Sawyer proposed."

Jenny pulled her daughter into her arms. "Congratulations, baby. I'm so happy for you both."

Just then, Sawyer padded around the corner. She raised an eyebrow and met the gaze of her future mother-in-law. "I take it that you find my proposal acceptable?"

Jenny reached for her and pulled her into the hug. "It's more than acceptable." She kissed Sawyer's cheek. "Welcome to the family."

***

The weather on Sage's birthday was 73 degrees and sunny. It was a perfect day for a bike ride. It was also a perfect day to take up cycling. Of Sawyer's three birthday gifts so far, she suspected that Sage might like her taking up cycling the most. Well, not really, but she did like it a lot.

When Sawyer rolled her new bike out of the garage, Sage thought it was a birthday gift for her. The bike wasn't nearly as high end as the one she rode, but she acted excited anyway. Sawyer had mounted before

Sage figured out what was going on. She chuckled. The relief that washed across Sage's face was priceless.

They'd taken off at a pretty good clip considering Sawyer hadn't ridden for years. Sage quickly peddled to the front position, but checked from time to time over her shoulder. Sawyer knew it was to be sure she was okay. She just peddled hard behind her and tried to hide her struggle.

"You doing okay back there?" Sage called out.

"Yeah," Sawyer huffed, "I'm good." She puffed. "This is a bit more of a workout than I anticipated."

Sage laughed. "It is, isn't it?" She sped up— intentionally. "That's why they call it a sport."

"Uh-huh." Sawyer chuckled as she glanced at her watch. "We probably need to head back pretty soon. Sorry, but I've got a quick errand to run before we head out." She huffed again and peddled hard to catch up. "Wouldn't want to be late for somebody's birthday dinner."

Sage peddled harder, laughing, as Sawyer struggled to keep up. "We certainly wouldn't."

***

The captain maneuvered his 140-foot three-level mega yacht into the Sarasota Marina and docked her with the skill and precision of a lifetime mariner. Sawyer sucked in a nervous breath as she watched. Everything was coming together.

"Your yacht's magnificent," Sawyer said as she took a quick look around. "Each level's so unique and luxurious." She grinned. "My fiancée will absolutely love it." She wrote out and handed the man his check. "Thanks for doing this on my schedule."

***

Sage hugged her mom and dad goodbye. "I wish you guys were coming with us," she pouted. "We always go out to dinner on my birthday."

"You know we want to, sweetie" Jenny said, "but I don't think your daddy's up to it. He's just a little too confused this evening." Jenny sighed and kissed her daughter goodbye. "We'll have birthday cake when you get back home."

"I know," Sage said, "but Daddy just doesn't seem that bad tonight to me."

"Maybe it's just me," Jenny said. "I'm still a little spooked after the fire." She put her hand on her daughter's shoulder and gave her a nudge. "You two go on. Have a nice romantic birthday dinner and we'll see you when you get home."

"Okay," Sage said, "but we'll miss you," She slipped her purse strap over her shoulder and looked to Sawyer. "You ready?"

"I am," Sawyer said as she followed her down the walk. She opened the passenger door and walked around to slide in the other side. Timing was crucial. She'd have to stall for at least a half-hour. Sawyer started the engine. "Mind if I make a quick stop at the station on our way to dinner? I need to pick something up."

Sage smiled. "That's fine. We've got plenty of time." She shifted in her seat to look at her. "So tell me, Ms. Mysterious, where exactly are we going for dinner?"

"I guess you'll find out soon enough," Sawyer said. "It was gonna be a surprise, but I might as well tell you now. I got us last minute dinner cruise tickets." She shook her head. "I hope we have a decent table."

"Wow," Sage said with a wide smile. "I haven't been on a dinner cruise in years. I used to love 'em when I was a little girl." Sawyer already knew because Jenny had told her. Sage leaned across to kiss Sawyer's cheek. "You're so thoughtful."

Sawyer drove well below the speed limit as she made her way from the PD to the marina and pulled into one of several parking spaces reserved for police vehicles. They were right on time. She nodded toward the large yacht that was docked nearby. "There she is, *The Lady Katherine.*"

"Hum…I've never heard of that one," Sage said with pursed lips and a crinkled her brow. "She looks nice."

"Yeah, she does," Sawyer said as she took a quiet breath to settle her nerves—almost there now. She could barely believe she'd been able to pull something this big off without Sage knowing. She smirked for show. "Now watch, they'll seat us at some crap table on the lowest level." She shook her head in fake disgust. "I always put things off to the last minute. I should've made the reservation when I first had the idea."

"Oh now, come on," Sage said. "You're always too hard on yourself." She squeezed her hand. "It'll be wonderful, even if they seat us on the dock."

Chapter Twenty-Two

They were greeted the moment they boarded, offered a cocktail, and invited to have a seat on the sky deck. Their table below was currently occupied, but would be available shortly. There was no suggestion that anything was out of the ordinary. *The Lady Katherine* was masquerading as a floating restaurant. This was an example of getting exactly what you paid for.

Sage surveyed her surroundings. "Wow, this is a *really* nice boat. I'm surprised there aren't more people waiting for a table." She shrugged her shoulders. "Maybe it's so new that people just don't know about it yet."

Sawyer fought back a chuckle and tried to sound nonchalant. "Maybe. Who knows?"

"Well, I'm impressed that you found it," Sage said. She grinned and did a little dance with her shoulders. "Ooo-la-la...a fancy dinner on the water at sunset. What a fun birthday!" Sawyer loved to see her enjoying herself.

Just then, a crew member appeared out of thin air. Their table had become available. She was right on time. They followed her past a full service mahogany bar that had the most unbelievable Gulf panorama. They trailed down the stairs and into the elegant first-level dining room. Sage had barely stepped her foot inside the door when the room full of people—well over 100, including her parents—erupted.

"HAPPY BIRTHDAY," they screamed at the top of their lungs.

Sage got happy tears in her eyes and turned to Sawyer. "I love you so much." She threw her arms around her neck. "I don't know how you did this, but it's one of the nicest things that anyone has ever done." She scanned the room. "They're all here—even people you wouldn't know."

Sawyer grinned ear to ear. "I have to give credit where credit's due." She nodded to Jenny and Cathy. "I couldn't have done this without their help." Sawyer leaned down to kiss Sage on her lips. "Happy birthday. I love you, sweetheart."

At exactly 5:30, the engines turned over and the horn sounded. The mega yacht made ready to navigate her way out of the marina and into the open waters of the Gulf of Mexico. The guests mingled about and grazed on a wide assortment of free hors d'oeuvres and cocktails—all compliments of Sawyer. She smiled and watched Sage flutter about her guests. She was like a delighted butterfly with a ring finger that sparkled. The dinner bell sounded promptly at 6:30 and the guests returned to their tables. The executive chef stepped forward to announce the menu and welcome guests on behalf of the crew and their vessel.

"My God, Sawyer," Sage said. "You're spending a fortune."

Sawyer raised an eyebrow. "It's a special birthday." She leaned in for a kiss. "I didn't have a choice."

The band assembled and began to play–a classic mix of fast and slow. Sawyer stood and held out her hand. "Care to dance?"

Sage's eyes twinkled and she smiled. "I'd love to." She took Sawyer's hand and they made their way to the dance floor. Everyone else seemed to have the same idea at the very same time. The dance floor was crowded in no time.

Sage folded into Sawyer's body and followed her lead. They danced as one, like they'd done it for a lifetime. Sawyer closed her eyes. She had the woman she loved in her arms and they were dancing to the sexiest song. It was shaping up to be a very good night.

Sawyer was enjoying being enthralled by Sage when an unwanted hand tapped her on the shoulder. She opened her eyes, turned her head, and met John's gaze. Who the hell invited him? Her jaw clenched and she swallowed hard.

John bowed like the gentleman that she knew he wasn't. "May I cut in?"

Sawyer nodded and stepped back. She did what was proper on the dance floor. Her stomach churned as she released Sage's hand. Sawyer turned and walked away in silence.

***

Sage was instantly aware of the intensity of Sawyer's reaction. She glared at John. "This is gonna be quick. Damn you. You knew this would upset her and you did it anyway."

Sage pushed back to create extra distance between her body and John's and glanced toward the table.

Sawyer didn't head in that direction, but she hoped that maybe she'd circle back to sit with her parents, Amber, and Laurie. Nope—still no Sawyer. Most likely she was already at the bar. Sage managed to catch her mom's eye. The moment she did, Jenny stood and headed for the stairs. Sage escaped and met her there as soon as she could.

"Thanks, Mama," Sage said as their eyes locked in understanding. "I wasn't sure how easy it'd be to get away. I'll handle it from here on out."

Jenny's eyes loaded with concern. "I don't usually like to interfere in your life, but…."

"I know, Mama," Sage said. "You don't have to say a word." She shook her head. "I know and I knew better."

Sage climbed the stairs to the second level. After a couple moments, her eyes finally adjusted to the reduced lighting. She looked around fully expecting to find Sawyer slumped over a beer at the far end of the bar, but she wasn't there. She should have been ecstatic about that, but she wasn't. Instead, she was scared. Her fear felt irrational, but she couldn't help it. Sawyer hadn't been sleeping well lately and she'd been so on edge.

Sage climbed two steps at a time toward the sky deck and opened the door. Sawyer was there—one hand on the railing and the other on an unopened bottle of beer. Sage released the breath she'd been holding and joined her. Thank God she was alright.

"You didn't open it," Sage said softly. "I thought maybe you would."

Sawyer continued to stare across the almost calm water. "I didn't think it would please you if I did."

"I'm sorry," Sage said. "You were absolutely right about John." She leaned against Sawyer's shoulder. "I should've listened to you."

Sawyer turned and met her gaze. "I love you, but I won't share you either."

Sage tiptoed up and kissed her lips. "You'll never have to."

***

Sawyer padded through the dark kitchen in her boxers. She opened the refrigerator as quietly as she could. It hung in that position, lighting the room, as she studied the assortment of leftovers. The perfect midnight snack had to be in there somewhere.

Jenny came around the corner. "I thought that might be you." She shook her head and smiled. "I can't believe you're still hungry after all that food."

Sawyer laughed. "I can't either." She resumed her search as Jenny continued.

"You know," Jenny said, "you made our daughter very happy this evening. She was happier than I think I've ever seen her before."

"She deserves to be happy," Sawyer said as she dropped a loaf of bread on the counter. A sandwich would have to do. She shut the refrigerator door and the room darkened.

Jenny was quiet for a moment and then resumed. "It was her choice, you know...to be alone all these years." Jenny adjusted her robe to cover more skin. "Sage could've had someone. Heck, she could've had John. She just chose not to." Jenny locked eyes with Sawyer. "Everything changed the moment you came into her life."

She reached up to pat her shoulder. "I just wanted to tell you that." She paused and then fell quiet again. "I also wanted to tell you, I'd be honored if you'd think of me as your mama too."

Sawyer pulled Jenny into her arms. She was going to be the world's best mother-in-law. "I already do."

***

Sawyer tried to slip back into the bedroom without a sound. She was sure Sage had just gotten to sleep and didn't want to wake her. Sage stirred and she knew that she hadn't been successful.

"Did I hear you talking to my mom?" Sage asked as she propped herself up on an elbow.

"Yeah, she heard me digging around in the refrigerator." Sawyer sat down on Sage's side of the bed. She chomped into her bologna sandwich. "Want a bite?"

Sage made a face. "No, not after all that food." She raised an eyebrow and then frowned. "I suppose you had another nightmare?"

"Yep," Sawyer said as she chomped again. "Not as bad this time, though. I think I'm getting used to 'em. I woke right up before it had a chance to get a good hold."

Sage sighed. "That's not necessarily an improvement."

Sawyer swallowed the last bite and flopped down beside her. "Oh, no—I think my therapist has joined me in the bedroom again." She raised an eyebrow. "We simply must stop meeting like this, my dear."

Sage scowled. "I was just concerned." She punched her pillow with her fist and flopped over to face the wall. "Just forget I said anything."

"Come on, baby," Sawyer said. "I was just kidding." She scooted over and put her arm around Sage. "I know you're worried." Sawyer was sick and tired of lugging around her baggage. She was even more tired of therapy in the bedroom. "Come on, Sage. I want to know what you think. I was just trying to be funny. Come on...."

Finally Sage flipped back over. She adjusted her nightgown for coverage and propped herself back up in the bed. Her eyes found Sawyer's. "I think I'd like an outdoor wedding."

Sawyer's mouth fell slightly open, bemused. She cocked her head.

"And," Sage continued, "I'd like an Illinois honeymoon."

Now the dots were connected. "An outdoor wedding should be beautiful in December," Sawyer said. "But Sage...." She sucked in and exhaled a breath. "You know I've never been back." Her eyes misted over. "I haven't been back for a reason—because I can't deal with it."

Sage's gaze was so gentle. "I know you think you can't, but you can. It's time to go back." She softly kissed Sawyer on her lips. "I think your nightmares are your subconscious mind's way of telling you that you're strong enough to acknowledge what happened to you, to feel your pain, and to move on." She smiled a tender smile. "It's time, sweetheart. It's time to go home."

"God...I'll be such a mess." Sawyer shook her head. "You'll have to scoop me off the pavement."

"I will if I need to," Sage said quietly. "We'll face it all together and move on."

Chapter Twenty-Three

In some ways, the three-month absence had seemed like a lifetime—a lifetime filled with a dichotomy of terrifying nightmares and beautiful dreams. Amber rested her hand on the sturdy fire door as she watched the woman she loved pull away from the curb in her car. She smiled and gave the door a tug. Laurie looked good in the orange bug. It suited her.

Amber had feared that she might never again be able to return—to this place, to who she'd been, to who she was at her core—a teacher. She inhaled and exhaled a deep breath. God, it was good to be back to the chalk-dusted air where desks shuffled, chairs scooted, and students learned.

All Amber could do was smile and reflect on the many positive changes that had occurred in her life since she last walked the two flights of stairs up to her classroom. It might strike some as peculiar that she could find positives in the horrors of her psychotic breakdown, but she could. For without that breakdown, Amber wouldn't have spent the many hours in therapy. And without that therapy, she wouldn't know the joy of feeling comfortable in her own skin. Without that breakdown, she wouldn't have Laurie, because their paths would never have crossed at that critical juncture in their lives. Yes, it might strike some as peculiar, but it wasn't. She flipped on her classroom lights, cracked open her worn colonial history textbook, and began preparation of the day's lesson.

Amber knew she was back in the groove when her students filed in. They'd barely gotten into her lesson plan when she sensed someone watching from the door. She was a teacher, genetically engineered to have amazing peripheral vision and eyes in the back of her head. She smiled and raised an eyebrow. "Come in, Ms. Jackson." She nodded toward the rear corner of her classroom. "There's an empty desk right there in the back row." She looked to the student in the adjacent seat. "Craig, would you open a textbook to the correct page for our guest?"

Laurie took the seat. Initially, she looked quite uncomfortable.

Amber took a breath and released it. "Okay, where were we?" She smiled. "Ahh, we were just discussing...." She nodded to the long-haired kid in the last row. "Craig?"

He stuttered a bit and then spoke. "We were discussing the separation of church and state in colonial America."

"Indeed we were," Amber said as she crossed the classroom and stood before the desk of a husky blonde. "And something related to this topic troubled our friend, James Madison." Her eyes widened. "In fact, it troubled him so much that he went into politics. That something was...." Amber nodded to another student. "Susan?"

The girl smiled because she knew the answer. "It was the imprisonment of the local Baptists."

Amber smiled back. "That's right. And our friend James Madison partnered up with a fellow Virginian by the name of..." She looked across her classroom. "Anyone?" No hands went up. "Thomas Jefferson. So tomorrow, we'll begin our discussion of how these two men shaped the relationship between church and state in America." The loud buzzer buzzed and the shuffling began. "Read chapter 13," Amber called out as the herd of seniors headed for the hallway. She walked to the back of her classroom.

Laurie stood and met her halfway. She held out a brown paper bag. "You forgot your lunch." She met Amber's gaze. "And...I've never been as proud of you as I am right at this minute. You're really something." She shook her head.

Amber could tell that Laurie was about to cry.

"And for the life of me," Laurie said, "I don't understand how someone as smart as you would give someone like me—an old, high school dropout—a moment's notice.

Amber's gaze lingered. The buzzer buzzed and second-hour students began to meander into the classroom. She smiled a tender smile. "I'm afraid we'll need to continue this discussion at home. Thanks for bringing me my lunch."

***

Sage wore attire totally unsuited to do what they'd just done–hiked through a stretch of untamed Florida wilderness. Sawyer's attire was equally out of place. The setting, the attire, and the pose were to be a playful twist on tradition.

The photographer stood back to survey the landscape of her next shot. "Okay Sage, now hike up that beautiful blue gown and take a really wide stance so that you both don't go tumbling down the hill." She crossed her arms. "Good." The lens cap came off. "Okay Sawyer, straighten your tie and relax. Just let Sage dip you way back. It'll feel a little weird, but just go with it." The camera was up and ready for the perfect shot. "Okay Sage…here we go…dip Sawyer back and get ready to kiss her like you mean it—okay now, go." Click–click–click. "Perfect."

Sawyer groaned and struggled to regain her balance and stand upright. She looked into Sage's eyes—exhausted—certain that she was about ready to collapse. Sawyer lay back against a banyan tree to rest as the photographer twisted on yet another lens. "God, will it ever be over?"

Sage sighed. "It has been grueling." She leaned back against the tree with Sawyer. "Four hours is a long time to be posed and propped."

The photographer smiled and encouraging smile. She put her hand on both their shoulders and gave them a nudge forward. "I know you guys are tired, but you'll be happy we did this when you have lots of gorgeous proofs to pick from." She adjusted her neck strap. "Okay, just one more shot and then we're done." The lens cap slid into her pocket. "Sage, I want you to sit sideways over there in front of the banyan tree so that I can get a good shot of the water and sandy shoreline." She gently tugged Sawyer into position. "Okay Sawyer, I want you to crouch close behind Sage and square your body with the camera." The photographer squatted down to sight her shot. "Good. Now Sage, I want you to place your hands gently on Sawyer's chin." The camera rose to eye-level. "Now, sweet and tender, I want you to ever-so-delicately kiss her on her cheek." Click–click–click. "Perfect. We're done." She grinned. "You're gonna love these shots! I'll call you next week."

***

Laurie had already shifted to the passenger seat by the time Amber came out the front door of the high school and made her way down the front steps toward the car. She slid in behind the wheel—adjusted the mirror up, moved the seat back, and of course, repositioned the flower that rode in the small vase attached to her dash. Her eyes met Laurie's. "I'm with you because I love you." She looked over her shoulder to check for oncoming traffic. "And it troubles me that you think so little of yourself." She pressed down on the accelerator and the little bug chugged forward. "It troubles me a lot, and I've been thinking." They drove the rest of the way home in silence and pulled into the carport. Amber reached into the backseat and retrieved her leather satchel. She slid the strap over her shoulder and got out. God, it felt good to carry books again.

They rode up. Laurie unlocked the door and they stepped inside. "So, does the teacher have homework this evening?"

Amber rolled her eyes and smiled. "The teacher always has homework." She shook her head. "Maybe one of these days I'll figure out how not to." She patted her satchel. "But I'm not there yet." She set it down on the breakfast bar and headed for the refrigerator.

Laurie chuckled. "I think I've already fallen down on my new job."

Amber paused her search to look up. "What are you talking about?"

"I should've prepared a healthy after-school snack for my girl," Laurie said as she pressed herself into Amber's arms.

Amber bent down to kiss her. "God, am I ever gonna like being spoiled."

"Not as much as I'm gonna like spoiling you," Laurie said. Her voice trailed off. "You said you'd been thinking." She looked into Amber's eyes. "About what?"

"Snack first, discussion later," Amber said. She slopped a glob of jelly onto her peanut butter and squished it around. "Because I've talked all day and I'm hungry." She took a bite. "Don't worry." She kissed Laurie's forehead. "It's nothing bad."

Laurie watched Amber until she swallowed her last bite.

Amber smiled and held out her hand. "Okay, let's go."

Laurie took it and they headed for the bean-bag. She settled in front and laid her head back against Amber's shoulder.

Amber slipped her arms around her and held her close. "So I've been thinking."

Laurie's gulp was audible.

"I've been thinking," Amber said softly, "that we don't really need you to find a job. I make plenty to take care of our bills."

Laurie crinkled her brow. She was obviously trying to figure out where the conversation was going. "Okay…."

Amber met her gaze. "I thought you might like to go back to school." She smiled a playful sort of smile.

"It'd be fun, you know. We could do our homework together."

Laurie began to babble a myriad of excuses about why going back to school was a crazy idea. Amber listened, but her words lied. They didn't convey what she really wanted; they only showed her self-doubt that slithered out of fear. The truth was hidden in the twinkle of her eyes. At first, Laurie was surprised—surprised that anyone would actually think she was smart enough to learn. But then, she was delighted—delighted at the realization of an opportunity to pursue a lifelong dream.

***

Sawyer was never so glad to have taken the day off as she was today. Just the thought of changing into uniform for her 3:00 to 11:00 shift was painful. She dropped her navy trousers to the floor on top of their white oxford mate and fell back onto the bed. "Are you as tired as I am?"

Sage groaned. "God, yes. Even worse, I don't think I have a solitary muscle that doesn't hurt." She turned her back to Sawyer. "Unzip me?"

Sawyer felt her libido revive and rise. "You bet." An ornery grin traversed her face. "Can't quite reach you though. Back up just a little bit more."

Sage stepped back against the bed. "Better?"

"Oh yeah," Sawyer said. Her response was instantaneous. The zipper unzipped and the dress topped the trousers on the floor. She pulled Sage down on top of her.

Sage squealed. "I thought you were tired…hey, wait, I need to hang…umm, to hang that up…."

Sawyer laughed. "Tired, who's tired?"

Sage slipped down to touch Sawyer. "God, you're wet."

Sawyer arched into her. "Touch me like that and I'll be gone in 60 seconds."

Sage lightened her touch. "I want you to come in my mouth."

"Then you'd better move in that direction," Sawyer panted. "Because the train's leaving the station."

***

The aroma of frying chicken hit Sage the moment she stepped onto her parent's front porch. She salivated as she dug out her key. Her mom had always been a wonderful cook.

"Come in, sweetie," Jenny exclaimed. "What a nice surprise. I didn't expect to see you today."

"God, it smells good in here. I might just have to stay." She closed the door behind her and glanced over to the puzzle table. "Daddy's not home yet?"

Jenny's smile faded. "No, not yet. The bus drops him off a little after 6:00."

Sage pulled her mom in for a hug. "Still feel good about your decision to send him to adult daycare?"

"Yeah, pretty much," Jenny said. "I know it's for the best. I just miss having him around, that's all." She headed back to the kitchen.

Sage followed. "I know it is, Mama." She kissed her cheek. "These are hard times. I wish I could tell you it was gonna get easier."

Jenny looked up from the stove and met her daughter's gaze. "They are hard times, but happy times too." She smiled. "My sweet girl's gonna get married in a couple weeks. She's gonna get married to my other sweet girl."

***

Sawyer exited the bakery and mentally checked another item off of her lengthy wedding preparation list. She'd never done this before and was amazed at all there was to do. No wonder couples enlisted the service of their parents and a wedding party to get it all done. She chuckled to herself. Sage didn't seem to be bothered by any of it. Actually, she seemed to be enjoying herself—maybe because, even if only for a little while, her mind was off her parents. The to-do list once again filled her mind—invitations—check. Location reserved—check. Minister—check. Airline tickets—check. Attire—check. Wedding cake—check. Caterer—check. Photographer (ugh)—check. Music—check. Wedding party gifts—check. Her brain screamed. She'd forgotten to call to make their hotel reservation. They were going to Danville, Illinois for their honeymoon. (Ugh!) No wonder she'd put it out of mind. She dug her phone out of her jacket pocket, swiped, and dialed.

Chapter Twenty-Four

Both Sage and Sawyer wanted a tranquil wedding held in a place enveloped by nature with a breathtaking view of the water. Marie Selby Botanical Gardens, 14 acres nestled between bricked residential streets in the heart of Sarasota was perfect. The gardens were a community treasure, one they'd taken to enjoying on lazy Sunday afternoons. It had been an easy first choice for their nuptial. They were thrilled when even on short notice their December date had been available.

"Getting close now," Sawyer said as they strolled past the picturesque grove of banyan trees.

"I know," Sage said. Her voice quivered a little. "Really close. I just hope we haven't forgotten anything." She bent down to look more closely at a tiny exotic flower.

Sawyer smiled. God, she was beautiful. "So, you're meeting Zane and Jaina at the airport tomorrow at 12:30, right?" She reached down to hold Sage's hand. "And your mom's okay with having all three of them stay in her extra bedroom?" She shook her head. "It's been a longtime since she had a three-year-old in her house."

"Yeah, she's good with it," Sage said softly. "In fact, she'll love it."

Sawyer detected the hint of sadness in Sage's tone and pulled her close. She slipped her arm around Sage's

219

waist as they continued their walk into the open area where their reception would be held. They paused to gaze across the water. A bit farther and they came upon the secluded clearing. Amazing how it was almost completely surrounded by banyan trees—their favorite place in the gardens. They paused again in the shade of the most majestic banyan of them all.

"You think we should have a few extra chairs set up?" Sawyer asked. "What if 150 isn't enough?"

Sage nodded. "Yeah, maybe we should. I'll call tomorrow and make the arrangements." She laid her head on Sawyer's shoulder.

Sawyer nuzzled her hair and kissed her forehead. "This is where we'll say our vows."

"Yeah," Sage said softly. "I know." Her eyes looked up. "I love you, Sawyer."

Sawyer kissed her lips. "I love you too."

***

Zane lifted her daughter out of the car seat and handed her to her other mom. BK giggled with delight as Jaina playfully rubbed their noses together. Zane stood for the moment, mesmerized. She loved to watch her wife with their daughter. They were the loves of her life. Zane groaned as she hefted their bags from the trunk and loaded them onto the luggage cart. "Pack the kitchen sink for this trip, darling?"

Jaina paused the nose rubbing to look over her glasses and smile at her wife. "No, Pastor Winslow, only the bathtub." She tiptoed up for a kiss. "I didn't think we'd need the kitchen sink this time."

Zane caught her little girl's eye. "What am I gonna do with your mommy, Bonnie Kate? She's so silly." She leaned down for her own nose rub.

BK giggled in delight.

***

It was down to the wire now. So much to do and very little time left to get it done. It didn't matter. Sawyer and Sage hadn't seen much of Amber lately and both were determined to work in lunch. Sawyer leaned back, stuffed full of snow crab. Amber stealthy unsnapped her shorts, and then did the same.

Sage chuckled as she looked across the table, first to the twins and then to Laurie. "Can those two eat or what?"

"Oh yeah," Laurie snickered. "It's always been that way. When they're not eating a meal, they're snacking in-between." She shook her head. "If I ate like that I'd be a blimp."

Sage giggled. "Well, I'd be a hippo."

Sawyer suppressed a laugh. She met Amber's gaze and together they slowly shook their heads. "Right here you two," she said. "We're right here and we can hear you."

The four laughed and the mood was light.

Amber caught Sawyer's eye. "So, you ready for the big day?"

Sawyer reached over to hold Sage's hand. Their gaze lingered a moment, then she looked up. "We are. How about you? All ready to be my Best Woman?"

Amber rolled her eyes. "Of course I am." She squeezed Laurie's hand. "Who knows, maybe we'll give you the chance to return the favor one of these days."

Sawyer grinned and winked at Sage. "See, I told you before long they'd be thinking about getting married."

***

Sage had worried that she might not make it to the airport on time when lunch had lasted so much longer than planned. She'd managed though, even if it was at the last moment. She smiled as she thought about Amber and Laurie. They'd seemed so happy together. Everything was working out just fine.

The PA system crackled with the announcement she'd been waiting for. "United Airlines, 3511, non-stop from Indianapolis to Sarasota-Bradenton...."

Sage picked up her pace. The gate was a good five-minute walk down the corridor. She made it just as the first passengers stepped inside the terminal—watched as they made a beeline for the luggage carousel—but still no Zane and Jaina. She checked her watch. Could she have met the wrong flight?

There they were. Thank God.

"Hey there," Sage called out as a wide grin spread across her face. "It's good to see you guys again. We really appreciate your making the long trip."

Zane squatted down to her daughter's level. "This is our friend, Sage." She looked up. "Sage, I'd like to introduce you to our daughter."

Sage could hardly believe the string of words that flowed from the young child's mouth. "I get to sprinkle the flowers when you get married to Sawyer." The child looked to Zane. "Right, Mama?"

Zane beamed with pride. "That's right, sweetie." She gave her little one a squeeze. "And you'll be the prettiest little flower girl in the whole wide world."

Sage thanked her friends once again for going to so much trouble. It was a long and costly trip. It wasn't like there weren't other ministers in the area, it was just that she and Sawyer didn't really have a church. They'd gotten to know Zane at homecoming and she was the one they'd wanted to marry them.

"I told you, it's no trouble," Zane said. "My goodness, we would've attended anyway." She raised an eyebrow. "I assume we'd have been invited."

Sage made a face. "Of course you would have."

Zane smiled. "Good." She lifted her daughter onto her shoulders. "Come, sweet girl. Let's go find your mommy's bathtub."

Sage looked to Jaina. "Bathtub?"

Jaina shook her head and smiled. "It's a long story."

***

The luggage was located in short order. Before long, they were on their way to the Carson residence. Sage was certain that they were late enough that dinner might be waiting on the table. She smiled, certain that it would once again be all of Sawyer's favorites. She loved that her mom loved her future wife.

Jenny welcomed her guests at the door and, as anticipated, they immediately sat down for dinner.

"She's well-behaved," Jenny said as she watched the little girl at her table. "I remember when Sage was that size."

Jaina stroked her daughter's hair and met Jenny's eye. "Thank you." She looked to Zane and smiled. "She's the joy of our life."

Sage watched as well. "Is it hard to juggle everything? I mean, you both have full-time jobs."

Zane looked pensive for a moment. "It might be if we didn't have my moms nearby."

"Yeah," Jaina said as she took a sip of coffee. "It'd be bad without Nancy and her wife." She set the cup in the saucer. "Although, we do try not to take advantage of grandmas who'll provide childcare on zero notice."

"I'll bet they love every minute of it," Jenny said with the softest smile. "I know I would."

Sage inadvertently caught her mom's eye. She knew what she was thinking—that she wished she had a grandchild. It was no surprise that she'd said it out loud. It was Sage's shortcoming as her only daughter and she was sorry. She was sorry, but she couldn't have considered having a child with John. She just couldn't. Now at 40, Sage wasn't sure there was enough time. She hadn't even broached the topic of having children with Sawyer.

***

Laurie rocked the mid-century rocker as she watched Amber dress for the wedding. "God, you're a handsome woman."

Amber paused–trousers half-on, half-off. "Thanks." Both she and the maid of honor would wear navy with mint green. "You're not so bad yourself." She gazed a moment before her dressing resumed. Laurie was absolutely stunning. The red form-fitting dress had been a perfect choice for the wedding. Amber stepped over and gently kissed her lips. "You doing okay today?"

Laurie's expression became thoughtful. She inhaled and exhaled slowly. "Yeah...I'm doing fine." She held Amber's gaze. "It's sweet that you asked me."

***

The chairs had been arranged in perfect rows with 60 on each side of the wide aisle. The ushers, all of whom obviously worked with Sawyer, wore their blue dress uniforms. Sawyer's guests were seated to the right and Sage's to the left. Immediate family and close friends were seated in the front row. The altar was adorned with a beautiful arrangement of exotic flowers and a stringed quartet played softly in the background. It was 5:00 in the evening—a time for romance–a time for the commitment of a lifetime.

The music stopped. The guests looked over their shoulders and down the center aisle to the pastor who was reverently making her way toward the altar. She wore a black robe and a white clerical collar. Her white stole was special. It had been embroidered in gold and blue with intertwined wedding rings and a cross. It proclaimed the significance of the ceremony.

Zane stepped up to the altar and turned to face the wedding guests. All the seats were filled. The number of Sarasota's finest, all in perfectly pressed dress uniforms, was staggering. "Good evening. I am the Reverend Zane Winslow and it is my honor to have been invited to journey from Illinois along with my wife and daughter to officiate this wedding. Today, two very special people will be joined in the bond of holy matrimony. Sawyer and Sage have asked that I welcome you to this, their special place. They are overjoyed that you have chosen to be present as they vow to pledge their lives to each other."

Zane nodded and the string quartet began to play. Cathy made her way toward the altar from the left. Amber made her way from the right. They nodded to each other with recognition. BK carried a small basket filled to the brim with rose petals. Under the close supervision of her mommy, she dropped the petals down the center aisle, and around the altar. Zane couldn't help but smile. She nodded again and Sawyer and Sage assumed their positions at the rear of the outdoor sanctuary. Sage was on the far left. Sawyer was on the far right.

Sawyer was smartly dressed in uniform. Sage wore an elegant mint green gown. Photographers stood ready at the front of each aisle to snap the perfect shot. Zane nodded and the quartet began to play "The Wedding March." On the first note, Sawyer and Sage looked across the sea of guests and locked eyes. Their entry would be from opposite sides of the room as equals–separate and alone. It would need to be perfectly synchronized. You could've heard a pin drop as they walked deliberately forward and met at the same moment before the altar. They faced each other—each lost in the depths of their lover's eyes.

"Friends and family," Zane said as she raised her arms high above her head, "we gather together on this beautiful warm December evening to join these two strong women in the bonds of holy matrimony. Sawyer and Sage have come with joy in their hearts and in a spirit of celebration. It is their hope that you have done the same. Their vows are their own." She nodded to Sawyer.

Sawyer met Sage's teary gaze. "This evening, we are surrounded by all the people who love us and it is in their midst that I choose you to be my partner and my wife. I vow to always be in your corner, to protect you, to encourage you, and to love you for all time." Sawyer smiled tenderly.

Zane met Sawyer's gaze. "Do you have a ring to symbolize your commitment? If so, please place it on Sage's finger as you say her name and these words: with this ring, I thee wed."

"I do," Sawyer said as she looked to Amber. Amber placed the beautifully engraved golden band in her palm.

Sage's hand trembled as she held her finger out to Sawyer.

"With this ring," Sawyer said softly, "I thee wed." The wedding band slid on easily next to her diamond.

Zane looked to Sage with a warm reassuring smile. "It's your turn," she said softly.

Sage held Sawyer's gaze. With a trembling voice she vowed, "Sawyer, I promise to listen to you, to laugh with you, and to comfort you. I'll always share your dreams and encourage you to reach your goals. You'll be my only one. I promise to be your partner, your wife, your lover, and your friend for as long as we both shall live."

"Do you have a ring to symbolize your commitment?" Zane asked. "If so, please place it on Sawyer's finger as you say her name and these words: with this ring, I thee wed."

Tears rolled down Sage's cheeks as she looked to her friend. Cathy squeezed her hand and then placed the matching golden band in her palm. Sage choked back a soft sob as she said the words and slid it onto Sawyer's finger.

Zane raised her arms high once again in proclamation. "This evening, brothers and sisters, you and I have witnessed Sage and Sawyer pledge their lives to each other before God, friends, and family." She paused and gazed warmly into the two pair of anticipating eyes. "Now, the moment we all have been waiting for.... By the power vested in me through ordination and by the state of Florida, I pronounce you, wife and wife. You may each kiss your bride."

Without a moment's hesitation Sawyer swept Sage into her arms. She held her close and sealed their vows with a kiss of passion.

Zane turned the newlyweds to face their guests. She took hold of their clasped hands and raised them high. "What God has joined together, let no one put asunder." She grinned and was the first to give them a hug. "Congratulations."

The music commenced, Sage slipped her arm through Sawyer's, and they marched as one down the center aisle.

Chapter Twenty-Five

The orange sunset glowed over the water as the wedding party and guests wended toward the reception area that had been set up in the clearing by the bay. A banquet of food and drink, including a wedding cake, awaited them. Sawyer and Sage were high on adrenaline and, of course, love. Tonight would be a night for celebration. Tomorrow morning, bright and early, they'd fly north to Illinois for their honeymoon. Amber clinked her glass with her spoon. The crowd silenced as she made a toast. The couple cut the wedding cake. The evening's festivities were underway.

Cathy pulled Sage aside the moment she was alone. She put her arms around her and gave her the biggest hug. "It was a lovely ceremony. We're so happy you found each other. Mike told me this morning that he didn't think Sawyer would ever settle down." She shook her head and smiled. "I must admit, I thought the same about you."

Sage glanced over at Sawyer. She was chatting fast and furious with Mike, probably about some new police gadget or protocol. Sage couldn't help but smile. "I guess we were just waiting until our paths crossed."

Cathy smiled too. "I guess you were." She fell silent for a moment. "It'll sure be weird without you on the unit." There was a touch of sadness in her tone. "But

I'm happy for you. I know you'll do great in private practice. Sarasota's a prosperous area and with your skills...." She shook her head. "Well, the sky's the limit."

Sage took a deep breath. It was a huge leap to go out on her own. Yet, it seemed like the thing to do. It was all coming together. "Can you believe my caseload's already full? I won't see my first client for over two weeks and I already have a waiting list."

Cathy patted her friend on the back. "You know, I'm not surprised at all."

***

The DJ set up to play alongside the large portable parquet dance floor—a classic mix of fast and slow. It was in the mid-70s with a light breeze. The sky was filled with stars, a perfect night for dancing. The lights outlining the perimeter of the dance floor flickered. It was time for the first dance and the guests gathered around to play their part. Each guest held their sparkler at the ready as Sarasota's finest moved through and lit them one by one. Within moments, the glimmer of multi-colored sparklers reflected off the floor. Sage placed her hand in Sawyer's and they made their way to the center as the DJ put on their song—*Could I have this dance for the rest of my life? Would you be my partner every night?* They danced as one.

"It went well," Sawyer said.

Sage nuzzled close. "It did."

Sawyer tipped down to kiss her wife. "I got such a kick out of watching your mom and dad today." She chuckled. "All romantic and snuggly. That'll be us when we're in our 70s...80s...90s."

***

Amber watched Laurie watching the newlyweds on the dance floor. "You still doing okay?" She reached over and took her hand into her own.

Laurie smiled and met her gaze. "Yeah, I'm still fine." She gave Amber's hand a squeeze. "You're so sweet and considerate." She laid her head on Amber's shoulder. "Sometimes I have to pinch myself to know you're real."

Amber continued on. "Because if you weren't okay, you could talk to me. You know that, right?"

Laurie took a breath. "Yes, sweetheart. I know." She brushed a stray lock of hair from Amber's eyes. "I'm happy for Sawyer. She found the love of her life—just as I've found the love of mine."

Amber stood and held out her hand. "Dance with me."

Laurie's eyes twinkled and she smiled. "My pleasure, handsome."

***

Sage walked over to join her mom and dad. She was pleased that they were having such a good time. How had she gotten so lucky? She had them for parents and now she had Sawyer. It just seemed like so much more than one person deserved. "I love you guys." Sage kissed both their cheeks. "And I want you to know how very special you are. Some still might have difficulty with their daughter marrying another woman." She shook her head and smiled. "But not you two, you guys are all about it."

Jenny crinkled up her brow. "We love you and we love Sawyer. I can't imagine not being thrilled that you vowed to love each other."

"Like I said, you two are special." Sage stood and held her hand out to her dad. "Care to dance with your daughter?"

Bob beamed with pride. "I'd love to, sweetheart."

***

The dance floor was crowded as the daughter-daddy duo made their way to the center. Sawyer watched them for a couple minutes and then caught Jenny's eye. She smiled and Sawyer could tell that Jenny knew what was coming.

"Care to dance?" Sawyer said. She cocked her head and a raised an eyebrow.

"I thought you'd never ask," Jenny said as she followed her daughter-in-law to the corner of the dance floor.

Sawyer took her mother-in-law in her arms.

"It was a beautiful wedding," Jenny said as she recovered from a twirl.

Sawyer smiled. "Yeah, it was."

She caught Sawyer's eye. "And you're okay with the trip to Danville?" She shook her head and uttered a little sigh. "Sage can be kind of strong-willed sometimes."

Sawyer resisted the urge to laugh out loud. Jenny wasn't telling her anything she didn't already know. "Yeah, I'm okay. Sage feels like we need to do this and I trust her." She shook her head. "I'm just glad we're spending our wedding night at the condo." Sawyer winked. "I'd hate to disappoint her." They laughed the easy laugh of in-laws who loved each other.

***

Sawyer startled awake, gasping and drenched in sweat, gripped again in the terror of a nightmare after the most wonderful evening of her life—an evening chock-full of romance, lovemaking, and beautiful dreams. Why did something so beautiful have to end with a nightmare? God, what she wouldn't give for a good night's sleep. She sat up and held her dampened head in her palms.

"I'm sorry, baby," Sage whispered through the dark.

"God Sage, will they ever stop?" Sawyer asked. Misery dripped from her every word. "I'm just about at the end of my rope."

Sage reached up and rubbed her wife's back. "I hope so, sweetheart. I hope they stop really soon."

***

Amber shut her eyes and tried desperately to clear her mind. She lifted herself up in the bed to look at the clock. It was 3:00 a.m.—three hours since Laurie had rolled over after they'd made love, three hours since Laurie promptly fell asleep, three hours since Amber shut her eyes and tried, and three friggin' hours since she couldn't get Sawyer's trip back to Danville out of her mind.

Laurie stretched and then rolled over. She slipped her arm around Amber, then under her shirt. "You're still awake."

"Yeah," Amber said, "I can't stop thinking about SD—about the trip. God, I want to, but I can't get her out of my head."

"She's your twin, honey," Laurie said as she raised up to look into her lover's eyes. "She's going back to a place that scares you both half to death. Of course she's on your mind."

"I know she'll be okay," Amber said as she tugged her shirt up to give Laurie easy access. "Sage is really good at what she does. I know that first-hand." She shook her head. "I was a mess. You can't imagine how much she helped me. She's really good, and if she thinks SD needs to do this, then she probably does. It's just...." Her voice faded off.

"You're worried...and you're scared," Laurie said tenderly.

Amber's voice trembled. "Yeah." Tears welled up in her eyes. "I'm scared that we're not strong enough for her to do this." Her voice broke. "I'm just so scared."

Laurie pulled Amber close to rock her. She soothed her until she finally fell asleep.

***

Sawyer's grip on the steering wheel was so tight that she left the imprint of her fingers in the leather. This ride into Danville reminded Sage of another one not so very long ago—the night she'd been attacked by her father. It was like déjà vu. "You're gonna tell me what's got you so frightened, right?"

Sawyer clenched her jaw. Any tighter and her teeth would loosen. "Not now," she snapped. "I'm driving."

Sage leaned back in the bucket seat and took a breath. "I can see that." She tried to rein in her temper. God, Sawyer could push her buttons. "We don't have to do this." She pursed her lips. "As far as I'm concerned, we can turn around right here." She folded her arms. "Quite frankly, I'm sick and tired of the chill in the air and I don't mean the outside temperature."

Sawyer's shoulders relaxed a bit. "I'm sorry." She looked to her wife. "He's dead and yet I'm still terrified." Her jaw clenched even tighter. "I'm such a mess." She let up on the accelerator and the SUV slowed to enter the exit ramp. "I'll probably always be a mess."

"You know you need to work through this," Sage said. "You know it and I know it." She laid her hand on Sawyer's arm. "But you don't have to work through it with me."

Sawyer crinkled her brow—confused. "If I've got to do this, why in the world would I want to settle for less when I could have the best?" A slight smile crossed her face.

Sage chuckled and the mood in the vehicle lightened. "Good point." She raised an eyebrow. "You know I won't go easy on you." The truth was, she would. She'd go as slow and be as gentle as she needed to be. The only thing that mattered was that in the end, Sawyer was all right.

"Oh yeah," Sawyer said. "I know."

"So, do you know why we're here?" Sage asked, "instead of home on our couch?"

Sawyer's grip on the steering wheel loosened. Her facial muscles did too. "I think it's because you think my being here will help me find words that I can't find at home."

Sage nodded. "Uh-huh, that's part of it. Can you think of any other reason?"

Sawyer raised an eyebrow. Her expression said she didn't know.

Sage winked. "You let me know when you figure it out."

"Okay," Sawyer said. "I will."

***

Sawyer swung her legs over the edge of the king-sized hotel bed. Her breathing was labored and sweat was dripping down her face. She sat for few moments to catch her breath, stood, and then walked to the window. An icy glaze and possibly a few snowflakes glistened on the cars below.

Sage slipped on her nightgown and joined her wife. She slid her arms around Sawyer from behind.

"You married a trainwreck," Sawyer said softly. "Now the fucking panic attacks are back." They were exhausting. In a way, avoiding them by avoiding sex had been so much easier.

Sage squeezed around her belly and laid her cheek against Sawyer's back. "You're not a trainwreck, sweetie." She kissed her shoulder blade. "The fact that you had another panic attack tonight doesn't surprise me in the least. One step back, two steps forward is not uncommon at all." Her hand found its way underneath Sawyer's shirt. "You're too hard on yourself."

Coming to Terms

"Easy for you to say," Sawyer said as she gently removed Sage's hand. Her tone deepened. "I need to take a walk." She pulled on jeans and jerked on her jacket. "I'll be back in a little while."

"It's two in the morning," Sage said.

Sawyer pulled the hoodie over her head. "Yeah, I know. Like I said, I'll be back."

Sage dropped back onto the bed with a sigh. She flopped her arm across her eyes. She knew the door would slam at any moment.

***

The snowflakes pelted hard. The wind was stiff out of the northwest. Sawyer walked alone in the middle of the night. She walked alone on the dark and deserted streets of her childhood, her old stomping ground, trying to shake off...whatever. Her steps were at the epicenter of all the things that frightened her, and yet, at this moment, she wasn't afraid—not at all. She knew these streets—this town—these people. She knew them well.

Sawyer's mind drifted as the snow would drift by morning. It drifted to memories from long ago—to the grocery store where they'd shopped on Friday nights, to the basketball hoop where she'd never missed a free throw, to the best hill for sledding in the world. Sawyer smiled as a squad car slowed, took a look, and then drove on by. She thought of her dad, but only for a moment, then pushed his memory out of her mind. Being here, in this town of her childhood, a town whose development had been frozen much like her own, wasn't as bad as Sawyer had feared. Its familiarity was actually comforting.

237

***

Sage heard Sawyer slide the card in the door—heard it unlock. She laid silently facing the wall and listened to sounds that had become so familiar—pockets being unloaded on the dresser—jeans falling to the floor—a holster being gently laid on the nightstand. She waited in silence. In a moment, they'd talk.

Sawyer's voice eventually broke through the darkness. "I think I know the other reason."

Sage didn't move. "Oh, yeah?" Her voice was filled with emotion.

"If I'm here," Sawyer said, "I'm forced to face-off with the monsters that lurked in the darkness of my childhood. Only in this place can I fully realize that they no longer have any power over me." She sat down on the bed. "I'm an adult now and I can choose to turn on the lights."

Sage rolled over to her back and met Sawyer's gaze.

"Here…" Sawyer said. "I might realize that there was more to my childhood than just pain—that there was good as well as bad—that I am more than the sum total of my victimization."

Sage smiled. "That's right, baby."

***

Sawyer awoke to a sound she hadn't heard for 20 years—snowplows chipping away at the snow-covered pavement. She slipped quietly from the bed to peer out the window. The streets were white and the traffic crept.

The hustle and bustle of a snow day was all around. She smiled and considered where she'd go to buy coats, gloves, and most importantly, a sled.

Sawyer slid back under the covers and scooted toward her sleeping wife. Her hand just naturally found its way underneath Sage's nightgown. She caressed her breasts and twirled her hardening nipples.

Sage stirred. "Mmm…that feels nice."

Sawyer thrust her pelvis against her wife's thigh. A couple good pumps and she'd be gone.

Sage moaned. Her body arched upward and her breathing quickened. God, her whimpers of pleasure were such a turn on.

Sawyer slipped her fingers down Sage's abdomen and beyond.

Sage reached inside her Sawyer's boxers.

They stroked in mutual rythym until both stiffened, gasped in climax, and collapsed in each other's arms.

"Oh my God," Sage panted. "That was incredibly erotic."

Sawyer released a breath. "It was, wasn't it?"

***

Sage was in awe of all that surrounded her on this cold December morn—the nip in the air—the trees with their glistening branches—the snow plows. Danville, like Sarasota, had its own special charm. She'd never experienced anything quite like it.

"I can't believe it," Sawyer said. "You've really never seen snow up close and personal? Never?" She shook her head. "That's impossible."

"Nope." Sage grinned ear-to-ear. "Never seen it." She looked around. "It's breathtaking, isn't it?"

Sawyer's eyebrow raised in amusement. "Yeah, it's breathtaking alright. Come on now, hop in." She opened the passenger door for her wife. "Let's go find us some proper winter clothing." She headed around and got in the other side. "And a sled." She chuckled. "I know the best hill."

Sawyer shifted back into park before they got out of the driveway. The damn cell phone was ringing and she had to dig it out from underneath her layers. Finally, she found it and pulled it out. "Sawyer James...oh, hi Sis. Yeah, she's here, hold on." Sawyer handed Sage the phone. "I'll take a little walk around, give you two some privacy."

Sawyer stepped out of the SUV. The snow crunched and her mind was gone—to snowball fights with Amber—to poking charcoal buttons in a snowman's belly—to a daddy pulling his daughters on their bright red sled. She breathed in the frosty air as memories from her childhood once again blanketed her mind. She walked for a while, then slid back behind the wheel.

"Amber okay?" Sawyer asked as she turned the key in the ignition.

"Yeah," Sage said. "She just needed to know that you were okay."

Chapter Twenty-Six

They spent the day driving over the snow-packed streets of Danville. Sawyer was an excellent tour guide. She really knew her way around—almost like she'd never left. She pointed out all the places a visitor might want to see—the Lincoln sites, the state parks, Lake Vermilion, even the best hills for sledding. She pointed out everything. It was dusk before she drove them back up to their hotel. Her first nightmare slapped her down by midnight.

"Poor baby," Sage said. She sat up and wrapped her arms around her wife. "We're in the hotel, honey. You're okay."

Sawyer buried her face in her hands. "I'm not okay," she sobbed. "There's no way I'm okay. I'm a mess."

"No, sweetie," Sage said, "you're not." She ran her fingers through Sawyer's hair. "You're healing, baby. It just takes time."

Sawyer lifted her head. "I couldn't make myself go there today. I know you wanted me to, but I just couldn't."

"I know," Sage said softly, "but tomorrow we will." She had to be firm.

Sage was wide awake for some time after Sawyer fell back to sleep, thinking and worrying. She was trying

241

to imagine what childhood horror could have been worse than the abuse perpetrated by Mark James. It had to be awful and so traumatic that it scarred Sawyer and Amber for decades. She lay awake for hours—afraid—so afraid that she wouldn't have the skills necessary to help Sawyer finish what she'd forced them to start.

Eventually, sleep did come for Sage. When she opened her eyes that next morning, she immediately met Sawyer's gaze. There was little doubt that she'd been waiting patiently for her to wake up. She was sitting straight as a pencil on the sofa, dressed in her freshly pressed navy trousers and light blue shirt, ready to go...somewhere. The expression on her face was exactly the same as the day she'd first disclosed.

"I let you sleep," Sawyer said. "I know it took you a while to settle back down after I woke you up." Her eyes were sad. "I'm sorry."

Sage stretched and yawned. "Come here. I want my kiss." It was a nice one with a little tongue.

"You're all dressed up," Sage said. "What do you want me to wear?"

Sawyer forced a smile. "You're beautiful in whatever you choose."

Sage dropped her legs over the side of the bed. "Black slacks with my green sweater?"

"Perfect," Sawyer said. "It'll match your eyes."

***

The SUV exited the hotel parking lot, turned the opposite direction, and onto the four-lane. Sawyer was quiet. She wasn't particularly upset, just didn't have much to say. Sage didn't either. Truthfully, they were both a bundle of nerves.

Sawyer pointed out a three-story brick building as they drove by. "That's where we went to high school." She slowed the SUV. "I ran track on that field." She smiled as memories flooded her mind. "We were conference champions my sophomore year." The SUV continued for a stretch and then turned to the right. She pointed to a smaller red brick building with a playground on the east side and behind. "That's where we went to grade school." She paused again, remembering. "Amber broke her wrist on that slide." The SUV continued on. It turned several times and finally came to a stop in front of the Danville Police Department.

Sage was clearly puzzled, but said nothing.

Sawyer got out. She plugged the meter and then returned to the vehicle. They sat in silence. She was trying to summon her words. Before they came, a high-ranking police officer leaned down and peered into the driver's window.

"Oh my God," the officer said. "I can't believe it. SD, is that you?" Recognition twinkled in his eyes.

Sawyer grinned. "Yep, it's me." She cocked her head and raised an eyebrow. "What happened to your hair, big guy?"

The officer gave her shoulder a playful nudge. "Always the smart-ass."

Sawyer looked to Sage. "Want to get out?"

Sage nodded, opened her door, and stepped outside.

Sawyer extended her right hand. The officer took hold and they shook for the longest time. She turned to

Sage. "This is Bud Ramshaw. I was assigned to him when I was a Police Explorer in high school."

Sage nodded a "pleased to meet you" and Sawyer continued on with her introductions.

"Bud," she said, "this is my wife, Sage Carson."

"Oh man," the officer said, "are you ever all grown up now." His eyes sparkled as he shook Sage's hand. "You caught yourself a good one, Ma'am."

"Yes sir," Sage said with a smile. "I believe you're right."

Sawyer took notice of the insignia on Bud's uniform—a single gold bar. "I see you got yourself a couple promotions along the way." She grinned. "*Lieutenant* Ramshaw."

Bud grinned back. "Yeah, just a couple." He nodded. "I head up the detective squad now. How about you?" His gaze lingered—clearly wanting to know if Sawyer had grown up to be a cop. That would be what everyone would have expected of her.

Sawyer squared her shoulders and met his eye. "Sergeant. Sarasota Police Department. I just transferred from special victims to head up narcotics." She smiled with pride.

Sage was touched by the fondness in the Lieutenant's eyes. "Good for you." He grinned. "We wouldn't want that chain to be broken, now would we?"

Sage cocked her head. She had many questions, but remained quiet.

Bud motioned toward the building. "I think you'll still know most everyone. I know they'll want a chance to say hello." He invited the couple in with his eyes. "Want to?"

Sawyer looked to Sage then answered. "Sure, we'd love to."

They followed along and stepped inside. The Lieutenant set Sawyer up in the break room to entertain her visitors. They filed in, one, sometimes two at a time. It was like a member of the royal family had dropped by.

Sage watched, bewildered. Who remembered the high school kid who volunteered 20 years prior, even if that kid was as exceptional as Sawyer? A major piece of the puzzle was still missing. She watched and listened closely.

"Hey Bud, do we still have all the pictures in the back hallway?" Sawyer asked. "I want to show a couple to my wife."

"Sure we do," the Lieutenant responded. "Go on back. I'll get the one of you as an Explorer off my desk." He smacked the back of Sawyer's head with considerable familiarity. "You were one cute kid in uniform."

Sawyer's gaze dropped to the floor, embarrassed. "Thanks."

Sage was perplexed. And who kept a picture of that high school kid on their desk for 20 years? She realized Sawyer was on the move and followed. They made their way down one hallway, around the corner, and up the next. She knew it wouldn't be long now. Sawyer had come unbelievably far in just 24 hours. Coming to Danville had been exactly what they'd needed to do.

The photographs were on display in identical frames hung in perfectly straight rows. Each had an engraved gold plaque with all the important details—names, dates of service, and last rank held. It was a memorial to all who had served and to all who had walked these halls as brothers. The images were arranged four-deep from left to right, black-and-white to color.

Sawyer looked into Sage's eyes. She squared her shoulders. Her chest puffed out with pride. "I'm a cop." She smiled a thin smile. "A cop is who I am and all I ever wanted to be. It's also all that was ever expected of me." She straightened a frame that had jiggled slightly crooked on the wall. "I come from a long line of cops. You might say it's in my blood." Her voice caught in the back of her throat. She cleared it loose and pointed toward the wall. Her finger made a slow pass from the far left to the far right of an entire row.

Sage was surprised speechless. For a moment she couldn't do anything except stand with her mouth hanging wide open. She stared at the wall—James, after James, after James. She looked up and into Sawyer's eyes. "All of them, your family?"

Sawyer nodded. Another slight smile cracked the corners of her mouth. "Yeah, they are." She pointed to a fading black-and-white. "My grandfather." Her finger slid over to the next section. "My great-grandfather...my aunt...my uncle...my cousin...."

Sage zeroed in on the one that Sawyer had failed to point out—a color photograph taken at least 30 years prior. She pointed. "Your dad?"

Sawyer sucked in a breath and held it deep within her lungs as she clenched her jaw. "Yeah. That's a young Sergeant Mark James—before he went bad."

A tall man with graying hair and the deepest blue eyes turned the corner and made his way toward them. The two gold bars, railroad tracks, identified him as a Captain. Sawyer straightened up, squared her shoulders, and met his eye. They nodded in respect and recognition. He stepped close and extended his right hand.

Sawyer took hold. Her handshake looked solid. "Uncle Sawyer, Sir."

Captain James nodded and smiled an approving smile. "SD…it's been a longtime. I never thought we'd see you again." He patted Sawyer's shoulder. "You look good."

"Thank you, Sir," Sawyer said. "You too."

"Your sister, she's doing well?" the Captain asked.

"She is," Sawyer said with pride. "She's a high school teacher now."

"Ah," Captain James said with an interesting pause. "Good for her." He nodded and continued. "I've followed your career, SD. You've made us all very proud."

They stood in companionable silence. Minutes passed before either spoke.

"I never got a chance to tell you how sorry I was about your mom," the Captain said tenderly. "His eye twitched. The topic had made him nervous. "She was a good woman."

Sawyer nodded and swallowed hard. "Yes Sir, she was." She looked like she was struggling to maintain composure. Sage wished that she could help.

Sawyer fidgeted a bit and then looked to her. "I'd like to introduce my father's brother and my uncle, Captain Sawyer James." She glanced toward the Captain. "Sir, my wife, Sage Carson."

The Captain's gaze and handshake were warm— like family. "How about you two join us for dinner tomorrow night? Say, 6:30? We're out across the lake now, built a place there a few years ago. I think you'll like it."

Sawyer looked to Sage and then nodded. "We'd love to."

Chapter Twenty-Seven

A relaxing walk through the downtown was just what the doctor ordered that afternoon. Both Sage and Sawyer desperately needed a chance to unwind. The morning had been emotionally taxing. They held hands and window-shopped. Sage allowed a myriad of thoughts to stroll through her mind. There was just something about this place, something special. Maybe it was the crisp, cold air. Maybe it was the smell of freshly cut pine. It could be the crackling fire in the hotel lobby. Or maybe it was watching Sawyer rekindle her relationships with old friends and family. Whatever it was, it filled Sage with the spirit of the season. She sensed that it did the same for Sawyer.

"The lights are gorgeous," Sage said. "I like the way they reflect off the snow." She smiled. "It's like being inside a Christmas card."

"Yeah it is," Sawyer said. "Danville's always gone totally Christmas." Her eyes told the story as her mind drifted to another place and time.

"You feeling okay?" Sage asked softly. "You seem like you're holding up pretty well."

Sawyer glanced her way and smiled. "Yeah. I can hardly believe it, but I feel fine." She shook her head. "But I'll probably be flat on my face after our next stop."

"Maybe we should wait until tomorrow," Sage said as she reached down to hold her wife's gloved hand. "We could, you know."

Sawyer shook her head. "No, I want to get this over with. If we did it tomorrow, it would ruin dinner with my uncle." Her eyes locked with Sage. "I'm ready, just scared."

"Whatever it is," Sage said softly, "we'll face it together." She kissed Sawyer's gloved hand. "You're strong. Your strength never fails to amaze me."

***

The SUV slowed and turned into a neighborhood of bricked streets in the north end of town. It crept several blocks before signaling and turning into the driveway of an older two-story red brick home. Sawyer's eyes were glued to the front porch, the porch swing, and of course the front door. She turned off the engine and her hand moved up to bounce a curled knuckle against her mouth. She looked green around the gills.

Sage touched her arm. "You still okay? We really can put this off. There's absolutely no hurry. We've got all the time in the world."

Sawyer inhaled and exhaled several times in a row. "No, I gotta do it now." She swallowed hard. "I'm just afraid I'm gonna throw up."

Sage took several slow and steady breaths with her wife. "Come on, breathe with me. You'll be fine." She really wasn't sure of that, but Sawyer must have believed her, because in a few minutes she was fine.

Sawyer stepped out of the vehicle and Sage settled in at her side. Together, they walked hand-in-hand up the steps toward the front door. They stood in silence before Sawyer finally rang the bell.

An older woman, probably in her mid-80s, peered through the screen. Her eyes lit up. She obviously recognized Sawyer and was delighted to see her. Sage smiled. Seconds passed and the twinkle in the woman's eyes transformed into an angry scowl. She glared at Sage. Sage's smile faded and she stepped back. What the heck? The woman didn't even know her. She was relieved when her gaze returned to Sawyer.

"Oh, Markie," Dorothy James purred. She kissed Sawyer on her lips. "I'm so glad you've finally come home." Her voice was disgusting—unmotherly. "How come you were gone so long?" The old woman shook her head. "Oh well, at least you're home now." She glared again at Sage. "But what did you have to bring her for?" She kissed Sawyer again. "You know your mama's all you need." She held the door open.

Sawyer looked like she was about to be sick. They stepped inside. She took a deep breath. "Grandma...it's me, Sawyer." She swallowed hard. "Mark's my dad."

Dorothy stepped further down the hall. "I suppose you'll want to take her in that room for a while." She shook her head and sneered. "Well, go ahead then. Have her if you want." Without another word, she spun and headed toward what Sawyer knew was her bedroom.

"I'm thinking Alzheimer's," Sage muttered under her breath. "I'm so sorry."

"Yeah, me too" Sawyer said. "Or worse...."

Sage rubbed her back. "Still doing okay?"

Sawyer pursed her lips. "Yep, let's get this over with."

They followed the old woman down the hall and Sawyer stuck her head in her open bedroom door. "If it's okay Grandma, I'd like to show Sage around the house."

Dorothy laid down her knitting needles and multi-colored yarn. She looked up and tilted her head. Her smile was almost seductive...sickening. "As long as you come back to see me when you're done."

Sawyer sucked in a breath and swallowed. "Okay Grandma, we will." Her mind flashed to things she almost remembered from long ago. She pushed them out of her mind, pushed the bile back down her throat, and went on.

***

Sage closed her eyes and intentionally slowed her breathing. She needed to be centered, to be fully present with Sawyer. Later, she'd have time to think more about what they'd just witnessed. She took hold of her wife's hand. They walked around the corner and down the hall.

Sawyer slowed as they approached the staircase. She stopped in front of a narrow wooden door. Once again they paused in silence. Sawyer was trembling. She took a breath and reached inside the right pocket of her trousers. She pulled out an old key ring. It was one Sage had never seen before.

Sage crinkled her brow. Sawyer hadn't even tried the knob. She'd already known the door would be locked.

Sweat began to roll down Sawyer's temple and bead up on her forehead. "They were my dad's. He had them in his pocket when he died." She flipped the key ring over and over. "There it is. That's the one." She inserted the rusted key into the old lock. The inner workings clicked and the knob turned.

Sage pressed her body close to Sawyer. She held tightly to her hand.

Sawyer tugged on the knob. The latch stuck like the door hadn't been opened in years. She tugged again. It opened. She held her breath for what seemed like an eternity. Finally, she exhaled, and then breathed again. She looked back to Sage with a look of pure determination and resolve. "Come in."

Such a small room—almost completely filled with bed with the exception of a nightstand, a lamp, and a solitary hard-backed chair. Vintage posters of naked women in lurid poses adorned the walls. Sage's gaze fell on the keyed lock on both sides of the door.

Sawyer noticed immediately. "Yep, always locked. The bastard had the only key." She paused to look around the room again. "God…." She clamped her hand over her mouth. The can of Coke was still there. "I'm gonna be sick." She ran for the bathroom.

Sage stood by the door and listened to be sure she was okay. What in the world had she gotten them into?

***

Sage knew what she needed to do. She sat down on the bed and focused on projecting calm. "Come sit with me."

Sawyer's eyes widened. She'd recognized the words and tone. "We don't need to do this."

Sage's gaze locked on. "Yes we do." She patted the bed beside her. "Come on, sit with me."

Sawyer shut her eyes and swallowed hard. When she opened them, she got up to shut the door. Her jaw and fists were clenched tight as she sat down.

"Sage, please, we don't have to do this," Sawyer said.

Sage laid her hand on Sawyer's bouncing leg. Her voice was soft and calming. "This'll be alright. You just need to trust me." She prayed that she was right.

"I do trust you," Sawyer said.

Sage stroked Sawyer's cheek. "I know this will be difficult." She peered into her eyes. "And I'm so sorry."

Sawyer squared her shoulders. "You do what you need to do." She brushed a lock of red hair from Sage's eyes. "I love you."

Sage took a breath. "Okay, I want you to shut your eyes for a moment. Just let your mind go…back to that last day that you were in this room." She paused. "Be there, Sawyer. Be there with all your senses."

Sawyer shut her eyes. Her body stiffened.

"Tell me about it," Sage said softly. "Tell me every single detail."

Sawyer sat quietly for minutes before she spoke. "He was drunk. The bastard wanted everything that day. He wanted it all." Pain flickered in the blue of her eyes. "Being fucked was the worst. We used to always try to satisfy him with girl-on-girl. We'd just block out that we were sisters and put on a show." She sucked in another breath. Her fists tightened and loosened repeatedly. "The room was dark. It always smelled like his sweat and beer." She cracked her knuckles, one at a time. "He was back by the wall that day." She nodded toward the bed. "I was in the middle. Amber was on the outside. His arm laid across us as he reached for his can of Coke." She curled her upper lip and nodded toward the nightstand. "Probably that one. He always had to have a Coke and a cigarette afterward." She began to cry. "I heard a loud pop. For a minute, I thought it was him just opening the can…but it wasn't." She held her breath—too long.

Sage rubbed Sawyer's back in soothing circles. "You're okay, sweetie. You need to breathe."

Sawyer gasped for air and continued on. "The bastard recognized the sound. He knew…and smashed his way out of the bed."

Sage kept rubbing. "Come on, baby. Slow breaths, breathe in and out."

"He scrambled for his pants and dug out the key." Sawyer's eyes widened as if she'd seen a ghost. "He opened the door." She released an audible gasp. "God…her blood was everywhere…shot herself in the head."

Sawyer brushed tears away with her thumb. "My mom…just outside the door. We had to step over her to get out." Sawyer swallowed hard. "If we, no, if I hadn't been so weak, she'd still be alive."

Sage was struggling to hold it together. She had to finish what they'd started. "Why you and not Amber?"

Sawyer stared off at nothing in particular. "We look the same, but we're different. You know that. Amber's always been a gentle soul. She's more fragile." Sawyer locked eyes with her wife. "It was up to me to protect her. I was the oldest, if only by a couple minutes." She breathed in and out. "That's why I always made sure it was me he fucked. I knew Amber couldn't deal with it."

Sage felt her eyes fill with tears. "So you had enough strength to deal with him, then and now."

Sawyer nodded. "Yeah, I guess I did."

***

Sawyer had a good night. Their lovemaking was relaxed and easy. Her sleep was free of nightmares. She could barely remember the last time she'd gotten eight hours in a row. Sage had definitely known what she was talking about. Sawyer wished she'd come home years ago.

"I'm starved," Sawyer said as she took in a whiff of the steaming hot pancakes. They were piled high, just the way she liked 'em. She dropped three pads of butter in the center and heaped on the maple syrup. "Want one?" she asked as she forked her first huge bite.

Sage smiled, but rolled her eyes. "No thanks. I'm good with my oatmeal." She shook her head. "You wouldn't find me as sexy if I gained 20 pounds."

"Oh yes I would," Sawyer said as she forked a bite three layers high. "But it wouldn't be as good for your health." She winked. "So stick with the oatmeal." Sawyer took a swig of coffee. "Dinner at Uncle Sawyer's tonight and the cemetery this morning?"

Sage nodded. "Sounds good." She finished off the bowl and met Sawyer's eye. "Just curious…have you figured out what triggered your panic attacks yet?"

"I think so," Sawyer said. It no longer felt like a forbidden topic. "I'm pretty sure it happened when Laurie leaned over me to get her Coke that night. She popped the can open and for some reason it flashed me back to that day. The sound must have reminded me of the shot." She looked up. "You were right. It never did have anything to do with sex. That was all in my mind."

Sage nodded with a slight smile. "I think you're on target. How about your nightmares?"

"I don't know about them yet," Sawyer said, "but I'm working on it." She looked up. "Do you?"

"Yeah, I think so," Sage said with a look. Sawyer knew she'd tell her if she wanted.

"Don't tell me," Sawyer said. "Let me figure it out."

Chapter Twenty-Eight

It was a calm but extremely cold morning. Snow and the occasional icicle clung tightly to the branches of the naked trees. Until this trip, 10 degrees below zero had been beyond Sage's imagination. Now she knew from personal experience what it meant to be dead cold. Supposedly, this was an extreme cold snap for this early in the season.

The SUV turned into the cemetery and bounced through potholes the size of moon craters. Had the snow-pack on what she assumed was a road been more than the six inches deep, Sage was certain they would've fallen in—never to be found. They thumped through another section of deep ones as they climbed the hill toward higher ground. It was a very large, and other than the condition of the road, impressive graveyard. Sage spotted a huge pine grove in the distance. It was just as Sawyer had described her extended family plot. Sage pointed. "Is that it?"

"Yep," Sawyer said with a slight smile. "There it is." She took a slow, deep breath. "That's where we're all buried—one James laid to rest beside another." Judging from the size of the grove that Sawyer said her family had purchased, Sage doubted she was exaggerating in the least.

Sage nodded. "It's a pretty setting, peaceful with all the snow." A sad smile turned the corners of her mouth as her gaze shifted back to her wife. "You seem good this morning." She reached across and laid her gloved hand gently on her thigh. Sawyer had dealt with a lot these last couple days. Sage was pleased that she seemed to be doing so well.

"I am good," Sawyer said. She flipped the switch to turn up the fan on the heater and held onto Sage's eyes. "You've helped me so much." Her gaze moved off in the distance. "This visit has been overdue for a very long time."

The SUV bounced to a stop. Its doors groaned open in the frigid cold and both got out. Sage dropped calf-deep into the snow. She yelped as she went down.

"Sorry," Sawyer called out. "I meant to warn you about that."

Sawyer trudged around to help up her wife, then stepped back to open the rear door. She'd brought the bouquet of yellow roses for her mom. She lifted them from the seat reverently. The door slammed shut with a groan. Sawyer took hold of Sage's hand. It was so much smaller than her own. Together, they made their way up the hill and toward the stone. It was almost completely covered by undisturbed snow. Sawyer dug and brushed it clean with her glove.

Amber Ann James
1964 - 1995
Beloved wife of Mark

Sergeant Mark Dane James
1944 – 2014

KA Moll

Beloved husband of Amber

***

It was a peaceful place—silent and cold. Not a car engine, not a voice, and not even the chirp of a sparrow disturbed the resting ground of the departed. The stone was gorgeous—ornately carved, two feet high and three feet long. Sawyer could tell that her dad had chosen one of the nicest ones for her mom. She squatted down to break loose a fresh clump of frozen soil. She swallowed a lump in her throat as she rolled it in her palm. It reminded her that this was *their* burial site and *their* stone. She bent down to lay the yellow roses above her mom. Instead, she laid them in between—above both. She stood up and stepped back. Her gaze lingered on the stone.

Sage reached for her wife's hand and laid her head against her shoulder. "She was so young."

"She was," Sawyer said softly. "When she died." She paused and swallowed again. "And also when we were born." She shook her head with disgust. Her dad had always liked the young ones.

Sage stooped down and brushed away a little more snow. "Amber was named after her?"

Sawyer nodded. "And I was named for..." She drew in a breath and released it slowly. "My uncle...and my father."

Sage reached up to rub Sawyer's back through her coat. "Your parents conceived and raised two of the most amazing people that I know." Her tear frosted as it tried to fall.

Sawyer leaned down to kiss her. "I think I'm ready to go."

***

Sawyer slid one leg into her dress blues. She paused, crinkled her brow, and looked to Sage. "Are you sure about this?" Her voice was filled with uncertainty. "You really think I should wear my dress uniform to dinner at my uncle's? I assure you he won't be wearing his." She wanted to make a good impression. To her, to her family, the uniform was work clothing.

Sage scanned her almost-dressed wife. "Yes, I think you should wear your uniform." She peeled her t-shirt over her head and her breasts fell free. A smile crossed her face when Sawyer noticed. She reached back and hooked her lace-trimmed bra. "It's just like you said, being a police officer is who you are. Well, it's who he is too. Not once has he ever gotten to see you in uniform." She stepped to the mirror and began to brush her hair. "It'll please him. I know it will." She raised an eyebrow. "And then of course there's also an added benefit...for me. If you wear it, I get to feast my eyes on you in uniform for an entire evening." She smiled her seductive smile. "Who knows, it might get the old juices flowing again."

Sawyer chuckled. "Okay, you talked me into it." She slid in her other leg and joined her wife in front of the full-length mirror. "God, you're hot in that dress."

Sage raised an eyebrow. "I believe I'm noticing a pattern." She'd already known the dress was one of Sawyer's favorites. That's why she'd brought it along. Sage pressed back into Sawyer's crotch. "If it's black, clingy, and a dress...."

KA Moll

Sawyer grinned and slipped her arms around her. She cupped her wife's breasts in her palms. "If it's black, clingy, and a dress—on you—I love it."

***

Sawyer opened the patio door and stepped onto the enclosed deck. It overlooked a wide expanse of a frozen Lake Vermilion and the view was absolutely breathtaking. The home was equally impressive. Uncle Sawyer had done quite well for himself. She knew that everything he'd done, he'd done for his family. He was a father and a husband they could be proud of. She heard the door slide open behind her, and she turned and smiled.

Captain James held out two bottles of beer, both unopened. "Thought you might want a cold one."

"Thank you, Sir," Sawyer said, "but I don't drink anymore." She heard her words and knew she spoke the truth. She'd been enjoying sobriety for the longest stretch ever.

The Captain squared his shoulders and cocked his head slightly to one side. His eyes twinkled. "I'll have your Aunt Marge bring you a cup of coffee if you'd like. She just brewed up a pot of a blend we found at the local roastery. It's delicious, imported from India, kind of dark and oily with a hint of caramel. You'll like it."

"Sawyer smiled. "Yes Sir. I'd love a cup—black."

The older James slid the door open and called the coffee order out to his wife. When she didn't answer, he stepped inside. He was chuckling as she stepped back through the door.

Sawyer met his gaze, then raised her eyebrow and chuckled with him.

"Our wives are sure having a good time," Captain James said with the remnant of a chuckle. "Never heard such giggling." He shook his head. "They'll probably forget all about your coffee."

"That'd be okay if they did," Sawyer said with a smile. "Heaven knows I had plenty of absolutely everything at dinner." She looked up. "It was all wonderful. We really appreciate your hospitality." Sawyer looked toward the floor and then back up to meet his eyes. "And your kindness."

The Captain straddled a chair. He crossed his arms and locked gazes with Sawyer. "We can stop beating around the bush with each other anytime you're ready."

Sawyer furrowed her brow. She wasn't sure where the conversation was headed.

The older man's expression became more serious, almost somber. "SD...I know...."

Sawyer wasn't sure how to respond. All she could do was swallow. Thankfully, the door slid open and Sage stepped out to join them. Their eyes found each other and held on.

Sage set down the cup of coffee then lingered, much longer than would've been typical. She was predictable that way. Sawyer knew her wife would stay as long as it took for her to be sure that she was fine.

"Here you go, sweetie," Sage said. "I'll be in the kitchen with Aunt Marge if you need me. She's digging out some of your old family recipes. I'll fix you a couple when we get home."

Sawyer caught Sage's eye before she was gone. "Thanks," she said softly.

Sage winked. "Anytime."

Sawyer watched her uncle study her interaction with her wife. She'd been surprised at how well he'd done with accepting her lifestyle. She wasn't sure why, but she'd halfway expected him to have a problem. He hadn't, and neither had her Aunt Marge. They'd both been absolutely wonderful. She was beginning to realize that she'd based her negative expectation on nothing. She wondered if she did that all the time.

"Sage is a beautiful woman," the Captain said, "and very smart."

Sawyer smiled with pride. "Yes Sir, she is. I'm very proud of her."

They looked out across the frozen water and fell silent. Eventually, Sawyer spoke. There were things they needed to discuss.

"So you know," Sawyer said almost inaudibly, "that I was the one who shot him?"

Captain James nodded. "Yes, I know, and I also know that you did it to save the woman who's now your wife."

The code—duty and honor—made things so much easier. Sawyer too looked at the world through the lens of a cop. Again they fell silent, but finally she found her voice. "We stopped by the house yesterday to see Grandma."

Uncle Sawyer shook his head and sighed. "God, I'm sorry about that. I should have warned you."

"Well, I must admit," Sawyer said, "it was pretty odd." She looked up and into her uncle's eyes. "We weren't sure what to think about her…behavior."

Captain James sighed and looked down. "I suspected, even when I was a kid still at home. But when your grandma got Alzheimer's...." He shook his head and Sawyer could tell he was disgusted. "Well, then she lost whatever inhibition she may or may not have had. It all just hung out there after that." His eyes were sad as he took another swig of beer. "When your dad

got dirty with the meth and you guys moved into the house...." He swallowed hard. "I should have dealt with it then, but I was a coward." Sawyer thought her uncle was going to cry. "I just let it go on."

"They hid it well," Sawyer said softly, "because Amber and I never had a clue." She shut her eyes. "I actually didn't figure it out until yesterday when Grandma thought I was my dad."

"God, I'm so sorry," the senior Sawyer said again, "about them, about your mom, about everything."

Sawyer put her hand on her uncle's shoulder and met his eye. She knew in her heart that he'd done the best that he could. That's all anyone could ever reasonably expect of another person. The circumstances had been difficult for everybody. "Amber and I got through it." She sucked in a deep breath and exhaled. "We dealt with it—the sexual abuse. For the most part, we're fine now. My wife is a great therapist." She looked up, shocked by the loss of color in her uncle's face. She'd said something terribly wrong. "Uncle Sawyer?"

The Captain's kind eyes filled with tears. He turned away, but Sawyer heard emotion catch in his throat.

"Oh my God," Sawyer said, "you didn't know about Dad molesting us." She reached for her uncle's hand. "I'm sorry I just blurted it out."

Captain James clenched his jaw. "You have nothing to be sorry about." His fists clenched hard enough to restrict blood flow to his fingers. "If I'd known—God, I should have known." He looked into Sawyer's eyes. "I never would have allowed him to hurt you. I just thought his thing was with Mom." He stood. His knees and voice seemed weaker somehow. "Now I understand why you left. I mean…I knew you were traumatized by your mom's…." His words caught in his throat. "I knew that trauma had to be the reason you girls left." Their eyes met in understanding. "But I never understood why you did it the way you did, just slipping away from the cemetery before she was even buried." He stared across the lake. "Now I understand. You had to run while he was otherwise engaged and couldn't follow."

Sawyer nodded.

The Captain stood, then moved toward the door. "I have some items I want to give you," he said. "We found them tucked away in your mom's personal belongings—had to take them with it being a death investigation and all. I know you understand." His jaw tightened. "It didn't seem right to give them back to your dad so I saved them for you and your sister." Uncle Sawyer slid the door open. Sawyer watched him step inside. He seemed sad and so much older.

***

Sage carried the small packet to the SUV and then on up to the hotel room.

Sawyer hadn't been able to touch it, carry it, or even look inside. Her eyes clung to Sage's as she stood stripped down to her underwear in the middle of their hotel room. "I just can't." Tears sprang from her eyes. "I just can't read my mom's diaries and poke through her stuff." A couple quiet sobs. "I just can't." She looked pleadingly to her wife. "I need you to do it for me."

Sawyer's expression and demeanor broke Sage's heart. She pulled her into her arms, stroked her, and held her close. "Okay, sweetie. I'll take the first look."

Sawyer looked physically and emotionally exhausted. It was no surprise when she stumbled directly into the shower and then climbed in bed.

Sage took her turn in the bathroom after she'd finished. When she got back, Sawyer was already asleep. Sage wasn't disappointed. Sawyer needed the sleep and she needed the night off. Her parts were sore from having sex so many days in a row. She curled up in the chair beside the bed and cracked open Sawyer's mom's diary.

Two hours before sunrise, Sage read her deceased mother-in-law's last entry. It was dated December 21, 1995. It was probably written less than an hour before she'd taken her husband's handgun off the nightstand, attached a silencer, and blown her brains out. Sage had much to think about and much to share later in the morning. She gently closed the diary, turned off the bedside lamp, and snuggled under the covers next to Sawyer.

***

Sawyer knew that Sage had stayed up most of the night and needed to sleep. She'd been sitting quietly beside the bed—waiting—for hours. It was 11:00 before her wife finally began to stir and then opened her eyes.

"Hi, handsome," Sage said as she tried to stretch herself awake. "You look like you've been awake for quite a while."

Sawyer nodded. "Morning." She kissed her lips. "Did you stay up all night?"

Another stretch and a yawn. "Yeah, pretty much," Sage said. "Man do I ever have a lot to tell you."

"I'll bet you do," Sawyer said. She pursed her lips and sighed. "I ordered room service."

***

"So, my mom had no idea that my dad was abusing us?" Sawyer continued to shake her head in disbelief. She'd spent the last 20 years believing his fuck that last afternoon had been the reason that her mom had killed herself. All that time—believing it was because she'd been a failure—a coward—too weak to stop her dad in time to save her mother.

"No," Sage said, "I don't think she had any idea, none at all. She loved you and your sister very much." Sage smiled the most loving smile. "She thought you'd grow up to be a cop, like your dad and your Uncle Sawyer. She expected Amber to grow up to be a teacher, like her mom—your maternal grandma."

Sawyer looked up. "Maternal grandma?"

"That's right," Sage said. "You have lots of family your dad never allowed you to know. Their names and contact information are all carefully listed in the diary."

"Wow." Sawyer stared off. She was somewhere out the window. "Well if she had no idea, then why? Why'd she have to go and kill herself?"

Coming to Terms

Sage met the saddest blue eyes. She brushed away a lock of hair. "It had been a bad day for your mom—a day that just kept getting worse. She'd come home early from work, depressed and angry over something that had happened with a coworker." Sage laid her hand on Sawyer's thigh. "Your mom...." She paused and took a breath. "Well, I think she had some serious mental health problems." Sage had noticed Sawyer's mom's consistent pattern of highs followed by extreme lows over a period of years. "Today, we'd probably diagnose her as bipolar. I think she'd be on a fairly high dosage of medication."

Sawyer licked her lips as her face turned ashen.

Sage noticed the alarm in her eyes. "No—not schizophrenic. I said bipolar." She pinched her brow. "There are genetic components, but that's not all there is to it. There are environmental factors as well. Today, it's totally treatable. Don't worry."

Sawyer took another breath.

Sage continued on. "Your mom expected to find your dad home that day because she'd seen his car in the driveway. Instead of finding him waiting, she found an empty house. It seemed that way initially, anyway. She believed that you and your sister were at basketball practice."

"It was cancelled," Sawyer croaked. "Freezing rain."

"Your mom found something when she got home that day—something so bad that she couldn't cope." Sage's expression was puzzled and she shook her head. "It may have been a photo, but I couldn't tell for sure. Maybe it was left for her to find, or she found it by accident. I don't know that either." Sage looked into Sawyer's eyes. "Regardless, your mom found it and in finding it, confirmed what she'd suspected for some time—that your dad was having an ongoing sexual relationship with his mother."

Sawyer dropped sideways and laid her head on Sage's shoulder.

Sage could tell she was still listening. "She was devastated by your dad's betrayal. At that point, she kind of lost touch with reality." She ran her fingers through Sawyer's hair. "She really loved him. I think he was a good man at one time. Had it not been for the meth and of course his ongoing sexual relationship with his mother.... Oh well, we'll never know for sure." She paused, processing her own words. "Your mom heard sounds in your dad's workroom. The door was locked as usual. She assumed he was in there with your grandma. She got his handgun from the nightstand, clipped on the silencer, and went into the hallway. She wanted to position herself where they'd have to step over her body on their way out." Sage inhaled. It was the only sound in the room with the exception of Sawyer's soft sobs.

***

Sawyer opened her eyes and stirred. Sage stirred too and pulled her wife close. They snuggled and kissed good morning. It was the last day of their honeymoon. The bags were packed and waiting by the door.

"Thank you," Sawyer said softly.

Sage raised an eyebrow. "I'm not exactly sure what for, but you're welcome." She smiled a satisfied smile. "If you're thanking me for last night, you don't need to." She winked. "You can ravish my body anytime you want." She kissed Sawyer's lips. "It's one of the multitude of benefits of being married to me."

Sawyer chuckled. "The thank you is for…." She met Sage's gaze. "It's for changing my story." She twirled a lock of her wife's hair between her fingers. "Without you, I'd still be a drunk cop sitting at the end of some bar." Sawyer stared off and then looked back. "Worst of all, I'd be alone."

"Aw, sweetie," Sage said. "It's you who changed my story." She palmed Sawyer's cheek. "Your touch and your love awakened me. With you, I'm alive."

***

Sawyer stared out the window as Indianapolis faded into the distance. She felt the airplane bank to the right and then level off. They'd reached altitude and were headed home.

"I know you weren't excited to go to Danville for our honeymoon," Sage said softly. "Now, what do you think in hindsight?"

Sawyer gathered her thoughts. "It turned out to be a honeymoon to remember." Her eyes were tender. "You might say it was the honeymoon of my dreams."

Sage leaned back in her seat. "Speaking of dreams." She raised an eyebrow. "Or rather nightmares, which I might add, you haven't had for several nights now, any insight?"

"Yeah," Sawyer said, "considerable insight. I think inside I knew it was time to go back to Danville, time to visit graves, and time to rekindle relationships with family. I think the scream I was hearing was a younger version of myself—screaming to go home."

271

Sage nodded. "You might just be right." She patted Sawyer's thigh. "Think we'll ever go back?"

Sawyer laid her hand on top of her wife's and squeezed.

Their gazes met and she smiled

"Yeah," Sawyer said. "I think our kids will want to meet the rest of their family."

About the Author

KA Moll was born and raised in snowy central Illinois. The change of seasons touch her soul. She holds a Bachelor's Degree in Psychology and a Master's Degree in Social Work from the University of Illinois. In addition, she holds a Master's Degree in Counseling from Eastern Illinois University. She is a young retiree from state child protective services, where she supervised investigations of child abuse and neglect.

KA and her wife have been together for just under thirty years and counting. Their marriage is the wind beneath her wings. She enjoys golf, bridge, and of course–reading and writing lesbian fiction.

KA can be contacted at kamollwrites@gmail.com
Website: www.kamollwrites.com
Twitter: @ka_moll
Facebook: KA Moll

Other Titles Available From
Triplicity Publishing

Second Chance by Sydney Canyon. After an attack on her convoy, Marine Corps Staff Sergeant, Darien Hollister, must learn to live without her sight. When an experimental procedure allows her to see again, opening up the possibility for her to go back to the career that is deeply ingrained in her, Darien is torn, knowing someone had to die in order for this to happen. She embarks on a journey to personally thank the donor's family, but is too stunned to tell them the truth. When the truth finally comes out, Darien walks away, taking the second chance that she's been given to go back to the only life she's ever known, but she's not the only one with a second chance at life.

Twin Bridges by Tina Kunkle. Hadley Jameson had it all in New York City, top detective in her precinct, someone to love, and a beautiful brownstone on the East side. Life as she knew it was good, but then, in a matter of seconds, it all changed and the Big Apple she once loved, became the place she could no longer stand to be in. Landing a job as Sheriff in Twin Bridges was exactly what she needed. When steer start turning up mutilated, the investigation leads her to Dakota, the beautiful and spirited veterinarian and the careful wall that Hadley had built around her heart was in jeopardy of being taken down, one brick at a time.

The Half-breed & Soiled Dove by Tina Kunkle. In 1866, spring arrived early for the small town of

Spindle Top, Texas, and twenty-two year old Johanna O'Riley wasn't at all prepared for what it brought with it. One fateful morning, the tranquility and peacefulness was shattered by the loud sounds of gunshots and her Ma's horrific screams. In her blood soaked dress she laid her entire family to rest. The anger inside her grew with each and every shovel of dirt she threw on them. When Johanna finished, she stood on that hill top over-looking the three freshly dug graves and vowed to get revenge on the outlaws who took her family from her. She was willing to do anything to keep it, including dressing as a man to get it done, but the one thing she didn't count on, was the beautiful Isabella entering her life.

Meant to Be by Graysen Morgen. Brandt is about to walk down the aisle with her girlfriend, when an unexpected chain of events turns her world upside down, causing her to question the last three years of her life. A chance encounter sparks a mix of rage and excitement that she has never felt before. Summer is living life and following her dreams, all the while, harboring a huge secret that could ruin her career. She believes that some things are better kept in the dark, until she has her third run-in with a woman she had hoped to never see again, and gives into temptation. Brandt and Summer start believing everything happens for a reason as they learn the true meaning of meant to be.

Coming Home by Graysen Morgen. After tragedy derails TJ Abernathy's life, she packs up her three year old son and heads back to Pennsylvania to live with her grandmother on the family farm. TJ picks back up where she left off eight years earlier, tending to the fruit and nut tree orchard, while learning her grandmother's secret trade. Soon, TJ's high school sweetheart and the same girl who broke her heart, comes back into her life, threatening to steal it away once again. As the weeks turn into months and tragedy strikes again, TJ realizes coming home was the best thing she could've ever done.

Special Assignment by Austen Thorne. Secret Service Agent Parker Meeks has her hands full when she gets her new assignment, protecting a Congressman's teenage daughter, who has had threats made on her life and been whisked away to a Christian boarding school under an alias to finish out her senior year. Parker is fine with the assignment, until she finds out she has to go undercover as a Canon Priest. The last thing Parker expects to find is a beautiful, art history teacher, who is intrigued by her in more ways than one.

Miracle at Christmas by Sydney Canyon. A Modern Twist on the Classic Scrooge Story. Dylan is a power-hungry lawyer who pushed away everything good in her life to become the best defense attorney in the, often winning the worst cases and keeping anyone with enough money out of jail. She's visited on Christmas Eve by her deceased law partner, who threatens her with a life in hell like his own, if she doesn't change her path. During the course of the night, she is taken on a journey through her past, present, and future with three very different spirits.

Bella Vita by Sydney Canyon. Brady is the First Officer of the crew on the Bella Vita, a luxury charter yacht in the Caribbean. She enjoys the laidback island lifestyle, and is accustomed to high profile guests, but when a U.S. Senator charters the yacht as a gift to his beautiful twin daughters who have just graduated from college and a few of their friends, she literally has her hands full.

Brides (Bridal Series book 2) by Graysen Morgen. Britton Prescott is dating the love of her life, Daphne Attwood, after a few tumultuous events that happened to unravel at her sister's wedding reception, seven months earlier. She's happy with the way things are, but immense pressure from her family and friends to take the next step, nearly sends her back to the single life. The idea of a long engagement and simple wedding are thrown out the window, as both families take over, rushing Britton and Daphne to the altar in a matter of weeks.

Cypress Lake by Graysen Morgen. The small town of Cypress Lake is rocked when one murder after another happens. Dani Ricketts, the Chief Deputy for the Cypress Lake Sheriff's Office, realizes the murders are linked. She's surprised when the girl that broke her heart in high school has not only returned home, but she's also Dani's only suspect. Kristen Malone has come back to Cypress Lake to put the past behind her so that she can move on with her life. Seeing Dani Ricketts again throws her off-guard, nearly derailing her plans to finally rid herself and her family of Cypress Lake.

Crashing Waves by Graysen Morgen. After a tragic accident, Pro Surfer, Rory Eden, spends her days hiding in the surf and snowboard manufacturing company that she built from the ground up, while living her life as a shell of the person that she once was. Rory's world is turned upside when a young surfer pursues her, asking for the one thing she can't do. Adler Troy and Dr. Cason Macauley from Graysen Morgen's best selling novel: *Falling Snow*, make an appearance in this romantic adventure about life, love, and letting go.

Bridesmaid of Honor (Bridal Series book 1) by Graysen Morgen. Britton Prescott's best friend is getting married and she's the maid of honor. As if that isn't enough to deal with, Britton's sister announces she's getting married in the same month and her maid of honor is her best friend Daphne, the same woman who has tormented Britton for years. Britton has to suck it up and play nice, instead of scratching her eyes out, because she and Daphne are in both weddings. Everyone is counting on them to behave like adults.

Falling Snow by Graysen Morgen. Dr. Cason Macauley, a high-speed trauma surgeon from Denver meets Adler Troy, a professional snowboarder and sparks fly. The last thing Cason wants is a relationship and Adler doesn't realize what's right in front of her until it's gone, but will it be too late?

Fate vs. Destiny by Graysen Morgen. Logan Greer devotes her life to investigating plane crashes for the National Transportation Safety Board. Brooke McCabe is an investigator with the Federal Aviation Association who literally flies by the seat of her pants. When Logan gets tangled in head games with both women will she choose fate or destiny?

Just Me by Graysen Morgen. Wild child Ian Wiley has to grow up and take the reins of the hundred year old family business when tragedy strikes. Cassidy Harland is a little surprised that she came within an inch of picking up a gorgeous stranger in a bar and is shocked to find out that stranger is the new head of her company.

Love Loss Revenge by Graysen Morgen. Rian Casey is an FBI Agent working the biggest case of her career and madly in love with her girlfriend. Her world is turned upside when tragedy strikes. Heartbroken, she tries to rebuild her life. When she discovers the truth behind what really happened that awful night she decides justice isn't good enough, and vows revenge on everyone involved.

Natural Instinct by Graysen Morgen. Chandler Scott is a Marine Biologist who keeps her private life private. Corey Joslen is intrigued by Chandler from the moment she meets her. Chandler is forced to finally open her life up to Corey. It backfires in Corey's face and sends her running. Will either woman learn to trust her natural instinct?

Secluded Heart by Graysen Morgen. Chase Leery is an overworked cardiac surgeon with a group of best friends that have an opinion and a reason for everything. When she meets a new artist named Remy Sheridan at her best friend's art gallery she is captivated by the reclusive woman. When Chase finds out why Remy is so sheltered will she put her career on the line to help her or is it too difficult to love someone with a secluded heart?

In Love, at War by Graysen Morgen. Charley Hayes is in the Army Air Force and stationed at Ford Island in Pearl Harbor. She is the commanding officer of her own female-only service squadron and doing the one thing she loves most, repairing airplanes. Life is good for Charley, until the day she finds herself falling in love while fighting for her life as her country is thrown haphazardly into World War II. Can she survive being in love and at war?

Fast Pitch by Graysen Morgen. Graham Cahill is a senior in college and the catcher and captain of the softball team. Despite being an all-star pitcher, Bailey Michaels is young and arrogant. Graham and Bailey are forced to get to know each other off the field in order to learn to work together on the field. Will the extra time pay off or will it drive a nail through the team?

Submerged by Graysen Morgen. Assistant District Attorney Layne Carmichael had no idea that the sexy woman she took home from a local bar for a one night stand would turn out to be someone she would be prosecuting months later. Scooter is a Naval Officer on a submarine who changes women like she changes uniforms. When she is accused of a heinous crime she is shocked to see her latest conquest sitting across from her as the prosecuting attorney.

Vow of Solitude by Austen Thorne. Detective Jordan Denali is in a fight for her life against the ghosts from her past and a Serial Killer taunting her with his every move. She lives a life of solitude and plans to keep it that way. When Callie Marceau, a curious Medical Examiner, decides she wants in on the biggest case of her career, as well as, Jordan's life, Jordan is powerless to stop her.

Igniting Temptation by Sydney Canyon. Mackenzie Trotter is the Head of Pediatrics at the local hospital. Her life takes a rather unexpected turn when she meets a flirtatious, beautiful fire fighter. Both women soon discover it doesn't take much to ignite temptation.

One Night by Sydney Canyon. While on a business trip, Caylen Jarrett spends an amazing night with a beautiful stripper. Months later, she is shocked and confused when that same woman re-enters her life. The fact that this stranger could destroy her career doesn't bother her. C.J. is more terrified of the feelings this woman stirs in her. Could she have fallen in love in one night and not even known it?

Fine by Sydney Canyon. Collin Anderson hides behind a façade, pretending everything is fine. Her workaholic wife and best friend are both oblivious as she goes on an emotional journey, battling a potentially hereditary disease that her mother has been diagnosed with. The only person who knows what is really going on, is Collin's doctor. The same doctor, who is an acquaintance that she's always been attracted to, and who has a partner of her own.

Shadow's Eyes by Sydney Canyon. Tyler McCain is the owner of a large ranch that breeds and sells different types of horses. She isn't exactly thrilled when a

Hollywood movie producer shows up wanting to film his latest movie on her property. Reegan Delsol is an up and coming actress who has everything going for her when she lands the lead role in a new film, but there one small problem that could blow the entire picture.

Light Reading: A Collection of Novellas by Sydney Canyon. Four of Sydney Canyon's novellas together in one book, including the bestsellers Shadow's Eyes and One Night.

Visit us at www.tri-pub.com